C000054004

R.K. LANDER

Copyright © 2017 Ruth Kent. All rights reserved.
This work is registered with the UK Copyright Service: registration
No.:284712822

This is a work of fiction. All characters, names and events in this book
are fictitious. Any resemblance to real persons, living or dead, is purely
coincidental.

Cover art by kaprriss
Book coaching: Andrea Lundgren
www.rklander.com

Map of
Bel'arán

Dunes of Calrazia

Barrier Ridge

Valley

Meng Slün

Prairie

Govant Slün

Median Mountains

Golave

Kunger's Fort

Downlands

Cor'huden River

Lagan'Ár Delta

Court of Vorn'aste

Tar'Eastór

Duggan Sands

Southerly Sea

Falls

Hager Island

Chrystal Straits

Ice Lands

Chapter One

GREEN SUN

*"Past King Thargodén's great city fortress and further North, the Deep
Forest of Ea Uaré begins, homeland of the Silvan people. Villages lay
dotted over a map of sprawling woods and vales, deep valleys and jagged
gorges. There are no grand halls, manors or palaces here, only cottages
and flets, mighty talans even, but it is all wood and rope, stone and
bone, feather and fur for these are the elements of this land."*
The Silvan Chronicles, Book I – Marhené

She called him Fel'annár, Green Sun, immortal child with the heart of
a Silvan and the face of an Alpine; it was a face that would garner hatred,
kindle love, inspire loyalty, bring persecution, a face Amareth of Lan Taria
had protected for fifty-one years.

But the woodland creatures of Ea Uaré knew little of such things, only
that danger approached and that they should flee. Birds erupted into excited
song and wings unfolded, flapping furiously until they were aloft and they
flew higher, into the towering boughs of the Deep Forest.

A squirrel stood alert and utterly still, shiny brown eyes fixed on the path
below. He spat an acorn, thinking perhaps he might choke should he try
to run with it still in his mouth, and run he *did*, for the thundering noise
was louder now and instinct sent him scampering up the bark and along a
sprawling, moss-laden branch and home, to wait in safety for the dissonance
to pass.

Silver-blond and chestnut locks streamed upon the playful wind, glorious
banners of liquid silk, in harmony yet clearly distinctive, just like the three
elves who bent low over the lunging necks of their galloping mounts, legs

bouncing off their heaving sides, elbows pumping, youthful faces infused with the joy of the ride, barely-contained anticipation for the coming of dawn and a new life.

As the path became more populated, some villagers shouted for caution as they dusted themselves off in the wake of the three mounted elves, but there was a gleam in their eyes and the hint of an indulgent smile on their lips. Others raised their arms and waved. "Hail the victorious Company!"

Giggles and guffaws accompanied the hoof beats and moments later, the three elves pulled sharply on their reins, sending a cloud of late summer dust into the air. The thump of boots upon the ground told the angry stable hands the riders had dismounted, but as the cloud dissipated, so too did their anger. Instead they smiled and nodded, taking the reins and guiding the heaving horses inside.

Fel'annár of Lan Taria smiled and nodded his thanks before lifting his face to the evening sun. He closed his eyes for a moment, feeling the warming light on his skin, soaking it up and he breathed deeply, a futile attempt to calm his excitement.

"Until the dawn," he said.

His two friends smiled back, eyes gleaming with the promise of adventure, of freedom and they clasped each other's dusty forearms. Fel'annár watched them for a moment as they made their way home to their mothers and fathers, brothers and sisters. His smile slipped and he turned, eyes drifting over Lan Taria, perhaps for the last time.

Slinging his cloth bag over one shoulder, he strolled down the main path towards his own talan and home – to the only family he had ever known, Amareth.

"Fel'annár!" shouted his blades instructor from across the field. "Don't get cocky, boy!" He smiled and held one fist aloft.

"No promises!" shouted Fel'annár with a grin before waving and continuing along the path.

"Good luck son," came the quieter, softer voice of the baker as he held out a hot loaf which Fel'annár took with both hands and a humble nod. As a child, Amareth would send him for bread every morning and if he was lucky, the baker would slip him some of the crunchy tips that had fallen off the loaves, sending him home with a pat on the head. Fel'annár would devour them on the way, brushing himself down before Amareth could admonish him for eating before breakfast but he would always forget to wipe the crumbs away from his mouth, his head too much in the clouds, full of warrior dreams.

A little further along, Fel'annár came across a pretty girl who stopped before him, a basket in her hand, a white cloth draped over the top.

"Fel'annár," she said, voice deep and husky.

"Dalia."

"I made you these," she said as she dragged the cloth away, hesitant eyes rising to meet him.

"Honey cakes," he exclaimed, and then walked up to her, slowly reaching out one hand to cup her cheek. He bent, softly resting his forehead against hers, an apology – or perhaps it was regret.

"Stay safe," she whispered, to which his only answer was a soft kiss to her brow. Her stubborn eyes watched him walk away, not for the first time, her basket in his hands.

The schoolmaster and a group of children made their way back from a trip into the forests. They held branches and flowers, stones and leaves and who knew what other, hidden treasures they had smuggled into their ample pockets. It brought fond memories of the good times. "Hwind'atór!" they shouted and Fel'annár beamed. Only the children and his closest friends used that nick-name – the Whirling Warrior. He waved and smiled a toothy grin and the boys waved back at him while the girls giggled and poked each other.

He passed the farrier and the pie maker, inhaling the blissful smell of pepper and pork that lingered in his wake, and then the Chief Forester and his apprentice who smiled and nodded their own silent goodbyes. A group of three lads he had once studied with walked past him, their stares cold but their lips mercifully sealed; it had not always been that way.

He was close to home now. He had said his goodbyes to everyone except Amareth, but as he stood before the tree that had housed him for fifty-one years, he thought perhaps he had been remiss. His free hand, rough and calloused, brushed over the bark as he climbed the stairs, a soft smile on his lips and a feeling of well-being in his heart, despite his fluttering stomach and the impending emotions of a stilted goodbye.

Amareth smiled down at him, loving yet disapproving eyes roving over the ruined mess of her braids in his hair. There was protection and love there but Fel'annár struggled to ignore the other emotions that lay discreetly behind her honey-coloured eyes, the ones she always tried and failed to hide from him.

Fel'annár could smell pea soup and he knew she would serve it with roasted nuts and soured cream, his favourite and as they ate, she would surely turn her eyes away so that he could not see her battle and he would bite his own tongue, again.

What happened to my mother? Who was my father? Why won't you speak?

Amareth did, indeed, serve him pea soup and it sat now, heavy and mellow in his belly as Amareth worked with his hair, weaved the tale of his life into each, skilfully crafted braid.

Child of Lan Taria, son of Amareth, Silvan warrior. Fel'annár knew she would not weave the heritage braid.

He himself had never been able to plait his hair. He could pull an arrow and shoot from a horse in a split second, splice an acorn perched on the furthest, highest branch – but he could not braid his hair, was as clumsy as a bear with a fiddle. He smiled at the image it conjured, tried to hold on to it but his mind was not cooperating and his memories slipped to the past once more, to the very first one he could recall. It was of a woman in the trees. He loved her, had carried her with him like a war shield through years of boisterous games, of mockery endured and battles fought on the cruellest of fields by the cruellest of warriors – children.

'You cannot be so beautiful. You cannot be Silvan and Alpine. You cannot be an orphan.'

The mockery had passed but his own questions remained.

'Fel'annár ... for his eyes are greener and brighter even than the Green Sun of the Deep Forest.'

Amareth would tell him the story of how he had been named, of his tragic mother's legendary green eyes, her Silvan legacy to her half-blooded child. She told him of how she had loved him and that she had died. It soothed him when his questions could not be answered.

"Amareth?"

"Um? she answered distractedly

"I spoke to Golloron today."

"Oh? she asked, hesitating, fingers momentarily stilling their movements.

"He said I will do well, that he has seen it."

"Our Spirit Herder is rarely wrong – you are happy then," she said, smiling as her fingers resumed their mesmerizing movements.

"Golloron said other things too," murmured Fel'annár after a while. "He said I would come to *know* myself. What do you think he meant?"

Amareth stopped her braiding once more, eyes closing in dread, only to open again when Fel'annár said no more. And then she spoke.

"I believe he means that you will come to understand your strengths and your short-comings, know your place in this world."

Fel'annár said no more. In how many ways could a question be asked? he wondered – he himself had surely tried them all – and failed but it didn't matter, he reminded himself. Nothing would sour his moment, the moment he had always known would come; the day in which he would ride out of Lan Taria and to novice training. A chubby face danced before his mind's eye, messy silver-blond hair loose and wild yet still, unable to dim the brightness of determined eyes.

'I want to be a captain. A Silvan captain.'

He had been five, oblivious of life and its wiles but this – this he *did* know and Amareth had smiled her stilted smile.

To deny the questions of a child who searches for his own identity is a dangerous thing, this Amareth knew; yet still, she had seen no other way, even now when Fel'annár stepped out into the world, away from Lan Taria, from her protective arms, her lies. She thought, perhaps, that the truth was too dangerous, indeed she never would tell him.

And yet the truth is like air, always finding its way upwards, to the surface. Amareth would never tell him and tomorrow Fel'annár would be gone. In his mind's eye, his unanswered questions faded into the receding mists of his childhood.

He would ask no more.

Chapter Two

INTO THE WORLD

*"To live with the certainty of death is a tragedy indeed.
The effects of Valley upon the mortal body are devastating. The closer
they draw, the longer-lived they become, but if they do not pass into the
Source, they are condemned to live their years in horror and growing
madness, for who can withstand the sight of one's own body as it slowly
succumbs to decay? Who can fathom the injustice when faced with the
beauty and untainted flesh of the elves?"*
The Silvan Chronicles, Book I. Marhené

Sunlight caressed the early autumn boughs, only a little of it filtering through to the loamy, leaf-strewn ground below. A beautiful, colourful end to another season in Ea Uaré, great forest of the Silvan elves.

But here, the dying beauty of summer was marred by a sight not often seen so far south.

"I never thought they would look quite so – *rotten*," a deep, rumbling voice cut through the stunned silence; Ramien, the Wall of Stone.

"Hardly surprising, given the stench," said a strangled voice through clenched teeth. "Its face is almost completely – eaten away," he added. The Wise Elf's lip curled in disgust but his eyes sparkled in curiosity; he'd never seen a Deviant before – none of them had.

"Is it male, do you think?" asked Fel'annár, eyes travelling over the putrid body. Disgust, curiosity; *pity*.

"Probably, I'm not looking though," said Ramien and Idernon snorted.

"It's hard to believe this was once human. That this was once a man with a wife, a family, children. Is it worth it, I wonder – the promise of immortality?

Is it worth the risk of failing and becoming – *this*?" asked Fel'annár, his eyes unfocussed.

"Who can say," said Idernon as he stood, brushing down his brown leather tunic, eyes still on the carcass of the Deviant. "When you are immortal, it's not easy to imagine mortality – the tragedy of it, I mean," he trailed off.

"Tragedy or no," said Ramien as he stood, towering over Idernon, "I'm not touching it."

It was Fel'annár's turn to snort as he, too, stood. "Get used to it, Ramien. When we are warriors in the king's militia, we'll have our share of dirty work. Take this as practice. You don't want to lose your lunch before the entire troop."

"Lose my …,"

"Come on," said Fel'annár, clamping a bristling Ramien on the shoulder and distracting him from what would surely become an indignant rant.

The three friends set about collecting dry wood and before long, the Deviant had been burned. Mounting once more, they resumed their journey towards the outer city barracks and recruit training, their dream since fate had brought them together, had made them brothers.

"Is that how you imagined them to be?" asked Idernon, his eyes fixed on the path ahead, a slight crease between his brows.

"They are – *worse*, I think. They look dead, even though I know they are not – I wonder if they wish to be though," said Fel'annár, one hand stroking the flank of his grey mare.

"Who would blame them," exclaimed Ramien with a scowl. "Well, at least we've actually *seen* a Deviant now, albeit a dead one. I wonder what the Sand Lords are like …"

"I have always hated that expression," said Idernon. "It makes them sound noble and good. Sand *Monsters* would be a better term."

"Yet they *are* human Idernon," said Ramien.

"Then they are human *monsters*," answered Idernon curtly. "If they are not seeking immortality where it is not given, they are searching for water and taking it where it is not offered, pillaging our harvests and slaughtering our people in the process."

"They are certainly prone to brutality. Taking lives does not seem to bother them," said Ramien.

"Neither does it bother many *elves*, Ramien. Our own history is proof of that. There are monsters everywhere – it is not a question of species or race."

Fel'annár's eyes drifted to Idernon for a moment, nodding almost imperceptibly but Ramien remained sceptical.

A while later, when the thick forest had opened and become wooded meadowland, Fel'annár heaved a long, deep breath.

"The air has changed; it is—*heavier*," he said, almost to himself as his eyes drifted over the unfamiliar territory. It was brighter here and the sun felt warmer; it should have comforted him, but it did not.

"Aye, and the trees are fewer, I feel—*vulnerable*," said Idernon with a scowl, his eyes darting around nervously. As Silvan elves, they were not accustomed to such open spaces, despite the trees that still dotted the land. Idernon's horse skittered nervously beneath him, mirroring the Wise Elf's mounting unease.

"It won't be long now until we are in the realm of the City Dwellers," said Ramien. We are out of our element, brothers; I feel—*small*," he said, eyes glancing this way and that, as if he thought perhaps they would be ambushed.

"*Small?*" chuckled Fel'annár and Idernon smiled for the first time that morning. "Not *you*, you lumbering oaf! And anyway, who is to say these lands are of the *City Dwellers?* They belong to us *all*. I wager many Silvans find a place in the king's halls too, even at his *court*," speculated Fel'annár.

"*Silvan numskull!*" smiled Idernon. "We Silvans rule the woods, aye, but *there*, at *court*," he jabbed southwards with his finger, "it is only High-born Silvans and Alpines that impose their ways on us all; that, I *do* wager on."

Fel'annár held his friend's gaze for a moment, a scowl back on his face. It brought his own conflict to the foreground once more. A boy, a would-be-warrior who was neither Silvan nor Alpine. How was he to reconcile his duality in a world that discriminated against the Silvans? Yet chosen he *had* – he was Silvan, like his mother.

"We'll be treated like village idiots, fledgling bumpkins," mumbled Fel'annár, shaking himself from his dark musings.

Ramien laughed at his friend's petulance and Fel'annár startled at the sudden sound. "We *are* bumpkins, Felan!" he mocked good-heartedly. "We are as foreign to these lands as gruel at the king's table."

Fel'annár smiled lopsidedly, shrugging his shoulders as if to excuse his ill humour.

"Fair. We *are* bumpkins *and* we are Silvan," he conceded. "But these are *our* lands; it is not natural for the Alpines to rule them. What do *they* know of the forest? of *woodcraft?*"

"Nothing save for what they have learned, I suppose," conceded Idernon. "They wish for power and wealth and well they know that is achieved by those who make the decisions. From their seats of power, they legislate to their own gain, contrive so that everything that's decided upon favours them in some way. It's not good government but it is the only one we have," he finished with a hint of sadness.

Idernon had nothing more to say and so he watched as Fel'annár's face hardened, eyes fixed on the path ahead, anger sharpening his extraordinary features, a face that contrasted starkly with the browns, greens and purples of the Silvan people and their forest home. His hair was not dark but the colour of winter wheat and his features were not full and generous but chiselled and sharp, high cheekbones and strong, dark eyebrows lending him a feral beauty that Idernon well knew had, paradoxically, brought him nothing but strife. It was his eyes, though, deep pools of river moss that shone overly bright. There was a light there that was unnerving. Those eyes were the only Silvan trait upon an otherwise foreign face, one that had always set him apart from the rest.

"We Silvans will be in the *majority* at the barracks with the warriors though," said Ramien, his eyes looking to Idernon as if for confirmation. "The bulk of our king's fighters are Silvan, albeit our commanders rarely are, at least that's what they say."

"It makes no sense unless you look at it for what it is," said Fel'annár, fidgeting in his saddle, "discrimination, racism created to dominate – it is about *power*," he spat and Ramien nodded his agreement.

Strangely, Fel'annár had experienced such discrimination from his own people, the Silvan people. He had endured it until he had been old enough to accept his lot, and then he had found Ramien and Idernon. It had been the dawn of joy, the beginning of what Fel'annár now knew was his path, the path of a warrior, well, a novice warrior to start. Idernon's quiet voice brought Fel'annár back to the present.

"Calro wrote an excellent account of the days that followed King Or'Talán's colonization of our lands – a must read – I have it if you are interested," he said, eyes slipping to the side as if he were remembering the exact pages, the many tomes he had devoured on the history of Ea Uaré when it was still ruled by the Silvans. Indeed the Wise Elf had been thusly named for his insatiable quest for knowledge, one that had blossomed no sooner he could speak. Had he not become friends with Ramien and Fel'annár, his destiny would, perhaps, have been different; a scholar or strategist, perhaps.

"I don't need a book to keep my wits about me. We'd do well to stick together with the other Silvans," said Ramien, before adding, "mind you, if Felan here is mistaken for an Alpine, that may not happen."

Silence stretched awkwardly between them before Ramien realized he should not have said that.

"Forgive me," was all he said, cringing, wilting almost under Idernon's stern gaze that lingered on him for a little too long, and despite Ramien's considerable bulk, he almost seemed to shrink.

"Don't fret, Ramien. I am well past that," Fel'annár assured his friend, albeit he would not turn to meet his gaze. Ramien's eyes *did* linger on the profile of his friend, a profile that screamed *Alpine*, until the face turned and green eyes stared back – Silvan eyes. It seemed almost cruel that destiny should have contrived to make Fel'annár singularly Silvan in his ways.

By midday, their stomachs growled and rumbled louder than any war-bound Elven battalion and the wholesome fare their families had packed for them began to weigh just a little more heavily upon their backs. Finding a suitably shady patch, the three friends dismounted and slapped their horses upon the rump, watching as they pranced away in a flurry of swishing manes and bobbing heads. Meanwhile, Ramien set about arranging their food upon his blanket, his head cocked to one side as he pondered on where to place each dish. It was an endearing sight, mused Fel'annár with a smirk, because the elf was so tall and strong it did not quite fit to see him fussing over the details of their lunch. The absurd notion of the hulking Wall of Stone as a royal cook, pinny too short and rolling pin overly large soon had him chuckling quietly.

Before long, the three friends sat cross-legged, eager hands clutching at gravy-filled pies and crusty bread, cheese and cold meat. It was a feast not commonly seen upon the road, a testimony to their mother's devotion, to provide them with one, last, wholesome meal before military training and hardship. None of them spoke until there was little left and the sun had passed into the West.

They sat in silence for a while. Idernon looked upwards, into the boughs, his mind away on some such philosophical question, while Ramien sat against a tree trunk, head jerking forwards as sleep threatened to take him. Fel'annár stared at nothing, his right hand caressing the root of the oak tree he sat under, pondering on a new close combat move he was yet to try out.

On any other day, they would have stayed to nap and then hunt, camp and tell stories, but today was the first day they were truly alone in the world, and their home village of Lan Taria seemed further away than it ever had. They were excited yet apprehensive, eager to impress yet unwilling to draw attention to themselves, for Fel'annár's sake. He was a tough lad, but both Idernon and Ramien knew his weak spot. All it would take was for Fel'annár to be labelled as an Alpine and when that happened, he would struggle to check himself, and at the barracks, his irrational anger might well land him in trouble. It was the one thing that made him vulnerable, the flaw in his character that reminded them both that Fel'annár was not immune to mockery, even though he thought he was.

Thoroughly sated, they whistled for their mounts and were soon on the path once more, each lost to his own thoughts, of what they had left behind and perhaps more importantly, what was still ahead of them.

They purposefully chose to cross the meadow through a copse of trees, for it felt safer and Fel'annár smiled, eyebrows rising in delight for a nuthatch was singing in the boughs; these creatures were not easy to come across.

"A *nuthatch*!" he exclaimed, but contrary to the awe-inspired comments he had expected, Idernon shot him a warning look, one Ramien did not see.

"*Bumpkin!* —'tis not a bird you hear but the call of an elven *warrior*!" he hissed.

Ramien chuckled at the joke, slapping his thighs and throwing his head back, hair flying chaotically about him; but then he almost choked on his own saliva, for in front of him, as if from nowhere, appeared a glaring Alpine warrior, a short bow slung over his back and the intricate pommel of an intimidating sword peaking over his armoured shoulder.

Idernon had not been joking.

"*You* boy!" called the warrior. "What is your name?" His sharp, scowling eyes pierced Fel'annár, who hesitated for a moment before answering, resisting a sudden urge to swallow. When his voice returned, he felt nothing but shame for the weakness in it.

"Fel'annár ar Amareth."

The warrior's scowl deepened and he cocked his head in thought. "I know of no Amaron of *Alpine* heritage," he said, watching the youth carefully.

"Not Amaron, Sir, but Amareth, and *she* is Silvan, as am *I*."

"And what of your father?" A clipped retort.

Ramien and Idernon clenched their jaws and looked to the ground for it would do no good to rile this admittedly imposing warrior whose appearance surely meant they were close to the barracks; for all they knew, he might be one of their instructors. If only they could find an excuse to help their floundering friend out of the bind he found himself in—again.

"My father died, Sir."

"I meant his name you *fool*," the warrior said, still staring openly at the pale blond hair and moss green eyes.

"I . . ."

"Well, speak up, boy. You do *have* a father . . . ?"

Silence was the only answer the warrior received, and understanding lit his sharp grey eyes. "Did he die in battle?" he asked, "or perhaps you are a bastard? That is a pity, Fel'annár. Whoever he was, he was obviously of Alpine descent."

"I am *Silvan*," hissed Fel'annár too quickly, his emotions getting the better of him as they always did, the words bubbling out of his mouth quicker than his mind could restrain them.

"Ooohh! Have something against the *Alpines* then?" he mocked, his grin twisted and challenging, his own, blond hair as much a declaration of his heritage as any flag.

Fel'annár was mortified at his outburst but he would be damned if he was going to apologize for it. The warrior was an ass, unnecessarily sarcastic and scathing.

"Well, well, *Silvan*. Proud and impulsive – not good traits in a recruit. You will learn soon enough though," he said, his caustic smile softening a little, even though Fel'annár could not see it, for he simply looked away, embarrassed and annoyed at himself and this pig-headed warrior who had subjected him to impertinent questions and called him an *Alpine*, no less!

Twin looks of caution from his friends tempered his simmering anger and he schooled himself as best he could. He *had* been rash.

He decided that he would no longer avoid the inevitable questions, for that had led his errant emotions astray. He would call himself Fel'annár ar Amareth for that was his only name; he would say that his father had been Alpine, for that he could not deny; he would say that his father was dead for even if he weren't, to Fel'annár's mind he might as well be.

None of it mattered, it was of no consequence.
He did not care at all.

"You three! Briefing is in one hour. Do *not* be late," said Calenar, the Alpine warrior who had guided them to the barracks, or *Nuthatch* as the three friends had baptized him.

He knew how overwhelmed these Silvan village boys could be when traveling to the outer city for the first time. Life here shared few similarities with their routines back home, and these three, by the looks of them, were no different save for one, surprising thing; one of them was an Alpine.

As he made his way to his commanding officer's study, he could not help wondering about the strange blond boy who had claimed to be Silvan, despite the evidence. True his name, Fel'annár, he recalled, was clearly Silvan; only the Forest Dwellers would name their children after a *plant*.

Nay he *was* Alpine, however much it seemed to rile the youth. *Youth*, he snorted, he was barely out of swaddling cloths, and yet he *had* been the leader of the three, or so it had seemed to Calenar, in spite of the boy's outburst and ensuing anger. The others protected him and the warrior realized he was intrigued; with no father to call his own, the boy's face was simply extraordinary. He would be popular with the lasses—and with the lads he added with a sardonic smile. Yet it would not be easy for him with those looks and that temper. Lieutenant Turion would soon knock him into shape, and a few of the other recruits too, he wagered, for envy was an ugly thing indeed.

It was times like these that Calenar waxed pensive, for the battles on the northern borders were increasing alarmingly, the death toll spiralling almost out of control. They needed more recruits to become warriors so that they could travel North and work to stop the tide of Deviants and Sand Lords. He wondered if that was why he was sometimes so curt with them – so that he would not become too attached. They would fight and die all too soon and he must guard his heart – everyone had limits.

Shaking his head to rid himself of his dour thoughts, a recent memory came to him, just as he reached Lieutenant Turion's door. Calenar had been called many things in his life as an instructor, most of them unpalatable—

but never had he been likened to something as innocent and endearing as a *nuthatch!*

Still four days' ride from the mighty city fortress of Thargodén King, the training barracks were, nevertheless, a sombre place. Grey stone and dark wood dominated everything and not one item of decoration graced the walls or any other part of the long dormitory they had been assigned to. Ramien and Idernon inspected the depressing room in silence, while Fel'annár scowled, eyes desperate to latch on to the slightest manifestation of nature, a leaf or vine, anything to connect the room with the outside world. He had always had an affinity with the trees back home. His window would always be open, even in the thick of winter, as if he could not stand the press of enclosing walls, the separation of his immortal soul from the land beyond.

Their beds were basic. Thick woollen blankets lay neatly folded beneath a single pillow and a bedside table lay on either side; on one a jug of water stood, a simple drawer beneath while the other provided basic shelving for personal effects.

Idernon sighed and glanced momentarily at Fel'annár, watching as he sat slowly upon an unoccupied bed at the end of the room, the small window above it drawing him like a beacon.

Idernon's gaze sharpened on one long finger as it brushed softly over a green leaf that had invaded the crack between the stone wall and the wooden frame. It had always fascinated Idernon, that gesture that was so ingrained on Fel'annár and he wondered what it was he felt; it was something he did constantly and every time it was accompanied by that strange expression on his face—one that spoke of fascination and perhaps just a hint of confusion.

As they settled in and unpacked their meagre belongings, more new recruits were steadily arriving, stepping slowly into the room and looking around in trepidation. They were all young, all eager to fight the war that was said to be waged on their northern borders, the war they had never seen or heard. It existed though, for their warriors died and songs were sung.

They were excited too. For many it was their first time so close to the city, albeit it could not yet be seen. Still, there were Alpines here and that was a testimony to how close they were. True, most were Silvan and they stared now at the blond boys with mistrust in their eyes.

Idernon could see the darker elves' ill-concealed stares at Fel'annár, heard their whispering and strangled chuckles. It would be a matter of seconds before Ramien heard them too and when that happened …

"You," gestured the Wall of Stone towards a group of Silvan recruits. "I like a laugh and a joke. Tell me, what is the object of your humour?" he said, eyes landing heavily on one brown-haired recruit.

"We were wondering – about *him*," gestured the recruit, head nodding at Fel'annár. You don't get to see many poor Alpines. Maybe he wants to be Silvan – and who can blame him?" he asked, looking at his friends and sniggering.

Fel'annár scowled, glancing down at his simple linen shirt and worn tunic.

Before Ramien could answer, one of the Alpine recruits further away walked forwards, turning to the dark-haired Silvan.

"He is Alpine – you have a problem with that?" he asked them, jaw clenching as his friends reached his side.

But Fel'annár scowled. "I am Silvan," he said simply, blank gaze resting on the Alpine recruit that had thought to defend him.

The Silvan recruits stared dumbly at Fel'annár for a moment, before turning to the Alpine who was scowling back. "You are Alpine; and you want to be Silvan?"

"I *am* Silvan."

One of the Alpines from behind their leader snorted. "You think to fool us?"

"No. I am half Alpine, and *Silvan*." His eyes stared back challengingly.

"A half-breed – who reneges his Alpine culture – is no friend of mine. You would do well to stay away from us," said their leader."

Fel'annár smiled, but there was a menacing gleam in his eye. "That would be my pleasure."

The Alpine stiffened, before turning and walking away, to the other end of the room where he and his friends had taken beds.

The Silvan recruits turned to Fel'annár, their expressions now open and curious.

"I am Carodel of Silvervale," said one.

"Nurodi of Sen'tár."

"Oden of Lan Bedar."

Fel'annár nodded. "Fel'annár of Lan Taria," he said simply, before turning back to his pack, taking the last of his clothing out and putting it away in a drawer.

Ramien and Idernon turned, and then introduced themselves somewhat stiffly, for these recruits had tried and failed to antagonize their friend. They had made up for it but there was no friendship between them, not yet.

"How do I look?" asked Ramien as he held his arms out to the side, showing his friends his new uniform. It was simple and practical for a forest warrior. Black breeches that hugged the legs and equally black boots with no other qualities to mention. A brown, knee-length tunic and a reinforced, sleeveless vest completed the outfit. Black and brown, wool and leather and just like the barracks – not one item of decoration. Still, it was fine leather and although plain, was still a uniform, one Ramien felt absurdly proud of.

But of course, Ramien was no ordinary Silvan warrior. He was at least a head taller than Fel'annár, who was counted tall. His chest was broad and his waist thick, just like his legs – his nickname had not been given to him in vain. He was a Wall of Stone and his tunic – was too short, too tight, and his vest sat too close under his arm pits.

Fel'annár guffawed and Idernon smirked playfully.

"These fabrics were not designed for Walls of Stone, my friend," exclaimed Idernon, before Fel'annár continued with the light-hearted banter.

"Aye, and look at this." He laughed harder now. "The clasps on this vest are straining so hard they will surely pop open no sooner you sneeze!"

Ramien was disappointed, his scowl deepening as he turned to the voice of Idernon once more.

"Oh, oh, and what's this!" said Idernon as he lifted the back of his friend's skirt and flapped it around, revealing his taut backside. "One fart and you will be the laughing stock of the barracks!" he exclaimed, sending Fel'annár off into a wheeze of laughter, which only worsened as he watched Ramien dance out of the way, batting Idernon's hands from the hem of his tunic. The other Silvan recruits laughed as they watched the three friends, until a mighty yell from the open doorway shot through them, and they stood to mortified attention. Calenar, their superior officer stood arms akimbo, face grim and eyes twinkling in hidden mirth.

"You! Shut your mouths and get to the main hall—you're late!"

Red-faced and duly chastised, the three friends marched towards briefing together with the other village boys and the small group of Alpine recruits. Fel'annár was one of only four with blond hair, although none sported the silvery paleness that had always singled him out – even now he stuck out awkwardly, involuntarily drawing attention to himself, attention he always strove to divert.

Elant was their drill instructor. His job was to teach them military protocol; how to salute, when to salute, how to march, present their weapons.

Calenar would be their physical instructor. His was the onus of building their muscles and improving their endurance.

Faunon was the only Silvan on the training team, a scout the recruits looked at in curiosity and respect. This Faunon must be good, they reckoned, to be the only Silvan amongst the Alpine tutors.

There had been no mention of weapons training and one recruit had promptly asked why that was. Calenar explained that they could not yet be trusted to hold a blade in their hands. Alpine warriors were brave, but not that much, he had added with a smirk.

By the end of their first week as recruits, their muscles ached ferociously, and Ramien was provided with a new set of clothing to accommodate his ever-growing bulk, triggering a round of light-hearted mockery which the Wall of Stone took with a rueful smile, earning for himself the respect of his fellow recruits. He was their Silvan giant, quick to rile and smile, always where the laughter was.

Idernon earned his own fame as a bookworm and was sometimes looked upon in puzzlement for it was not at all common for one his age to be so learned. But Idernon had an incisive and ironic sense of humour and for this, he was respected as a scholarly, witty elf and a generous companion.

As for Fel'annár, his corner of the room had turned almost completely green. Light green plants, dark green vines and wild, yellow flowers sprouted here and there, invading his bed, even sticking to the inner walls. An officer had once made to rip it all off but the baleful expression Fel'annár had turned on him had been enough to change his mind. He was a child of nature, they said, a true Silvan despite his looks, and some had even speculated he could speak to the trees, something most had laughed at good-naturedly. He was tough, sometimes quiet, sometimes as boisterous as they came. He was 'The Silvan,' they said, because that was what he had chosen, above his Alpine heritage. Fel'annár had accepted his new nick name with a smile and a shrug of the shoulders, but he bristled every time his instructors used the name, for their intentions were not so benevolent; it seemed Fel'annár was not to be forgiven for wishing to be Silvan.

They were always together, as close as brothers and yet so different; Ramien, the smiling giant, Idernon the witty sage, and Fel'annár, The Silvan.

With the third week came twisting cramps, dehydration and general exhaustion, for all except those of The Company, for unlike the others, they had subjected themselves to such physical training since they were children, especially Fel'annár, whose body was a silent witness to his relentless efforts. Idernon had often mused that training was Fel'annár's way of channelling his frustration over his aunt's refusal to answer his questions, his anger at his father for abandoning him and at his mother for dying.

Fel'annár bent at the waist, his legs descending in a perfect, straight line until his booted feet touched the ground once more; slow and precise. Righting himself, he shook his arms and then rolled his shoulders, waiting for his head to clear for he had been standing upon his arms for long minutes.

Sitting beneath a beach tree he crossed his legs and closed his eyes, left hand drawing lazy circles over the tree roots. He smiled a little and allowed his mind to wander where it would – there was no rush – he was free for the rest of the evening and here, away from the noisy barracks, he could train in his own way, far from prying eyes. The others were writing in their journals, composing letters to their families or playing games and placing bets.

Four of the longest weeks of his life had, paradoxically, flown by and he could not say they had been bad save for his rocky start with the Silvans – *and* the Alpines, he added pointedly.

He had managed to stay out of trouble for the most part and that was due to his own conscious efforts to blend in with the rest. He trained with the recruits and then carried out his own routine in the evenings when he was left to his own devices – admittedly with the help of Ramien and Idernon. It would not do to be caught performing his own movements, his aerial work – they would not understand.

His own chubby face floated before his mind's eye – a child with round sparkling eyes – eyes that dreamed of being a captain and here he was, forty years on, his dream still before him, the parchment of his story yet untouched, laid out invitingly before him. All he had to do was write on it – fill the pages and this was where it began.

At first, he had wanted to be a warrior – fight for the people, for his aunt, for Ramien and Idernon but then he had seen himself atop a mighty destrier, armour glinting in the midday sun, under a blood-splattered banner of victory. He remembered shedding a tear - not for the pride and glory that would come of such a heroic feat, but for the forest, for the lady in the tree, the first face he had ever seen. He had cried for the beauty of his woodland home, for the love it inspired in the deepest part of himself.

He had chosen to be Silvan, for half-breeds can surely choose, he had decided. All he needed to do now was overcome his own anger, the anger that led him to rashness. But how to achieve that when provocation was never far away? His new name—*The Silvan*.

His fellow recruits used it light-heartedly and that was all well and good, but that same name from the lips of his tutors was a veiled insult, as if they threw him bait and waited for him to bite down on it - trip him up purposefully for what fool, they would think, would choose the Silvan side and reject the glory of the Alpine elves?

"May I?" came Idernon's soft voice at his side, making Fel'annár jump.

"Your tracking skills are progressing," he said defensively as he fidgeted and then settled once more.

"I should hope so; Faunon is good," said Idernon as he lowered himself to the ground beside his friend.

There was silence for a while, until Fel'annár understood his friend would not ask him to speak and yet expected him to all the same—there was no escaping Idernon at times like these and so, with a heavy sigh, he gave voice to his thoughts.

"They think me a fool, for choosing my home, my heritage, for being Silvan and not Alpine – they think I hate them." If he had expected Idernon to comment though, he was wrong and he chanced a sideways glance at his friend, who was staring blankly back at him. His heart sank to his boots as he began to understand his friends' silence.

"You *agree*? You think I hate them – the Alpines?" asked Fel'annár, his anger becoming more apparent as realization sunk in.

"Do you?" asked his friend evenly, his eyes searching, "do you hate them?"

"Of course I don't. Idernon, I am Silvan and when I tell them that, they laugh and call me Alpine. I am proud of my origins, Idernon—why should I be pleased they call me Alpine?"

"I believe you miss the point," said Idernon carefully. He had always known this moment would come, the moment in which his friend would need to understand himself, the part Idernon had always seen so clearly.

"And the point is?" asked Fel'annár, his jaw working rhythmically.

"You are not angry because they will not see you as *Silvan*, Fel'annár. You are angry because they call you *Alpine*. Because your *father*, was Alpine . . ."

Fel'annár stared at his friend in disbelief. "I don't *care*!" he hissed, eyes suddenly wide and furious as he scrambled to his feet. "Is it too much to ask that I be called what I *am* and not what I am *not*?" No sooner had he said it, than he closed his eyes in defeat.

"And so you see," said Idernon calmly as he too stood, "What is it that you are *not* Fel'annár? Are you *not* half Alpine? Are you *not* as much a part of that race as you are Silvan? Why should it make you angry, if only because your *father* was Alpine?"

Fel'annár stared back at his friend in disbelief and betrayal, his head shaking from side to side as if he would deny the words Idernon had just said but he could *not,* and for some strange reason it made him even more angry. Taking a deep breath, he hesitated for a moment, almost as if he would speak, and then he stalked away towards the training fields, his gait stiff and controlled, anger rolling off him like fog upon the high plains of Prairie.

Idernon knew not to stop him for his friend had an ugly temper when his family was discussed. The unexplained absence of a father and the ensuing years of frustration could not be remedied easily and Idernon damned Fel'annár's aunt for her silence, a silence neither he nor Ramien had ever understood.

Lieutenant Turion sat alone and watched, not for the first time as the lone recruit worked through the basic stances of close combat, unaware that he was being observed.

Fel'annár, that was his name, he recalled. Green Sun—and he could see why, for the boy's eyes were blazing pools of spring moss, akin to the venerated woodland plant he was named after, a plant that only bloomed once, a flower of such beauty that many gave as tokens of esteem; indeed Turion's sister had one—she said it brought love and he would always laugh.

Fascinated, the lieutenant watched as one leg slowly slipped back, far behind the other, both arms stretched out in front of him, elbows bent, palms down, the muscles in his chest and arms flexing and cording. He stayed that way for many moments until he pulled back one arm, turning the palm skywards.

There was an intensity about the boy, an eye for perfection – he was intimidating.

He was good—nay he was excellent. But of course, Turion had already known that, not because he had seen this on the training fields, but because he had been here before, in this glade, the recruit's hidden spot.

He had obviously been training like this for a long while and Turion, experienced immortal warrior that he was, knew the signs of a troubled heart when he saw them. If he compared today with what he had seen on previous days, there was a sharpness to the boy's movements; slow, simmering anger that was being channelled into his movements. He had seen far too many cases of young warriors who had lost fathers to battle, mothers to the raids of Sand Lords or Deviants—he knew the signs of conflict, could read them on their young, inexperienced faces as easily as he could a child's bedtime story. Understanding them was part of his job, that and to make them the best candidates for warrior hood as he could. Turion had once turned down the opportunity to become a captain, to enter the venerable Inner Circle of Ea Uaré because had he accepted, it would have taken him away from all this. It was a simple yet rewarding life, one he had craved for after years of fighting in the field. It was a reward, he thought, for all those years of gruelling service in the North.

The recruit changed position, his extended leg slowly returning to its original position, before stepping diagonally, knees bent, arms tracing invisible ribbons in the air. Hypnotic. He was almost dancing, feet placed carefully this way and that, hands reaching forwards, sideways, palms moving up and down – it was a strange technique for it seemed that he would offer something, only to take it back, or perhaps he was inviting the enemy to tackle him, only to ward him off. There was a language behind the moves that Turion could not quite grasp. He wondered if the boy had designed the technique himself for as far as he knew, there were no combat masters in Lan Taria. But perhaps he was mistaken.

Fel'annár, what is your secret, child? he asked himself, his head cocking slightly to one side as he watched the entrancing moves of a fifty-one year old elf that was too young to have been taught such things.

Lieutenant Lainon popped into his mind's eye then and Turion smirked. They had served together in the North many centuries ago and then had both taken a step back from active duty. Turion had come to these barracks, still far enough away from the city, while Lainon had moved closer, a mere day's ride away from Thargoden's court.

He still remembered his friend's find many years ago, an astonishing young warrior who was now serving in the North. Lainon had boasted for months and Turion had endured it good-naturedly. '*Well, my friend. Perhaps it will be me to brag about my own find,*' he smiled to himself. He would wait a little longer, wait for one more sign lest he make a fool of himself. Yet time was a luxury he did not have. Just this morning, Turion had received orders from the city. News from the northern fronts was dire and novices were desperately needed. He was therefore required to send along his more advanced candidates to the next step of their training, to earlier promotion and the front lines. It was a sad fact of life in Ea Uaré, one that was all too easily forgotten in these, apparently peaceful parts of the forest. But one only had to look a little further away and towards the main path into the city to see the comings and goings of warriors, supplies, and the arrival of Silvan refugees. It had been bad even back when he was serving there, but now they were being forced to send *novices* to the conflicted areas. He closed his eyes in a rare show of emotion and then opened them once more, focusing on Fel'annár as he glided over the ground.

He would speak to the boy, he decided, help him if he could, and then he would send him away—to *war*.

Chapter Three

A SONG ON THE AIR

"There are three races of immortals. The Silvans of the great forests, the Alpines of the mountains and the Pelagians of the sea. And then there are Ari'atór – Spirit Warriors. They may be born of wood, stone or water but always with one purpose; theirs is the noble onus of protecting Valley, assuring the safe-passage of the elves that seek the sacred light of the Source – pass through it to the other side and bliss. Some take to arms and travel to the Median Mountains, to fight humans that seek the light and are turned to evil but others take to the souls of the Silvan people, for their connection with Aria's creation equips them with a wisdom that guides the spirit on the path of happiness. They are the Spirit Herders, revered and feared as much as their brothers in arms."
The Silvan Chronicles, Book I - Annex II: On the nature of the Ari'atór. Marhené

"Come."

"You wanted to see me, Sir," asked Fel'annár, standing rigid before his commanding officer. He was nervous, thought Turion, concerned perhaps that he had done something wrong.

"Stand at ease, novice," he said as he approached the boy from his spot before the window. "Fel'annár of Lan Taria, yes?" he asked.

"Correct, Sir."

"You are young for a recruit," he said almost conversationally, waiting for the boy to answer him.

"Yes, Sir," he said simply.

"Your tutors speak highly of you. You are disciplined, quick to learn and respectful to your superiors." He paused here, his eyes inviting Fel'annár to speak yet again.

"Thank you, Sir."

It was not enough. The boy was not forthcoming at all and so Turion took a more direct approach.

"Why do you hide what you know?" he asked, his eyes narrowing as he moved closer to the recruit, watching as his face dropped and then paled visibly—the question now was, would he lie and deny what Turion knew was the truth? It was a pivotal moment.

"I—I mean no disrespect, Sir," he said a little too fast; he was defending himself, realized Turion.

"I asked why you do it, Fel'annár. Why not allow others to see how good you are in combat? Surely you wish to do well, impress your tutors?"

"I do, Sir—but, but that would mean . . ."

"Drawing attention to yourself," murmured Turion, answering his own question even as he spoke and his eyes strayed over the boy's extraordinary hair. Fel'annár's eyes were wide, like a child caught stealing hot buns and Turion took pity on him.

"You are not in trouble, Fel'annár. I wish only to understand you. As your commanding officer, it is my place to ensure the best recruits become available for combat training, to protect our forest, and to do that I must first understand them, help them become the best warriors they can be. Do you understand?"

"I do, Sir."

"Then tell me. Why do you not wish to draw attention to yourself? You are popular with the other Silvan lads—I have seen little antagonism save with a few of the Alpine novices," said Turion. "Why do you stand in the shadows?"

Fel'annár dropped his gaze to the floor. He was uncomfortable and Turion's suspicions were confirmed. This boy *was* conflicted, for some reason he needed to understand, *wanted* to understand, and a thought suddenly occurred to him.

"Is someone bothering you?" he asked, watching closely for the reaction his words might provoke. "If they are, you seem more than capable of defending yourself—why would you hide yourself away for that reason?"

"I have no problems with my colleagues, Sir, for the most part. I am simply uncomfortable with attention."

"Most people crave it," commented Turion. "Or is it that you have had too much, of the *negative* kind?" he tried. His efforts were rewarded, for there was no mistaking the expression on Fel'annár's face.

"It must not have been easy—your childhood."

"No, Sir," said the recruit quietly; but he would say no more and Turion frowned. His hurts ran deep, he realized, and perhaps it was not the time to push him any further. After all, he had as much information as he needed to make his decision.

"Fel'annár. I am sending you to the city barracks for novice training. You leave in two days."

The downcast face transformed in an instant, the dark clouds of his troubled memories floating away, making way for a brilliant smile, face shining almost as brightly as his eyes; such passion in one so young, mused Turion and a shiver ran down his spine and it seemed a thousand ants crawled over his scalp. What drove a boy of this age to achieve what he already had and then wish to hide it all away? He would ask one more question, and then he would entrust the boy to Lainon at the city barracks.

"What is it that you want, Fel'annár?"

The recruit's eyes anchored calmly on Turion. There was no self-doubt, no shame, no hesitation. Instead, there was conviction, surety and single-minded determination.

"I want to be a captain."

The following day, the Silvan recruits enjoyed their first free evening in a while and they celebrated the day's surprising news in pure Silvan fashion. The Company was leaving for the city and novice training. There were questions in the other recruits' eyes, jealousy even. They had seen the three friends train and although good, they had not seemed inordinately so, except perhaps Fel'annár when they had been shown the basics of hand-to-hand. It was the news of the spiralling conflict in the North that helped them to understand; the army needed all the hands they could get and so, they thought, it would not be long before they, too, were called upon to move to the next step of their training.

Yet to the recruits, war was something they had not yet seen, could not really feel. They were still too far away from the Fortress and off the City Road. It was a distant certainty, a reality they had only just begun to prepare for, and nervous anticipation hung in the air.

For the moment though, they lay sprawled on the lawn before their dormitory. Bottles of wine both empty and full lay around them in varying states of disarray. Carodel, a young Silvan recruit with an artistic flare strummed a delicate melody on his lyre, a tune that did not match the bawdy lyrics at all, while Ramien danced a jig, miraculously managing not to rip his breeches in the process. Idernon too, danced a reel with a fellow recruit of dubious skill while the rest sat drinking and laughing.

Now, well into their cups, they swayed this way and that, even though they sat. Carodel leant forward with only a slight loss of balance and then peered into Fel'annár's eyes, as if he looked into a mirror and sat mesmerized at what he saw.

"Are you *really* Silvan?" he slurred.

Here we go again, thought Fel'annár, but surprisingly, this time there was no irritation, something only partially explainable by the copious amount of imbibed wine—indeed it was his recent argument with Idernon and then Turion's words just yesterday that had somehow bolstered his spirit, forcing him to see things from a different perspective. Why should he be ashamed of being half Alpine just because of his father? Why should he hide himself away? If he was to be picked on, then he would fight back and try not to get into trouble for it – but of course, that was the tricky part.

"I am—*half* Silvan" he said with a soft smile. "And before you ask, my mother died when I was too young to remember her. My aunt brought me up as her own son and I never knew my father."

Ramien and Idernon shared a stunned look before turning back to Fel'annár with wide eyes and slack jaws.

"Did your aunt not tell you of him then?" they asked.

"Nay, she never would. I would ask her incessantly whether he was Alpine, yet I could never get her to tell me a single thing about him. It made her nervous and she would change the subject. I have always known there is some family scandal involved, that he must have done something— *terrible*—to be banished thusly by the Silvans of my village; I think perhaps he was an outlaw," he mused as if to himself. "Either that or I was just not meant to be—an illicit child if you will—how would *I* know," he finished with a shrug, unaware of the way Idernon and Ramien watched him.

"Or," said Carodel, waving his hands in the air as if he were retelling a heroic ode from the Elder Chronicles. "Or maybe he was a mighty hero whose death is still too painful to be spoken of – or, or, a God who fell in love with the prettiest Silvan maiden of them all – no one ever speaks about the half-breed love children of the Gods!" exclaimed the tipsy Silvan. Ramien and Idernon closed their eyes and tensed their shoulders, anticipating the scalding reply that Fel'annár would surely provide. But only silence met Carodel's flamboyant words. Wine was poured and their goblets clanked and still, Fel'annár would not speak. Carodel's drunken imagination had grabbed Fel'annár by the shoulders and whipped him around – to a different perspective and he sat, shocked at the implications.

Someone filled his goblet and he took it to his mouth. He suddenly felt ashamed – at himself and his stupidity. He had led himself down the road of bitterness, had assumed the people's silence to be a consequence of his father's ill-doing. But Carodel's words, however unbelievable and fantastic they had been, opened up the possibility that their silence was not a consequence of his evilness, but a possibility that he had been good, and that he was missed – that he was not a monster that had abandoned his son.

Fel'annár shook his head and drank again. "Half-breed love child?" he asked with a smirk.

"*Ahh!* they all cheered and with a toast and a thunk of wooden cups, they drank once more, only a small part of the liquid making its way into their mouths. Idernon simply smiled but Ramien beamed and his teeth could not be contained.

"Hwind'atór," said Ramien as he sat forward clumsily "The Whirling Warrior. You are—destined for *great things*! he slurred. Gollo— Gollororollon—says it is so," he finished with difficulty, before slurping on his wine once more and sloshing it over his breeches.

"Golloron," corrected Idernon, just as inebriated as Ramien, even though he seemed completely in control of himself and his tongue.

"Golloron," he explained to the others, "is the Spirit Herder of our village. He says," he said pensively, creating an atmosphere of mystery and intrigue amongst the recruits and sending them into avid silence. "He says that Hwindo here has a great future before him. He has cast runes and has seen great battles, amongst other things," he trailed off, his voice now full of awe as he drank from his cup.

"What else? what else did he see?" asked one young Silvan, his eyes wide and sparkling in anticipation of the tale, for in the Silvan culture, Spirit Herders such as Golloron were feared and revered, for they were Ari'atór, Spirit Warriors, albeit their weapons were not of steel but of the soul.

"He has predicted that Fel'annár will be a great leader—perhaps even a *captain*," said Idernon with a proud smile, watching as the other youths nodded in awe.

"Well, there are few enough Silvan captains—it will be a welcome thing—we will all want to serve with you, Hwindo!" shouted Carodel.

"What a fine thing that would be," said Fel'annár, his eyes misty and far away, as if he could see himself upon a magnificent warhorse, leading his warriors through the troubled forests, just as he had dreamed of together with his friends since for as long as he could remember. "*Captain*," he said with deep respect.

Ramien slapped Fel'annár a little too hard upon the back, sending him reeling forwards and the Silvan recruits laughed hard, the solemn silence broken.

"To Captain Hwind'atór!" they shouted and then drank, before Carodel raised his cup once more.

"To *The Company!*" he shouted, and the merry little crowd exploded into cheering and laughter that carried on the wind and echoed throughout the glade until it reached the ears of their commanding officer.

Turion listened, and upon his face, a smug, self-satisfied smile spread wide enough to show his white teeth. He had a letter to write, and coin to collect from Lainon for *this* bet he would surely win.

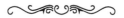

The Company left the following day amidst heart-felt goodbyes to Carodel and the others who sent them off with a cheer and a smile upon their youthful faces, in spite of their thumping heads and queasy stomachs. The Company would not be forgotten quickly, and from this first contact with the outside world, the lads from Lan Taria had made stronger ties than they could ever have imagined at the time.

As for Turion, he had handed Fel'annár a sealed letter which he was to deliver personally to Lieutenant Lainon, their next commanding officer, only this time they would be in the city barracks, close to the heart of Thargodén's realm. "You take it, Fel'annár. Your, *peculiar* looks make you the best choice," he had said dismissively. Fel'annár had frowned but Turion said no more, sending them off with a wave of his hand, as if he were happy to be rid of them.

Turion knew he would see the boy again, indeed he would make a point of following up on his find for he was sure there was the promise of command in this one.

That had been yesterday and now, as they rode through the outer settlements, ever closer to the city centre, they spoke excitedly to each other, their hearts hammering in their chests and their eyes bright with the thrill of adventure once more, only this time they did not walk blindly into the unknown and the thought was refreshing.

"So this, Lieutenant Lainon is to be our commanding officer," said Ramien quite unnecessarily as his eyes danced over the buildings they passed and the ever-increasing number of people that walked this way and that.

"His name is not Alpine, I believe," pondered Idernon, "yet neither have I heard it in our lands, and he would not be Pelagic, for they do not easily dwell where the sea cannot be admired."

"Ari'atór, then?" asked Fel'annár, the whites of his eyes momentarily visible.

The three friends shared a worried glance, for the Ari'atór were feared, even amongst the immortals, in part because there were so few of them, but also because their aspect was so very different from the Alpine, Pelagic or Silvan races, and if this was indeed an Ari'atór, why had he not taken the vow and left to protect Valley, as would be expected of him as a warrior?

"If we are right, I wonder why this Lainon is here, a lieutenant in the training barracks and not with his brothers in Valley, or serving as Spirit Herder," mused the Wise Elf.

"Aren't we rushing ahead of ourselves?" asked Ramien. "He may not be Ari'atór, and even if he is, maybe he was injured and is no longer fit for active duty in Valley."

"Perhaps it is as simple as that," admitted Fel'annár with a nod; "Ramien, ever the practical one, the voice of common sense," he added with a smile as they pressed on, all thoughts of the feared yet revered Ari'atór moving to the back of their minds for the moment—not forgotten, but merely postponed for truth be told, there was just too much to admire for eyes as young and inexperienced as theirs. There were buildings on the ground and talans in the trees. There were paths everywhere and people – so many people and so many colours.

"Well, Ari'atór or no, one thing is certain. We are now in the lands of the High-born—rich Silvan lords and merchants, Alpine councillors and legislators, wise healers and physics, famous musicians . . ." said Idernon with a flourish of his hand, before he was cut off by Fel'annár.

"And the most tantalizing lads and lasses!!" he said merrily.

"And that yes," smirked Idernon, casting a mischievous glance at Ramien and then Fel'annár.

"And weapons training!" added the Wall of Stone. "At last!"

"Aye. At last," echoed Fel'annár, for he above all of them, yearned to put himself to the test. He had only ever measured himself with his two childhood friends, and then those of his village. On that scale, he had nothing to learn, but here, in the city, where all the immortal races resided, where Lords and Ladies, lieutenants and even captains trained before riding out to defend the northern reaches, this was an entirely different matter. Here he would learn, he was sure of it.

The three friends soon fell into contemplative silence, for there was so much to think about, and the more they thought, the more butterflies danced and fluttered in their empty stomachs.

It was Fel'annár who broke that silence though, his gasp long and quite involuntarily, for before their eyes, not too distant on the horizon, stood Thargoden's city fortress, his seat of power.

Mighty pillars and spires of stone rose to the very heavens, all nestled together, harmonious despite their stark differences. Some towered over others, long and pointed while others were curved and irregular. There were colourful domes that gleamed in the early afternoon sun, and covered platforms seemed to hang precariously off the side of the rock into which the structure was built. It was strangely alien amidst this forest landscape, a massive, sprawling structure that stood arrogantly, defiantly amidst the trees of Ea Uaré.

Fel'annár suddenly wanted to be closer, to see the detail he knew stood upon the balustrades, that wound around the spires and decorated the mighty halls of carved rock and worked wood. He had seen it all in his books, the ornate gardens and the clever fountains. Oh, but the smells and the colours, the hustle and bustle of city life—lords and ladies decked in finery, warriors clad in skilfully-wrought armour. It was a strange thing though, he mused, for the architecture was artificial, so unlike the Silvan abodes of the Deep Forest that strove to emulate nature, sought to mimic its surroundings. This structure seemed designed to achieve the opposite yet even so, the trees embraced it, enclosed it in their protective boughs—so like the Alpines themselves, mused Fel'annár—welcome visitors. But what did the Alpines give back? he asked himself. What did they do to give thanks for their acceptance? The answer was not clear to Fel'annár at all.

He heaved a deep breath and his horse moved beneath him, as if impatient to be gone. He yearned to see it all but that was not meant to be, not yet. It was a cruel temptation that mocked them from afar; recruits did not reside there, he thought, not Sivan ones at least.

They sat for a while longer and marvelled at the extraordinary sight of Thargodén's city fortress, at a loss for words until common sense dictated they move, for they were surely close to their destination and it would not do to be caught in the dark.

Soon they were forced to ride single file to make way for the traffic; people, horses, carts loaded with merchandise, bound for the city and the king's table no doubt.

A distant shout demanded the road be cleared and the three recruits pulled over, watching in wide-eyed alarm as ten warriors thundered by in single file, bodies hunched over the reins, legs bouncing off the sides of their heaving steeds. They were dusty and bloodied, and two horses bore more than one rider.

"Wounded, from the North-east I would say," murmured Idernon, his sharp eyes finding the insignia on their leader's cloak as it billowed behind him.

Soon the warriors were gone, bound for the fortress, leaving in their wake a cloud of grey dust that lingered silently over the path as if it mourned their passing. Slowly, the people took to the road once more, quiet and sad and the din that had prevailed before was now muted and sparing.

It was the first time they had seen real evidence of the conflict and Fel'annár sat in quiet contemplation. There was a sad melody in his head, and a weight in his heart for these were a brave people, colourful and different, harmonious here amongst the workers and foresters and his head turned back to the distant fortress, knowing that it was different there, that many of these simple people would be frowned upon, scorned and mocked should they walk the halls of that place of power. How cruel, he thought, how utterly senseless. The passing of the North-eastern patrol had been over in seconds, but the impression it left on Fel'annár would linger always, for they had, quite unwittingly, shown Fel'annár exactly why he wanted to be a warrior, a captain. It was not about fighting Sand Lords and Deviants, it was about these people, their joy, their wish to live in this colourful harmony.

Following Turion's instructions, they turned at the market square, barely resisting the urge to dismount and run wild amidst the stalls of rich cloth, baubles and hot snacks. So many things to buy and no money to do so—thought Fel'annár, laughing at himself and his puerile ways but he could not help it, and even as they rounded the corner, his head was the last thing to turn to the fore.

"Bumpkin," said Idernon with a sly smile even though his own eyes twinkled in excitement, for he had spotted a book stall, where two elves sat and debated, or so it seemed to the Wise Warrior. He would return there, should he be given leave.

At the end of this path, they forked left and finally, their horses stood before the large, grey stone building that would be their home for who knew how many months. Just like their previous destination, it was bare and solemn in comparison to the distant fortress city and the teeming market they had just left. Yet it was still impressive in its enormity, the sheer magnitude of it stealing their breath for a moment.

Fel'annár glanced sideways, first at Idernon and then at Ramien, and with a steadying nod, they spurred their horses on until the thud of hooves became a clatter and they entered the open gates, their eyes following the high stone arch that floated above them until they were past it.

The courtyard was massive, closed in on two sides by buildings of varying shapes and sizes. Some were three or four floors high, while others were ground floor studies, for the commanders perhaps. There was a healing hall off to one side, something Fel'annár could immediately tell, for the smell that emanated from that place reminded him of scraped knees back home. He wondered what the other, longer buildings were for and he thought perhaps they would be store rooms—supplies for outgoing patrols or even armouries.

Warriors strode this way and that in varying states of urgency for some laughed and others hurried along with papers in their hands. Ramien spotted a lieutenant in a very fine uniform, and elbowed his friends, watching in awe as the commander's shiny boots tapped over the cobbles. Ramien wondered with a dreamy smile if he would ever have boots as fine as those, and then thought perhaps his feet would be too big.

Beyond the courtyard, the training fields sprawled endlessly into the horizon. There were hardly any trees at all and Fel'annár repressed a shudder for it made him feel cold. Warriors, novices and perhaps even recruits like themselves were sparring, their blades clanking and scraping together, while others moved back and forth in perfect formation, the fierce shouts of instructors and weapons tutors piercing the air, shriller than any woodland peregrine.

This was what they had come for. Their dream would finally come true; all they had to do was keep their mouths shut, learn as much as they could, and exert themselves to the best of their ability. They were infused with a sense of purpose and their brows set in determination.

Uniformed stable hands appeared, gesturing for them to dismount somewhat rudely, thought Fel'annár and so they slid off and whispered a quick goodbye to their mounts before looking around one more time in wonder, their excitement equal to their growing nervousness. They looked at each other and grinned in spite of it though, and then walked towards a large doorway, assuming that was where they would find this Lieutenant Lainon.

It was an imposing entrance where armoured elves in ceremonial uniforms stood at either side, their spears reaching almost to the top of the arched doorway. Ramien wanted to stop and admire the workmanship, but Idernon yanked on his cloak and whispered in his ear, "Don't you dare . . ."

No sooner had they stepped inside than a guard approached them, his hand held out towards them, albeit his eyes were riveted to the floor, as if his mind were elsewhere.

"Orders," he snapped.

"Only that we report to Lieutenant Lainon," said Fel'annár.

The guard looked up, but instead of leading them away, he froze where he stood, his eyes widening and his ears moving to the back of his head, momentarily smoothing out the lines upon his forehead. Righting himself immediately, he straightened his tunic as if he were embarrassed. "Yes, well, follow me," was all he said curtly.

Ramien smiled mischievously but not so Idernon, for he had not missed the guard's strange reaction. "It must be your good looks," he whispered to Fel'annár, who returned the smile with a cheeky wink of his eye.

The guard rapped upon a massive wooden door, then stepped aside as the two panes swivelled inwards and orange candle light spilled out, lending just a little warmth to the cold grey walls. There, at the back of the room, sat an elf at a table so large it made him look strangely small.

"Come."

The three friends walked forward, slower now, until they stood before the impressive desk. They did not quite manage to stifle their gasp as the elf looked up for the first time and revealed what they could only later describe as '*remarkable*' features.

His copper skin was the colour of autumn leaves and his eyes were oddly slanted, bright blue irises shining with power and keen intellect. He *was* an Ari'atór, Spirit Warrior—their conjectures had been correct.

Lainon too, stared back at them, his eyes moving up and then down, until they fixed upon Fel'annár's strange green eyes and did not move at all for a long while. It soon became embarrassing and Fel'annár shifted his weight.

"You have something for me," said Lainon simply, his voice too deep for such an exotic face, mused Idernon.

"Yes, Sir," said Fel'annár as he fumbled inside his tunic and removed the parchment Turion had given him. Holding out his hand, Lainon took it and unfolded it, his eyes latching onto the familiar script of his friend.

Lieutenant Lainon,

Before you stand three new recruits—and yes, they are Silvan, even the pale one.

I trust you will see fit to include them in your training programme. We have taught them all we can, but their level of skill is considerably beyond that of their fellow recruits, who will be joining you later.

I will see you soon, my friend. You found Farón, but I have found 'The Silvan.' Let it be known.

Lainon's mask of indifference slipped for a brief instant and his surprise danced across his strange face. It was quickly veiled though and the lieutenant folded the parchment, shoving it into his tunic. Indeed, he had found Farón, his best recruit so far who was now a novice warrior serving in the North-east. He was destined for leadership and Lainon had boasted his find to his friend. From then on it had been an ongoing game and Lainon was now intrigued by what Turion suggested was his own find. Yet what truly bewildered him was that his friend had not mentioned anything else—as if he had no ken at all of what Lainon was only now beginning to accept and a rush of freezing, icy shards travelled the entire length of his spine.

Was it possible that Turion had not realised? that he had not seen the resemblance? Folding the parchment, he stood, heart hammering in his chest—his face utterly straight and controlled.

"Come with me," he said flatly as he walked towards the door, his gait powerful, feline almost.

They passed recruits and novice warriors as they walked down multiple corridors, past mess rooms and leisure halls, bathing rooms and all manner of offices, and even an armoury the three friends yearned to investigate. But they could not stop for Lainon did not and so they matched his brisk pace until finally, they came to the sleeping quarters.

"The rest of the day is for yourselves. Wander freely. Your roommates will help you settle in. I will see you tomorrow when your training will begin," he finished, his eyes resting once more on Fel'annár before striding from the room, leaving them alone and bewildered.

"For the love of Aría," exclaimed Ramien with a sonorous rush of air. Idernon heaved a mighty breath of relief before sitting heavily on what seemed to be a free bed, and as for Fel'annár, he simply stood there, his mind elsewhere, and it took a shove from Ramien to bring him back.

"Funny eyes . . ." murmured Fel'annár.

"Well *you* can talk!" exclaimed Ramien, "but yes, he *is* strange and I for one will not be crossing him," he resolved as he moved towards an adjacent bed, claiming it as his own, but Fel'annár had not moved. He simply turned his head to his friends, eyes far away.

"The way he looked at me," he murmured.

"Well, maybe he *fancies* you," said Idernon as he inspected the bedding, oblivious to the strange turn his friend had taken.

"No, no it's not that. It was—it was as if—as if he *recognised* me."

Idernon and Ramien shared a worried look but Fel'annár turned away, his mind recalling Carodel's words. '*...maybe he was a mighty hero whose death is still too painful to be spoken of ...*'

No, his father was dead – he would think no more on it.

"Forward, forward, side, arc, down! *Again!* Forward, forward, side, arc, down, *Again!*"

They had been at it for hours and Fel'annár had no doubts as to why they wore only breeches and boots, for sweat dripped from his body as it had never done before. His throat was parched and his long hair stuck to his neck, albeit he had braided it just like the rest of his recruits, or so he thought; but then Fel'annár's hair had never obeyed the laws of nature.

Idernon and Ramien were in a similar state but the three were nowhere near their limits. Many recruits had faltered or even stopped, receiving the most spectacularly embarrassing tongue-lashings, both in the Alpine and Silvan dialects and all the while, the unnerving Ari'atór, Lieutenant Lainon, watched from afar, his face inscrutable and his gaze heavy.

"Stop. Five minutes for water!" shouted the instructor.

The recruits groaned and threw themselves to the floor while others ran to the barrels and scooped water into wooden bowls, drinking greedily.

Ramien turned to his friends and grinned, before jumping twice and showing them he was nowhere near exhausted. Idernon and Fel'annár laughed merrily as they drank sparsely, throwing the rest of the water over their heads.

One unfortunate recruit had drunk too much too fast, and was now paying the price as he vomited his water miserably. Fel'annár placed a hand on his heaving shoulder, but said not a word. It was enough though, to draw attention to himself and he soon heard his name called—his *new* name.

"*Silvan!*"

Slowly, Fel'annár turned to see a smirking recruit with two others at his shoulders.

They stared impertinently, the spark of spiteful challenge in their clear, grey eyes; *Alpine* eyes.

Within seconds, Idernon and Ramien were behind their friend, staring just as intently, searching the newcomers' faces for any signs of ill-intent— and finding it.

From afar, their tutor, realising there was a potentially dangerous situation unfolding, made to break them up, but Lainon's strong hand stopped him.

"Wait," he ordered simply.

"They may fight," said the flummoxed tutor but Lainon interrupted him.

"I take responsibility, just wait."

"What is it you want, *Alpine*?" asked Fel'annár.

"Oh, just a question, nothing of import. Tell us—why an Alpine wishes to be *Silvan,*"snorted the recruit with a wave of his arm. "Are you *ashamed*?" that annoying smile still plastered falsely on his pale, angular face.

"I *am* Silvan," came Fel'annár's measured response. The two Alpines at the recruit's shoulder shuffled nervously.

"Oh yes, yes, we can see that—look here. Long, long hair of pale silver wheat, skin whiter than white — you are no *Silvan,*" he sneered, "well save for those queer eyes."

Fel'annár bristled, for his eyes were those of his mother. "Think what you wish, Alpine. It makes no difference to me," he ground out, hands balled into fists at his sides despite his attempts at remaining calm.

"Oh, but it *should* — see we think you are a *half*-breed," smiled the recruit, his eyes searching for proof that he had, perhaps, riled the youth.

"And your point is?" asked Fel'annár, battling to keep his voice calm and his fists from striking out.

The smirk vanished and the recruit walked towards The Silvan until he was almost nose to nose, for his tactic had failed and in its place, frustration and anger came to the fore.

"You are arrogant; can you not just answer a simple *question*, boy?"

"And what is the *question*?" asked Fel'annár, his eyes never faltering from those of his antagonist.

"Pray I do not need to fight alongside you on the battle field, *half-breed,*" spat the elf, his face now twisted and wild.

"You may have to, one day," answered Fel'annár, his antagonist's comment somehow ameliorating his aggressive emotions rather than exacerbating them.

The recruit glared at Fel'annár, his eyes gleaming with irrational hatred but the green eyes that stared back at him were feral and unnerving; it was not long before the recruit turned away, the intensity of it too much.

"Pray I do not, for you will find no help from me," he sneered.

Fel'annár simply smiled through his victory, watching as the Alpine and his group of friends walked away, his own fists slowly loosening.

"Well done," murmured Idernon, as Ramien's massive hand slapped him on the shoulder.

On the side-lines, the tutor turned to Lainon then, a question ready to burst in his wide eyes.

"That is Turion's find. They call him The *Silvan*," said Lainon.

"Well, for one so young and—*green*—he holds himself well," said the tutor, still watching as Fel'annár sat with his friends.

"Yes, he shows potential. He shows the promise of *command*," mused Lainon.

"Well, we could do with more *Silvan* officers," said the tutor, turning to leave.

"One more thing," added Lainon, "watch and report—to me only. There is a song upon the air," he said softly, his eyes losing focus as he cast them sideways and towards the forest. "It comes from the trees," added the Ari'atór, almost to himself now. The tutor watched him for a moment, used as he was to his colleague's strange ways, before nodding and striding back to the group. Far be it from he to distrust the word of an Ari'atór.

Lainon looked back at the group of recruits but his eyes remained distant as he listened once more.

'*Tis a song of welcome . . . a proclamation.*'

If they had thought their training harsh at the village barracks, this was plain torture to some yet still, it did not push Fel'annár to his limits. More physical training, endurance training, climbing and rescue protocol was honing his body so that he was fitter than he ever had been. In the little free time he had, he concentrated his efforts on centring his mind, disciplining himself to focus on the task at hand and not be side-tracked with other thoughts and emotions. It was a technique he had first read about in the War Tomes, an ancient Alpine treatise on warrior training. He had practised it every day since then, even if he was not going to train. It had become a part of his life, a part of his training routine he had not been able to keep up these past weeks, for should he be seen, the questions would come and so he came here, secretly, with the help of Idernon and Ramien.

Cross-legged upon the grass, he closed his eyes and emptied his mind. Straightening, he stretched his back and rolled his shoulders, breathing deeply. Standing slowly, he doubled backwards until he stood upon his hands, his arms straight, legs skywards. Concentrating, he stilled the tremble of muscles until he was completely still. This was how the three Alpine recruits found him.

"What is he *doing*?" asked one with a malevolent sneer.

"Perhaps he wishes to join the king's *buffoons*," chuckled another.

"You would do well, *freak*," said another, watching their victim expectantly.

Fel'annár bent from the abdomen, his legs straight until he stood elegantly, his plaited hair falling back into place. His face was rigid and tight, his mind slowly returning to his present predicament.

Circling now, one elf reached out and flicked the end of a side plait. "You are pretty, there is no denying," he murmured as the others jeered. "Lovely hair and striking eyes, perhaps it is not the king's buffoons you should join but his *courtesans*—they do say our lord enjoys a bit of this and a bit of that . . ."

Fel'annár felt his anger surging from the depths and he calmed himself for his mind threatened to rebel against his own will and beat the fools to a pulp. Instead he remained silent and watched, mind analysing his own position, his attackers' positions, their clothing . . .

"You do not defend yourself, *Silvan*. Have you no words for me today, no witty rebuke?"

"Witty? Nay—only that you will have no satisfaction from me—I will not *hit* you, Borhen," he said but there was a gleam in his eye.

"Oh—am I not good enough for you then? You think you are better than a pure-blooded Alpine warrior?" said the blond recruit.

"You are a warrior, yes, and—I will not strike you, whatever your race," said Fel'annár, his eyes fixed upon Borhen, no emotion apparent on his face at all, only a subtle warning that the Alpine failed to see.

"You sound like Lainon," said his antagonist with a curl of his lip.

"*Lieutenant* Lainon—have you no respect?" growled Fel'annár, his voice dangerously low, his control slipping.

"*Respect*?" spat Borhen. "Here's the thing. We don't like you, *boy*. You are a freak, a bastard, a half-breed," he mocked, his mouth so close to Fel'annár's ear that his silvery braids danced with the insults. The words brought memories long buried, repressed but still there.

Across the field, Ramien tapped Idernon on the shoulder and nodded to the far edge of the green, close to the tree line, drawing the attention of the other recruits behind them. Sharing a panicked look, they ran off, even though they knew that by the time they arrived it would be too late.

"You are strong," said one Alpine as he slapped Fel'annár's taut abdomen a little too hard. The leader nodded at his friend who moved to stand behind their victim, but to Borhen's utter surprise, instead of enjoying a pained cry from The Silvan as his friend punched him in the kidney, a shock of silvery hair flitted past his face, only to be replaced by his friend's panicked eyes as he lurched forward to the ground, falling clumsily with a sharp cry.

After a moment of confusion, another Alpine took Fel'annár from behind in a neck lock, but before he could pull backwards and throttle him, the Silvan had grabbed his attacker's free wrist and moved back out from under his attacker's arm, twisting the limb behind the Alpine's back and forcing him to the floor lest Fel'annár dislocate his shoulder.

Borhen was livid. He had expected the slap of skin against skin, a split lip or a broken nose, grunts and gasps of pain and yet there he was, the only one standing before the strange elf. He would not stand for it and so he reached back and swung his fist straight at Fel'annár's emotionless face. But it never made contact and he felt his wrist squeezed painfully. Before he could reason what had happened, his entire body followed his fist and he was on his back, looking up at a fierce warrior with wild hair and dangerous eyes who pinned him to the floor with nothing but a warning glare.

Borhen complied with the silent command.

Slowly, the three Alpine recruits regained their feet, staring all the while at Fel'annár in something akin to horror, not even aware that a crowd had gathered behind them. One cradled his wrist while the other rubbed his shoulder. Borhen though, simply sneered, touching his forehead and checking his fingers for blood.

"You see," said Fel'annár lightly as he approached Borhen until his face was but inches from the now completely serious Alpine. "I told you I would not *hit* you," he said with a subtle smile, and then stalked past the seething elf, nodding at Idernon and Ramien.

As they walked back to the barracks, Fel'annár said nothing at all; the recruits though, had exploded into excited chatter, gesticulating wildly as they spoke of wrist controls and how to unbalance your opponent. The news would not take long to travel back to their commanding officer and Fel'annár would surely be in trouble, yet the days passed by and still, nothing had happened. Fel'annár had not been summoned to Lainon's office and the recruits had simply followed their routines, albeit the atmosphere in the barracks had changed. Before, there had been hard work and camaraderie, but now, there was excitement, especially amongst the Silvan recruits.

Fel'annár had inspired them and Idernon smiled, for he had, in some small way, become a leader—the leader he had always known resided inherently in his dear friend, latent—until now.

Chapter Four

PRINCES OF EA UARÉ

"…and so, Or'Talán of Tar'eastór rode to Ea Uaré and was proclaimed
King, for the Silvans were accepting of him and he in turn, loved them
well. He ruled and died upon the dunes of Calrazia and his son, Thar-
godén, took the throne. Brave and strong, our new king took a noble
Alpine lady as his queen. She gave him two sons and a daughter before
departing for Valley: Rinon, Handir and Maeneth.
Lord Band'orán, brother of King Or'Talán never seconded the rightful
king, his own nephew, and began a new movement, one that sought to
bring Alpine splendour to the forests of Ea Uaré.
It was then that our land became divided …"
The Silvan Chronicles, Book III. Marhené

Far away, towards the North and the troubled lands, a blood-curdling
scream turned into a hoarse wail, waves of agony piercing the very souls of
those that tried to help the warrior. But there *was* no hope; this, Rinon knew,
even though he was not a healer.

And so, he sat there, looking down upon his life-long friend, his own
uniform torn and stained. Reaching out with a bloodied hand, he clamped
down desperately against the shoulder of the writhing warrior.

Let it stop, he begged to himself, *let the suffering stop – it is enough – it is*
too much.

But Rinon knew that it wouldn't, as did the healers who watched on
helplessly – another commander, another broken family. The warrior's breath
shuddered to a halt as another wave of excruciating torment wracked his
frame and it seemed all the muscles in his body tensed involuntarily, lifting

him for a moment from the soiled bedding. Spittle flew from his lips, as another howl of brutal agony swelled in his chest and then split the heavy silence once more. Tears welled in Rinon's eyes as his hand pressed bruisingly against Har'Sidón's shoulder, eyes unwilling to register the mangled flesh and shattered bone, the ruined remains of his legs.

How could it be, he asked – that one so skilled and powerful – could be reduced to *this*? He had laughed and cried with this warrior. Had witnessed his troth, saved his life, drank cups with him. How could it be that he lay here now, upon the borders of Valley, screaming and writhing – incomprehensible agony his last, bitter taste of life.

Let it stop – please- let it stop. It is enough…

Another cry escaped the broken captain but this time it was weaker, his voice failing, mouth frozen wide, eyes open yet unseeing – glazed, absent.

Healers were atop him, around him, pressing him down but Rinon's eyes were anchored on his friend's face, watching as Har'Sidón's head lulled to the side, the muscle beneath Rinon's hand softening.

"Har…" his own voice broke, eyes welling in crushing pity and sudden panic for his friend was slipping away in the wake of ill-deserved suffering.

A hand shot up and latched onto Rinon's collar, pulling him down with surprising strength until Rinon's face was inches from that of his dying friend. But no words passed Har'Sidón's lips for his breath had caught in his throat and would not be loosed, eyes bulging in sudden surety and utter terror.

Rinon watched through a watery haze as the immortal light in his friend's eyes slowly petered out, leaving them dull and blind, eyelids drooping half-shut as his chest shuddered, and then was still.

The healers froze, hands hovering over cooling flesh, watching as Rinon's head fell heedlessly against the smooth forehead of Captain Har'Sidón, commander of the Northern patrol of Ea Uaré.

Rinon slowly moved back until he looked down on his friend's lifeless form and even though he cried, his jaw clenched and his eyes sharpened until they were piercing shards of ice.

"We will leave you for a moment, my Prince," came the soft voice of a healer, his strong hand squeezing Rinon's shoulder in sympathy before moving away.

Rinon's mind showed him his friend's bride, his children, eyes begging for answers yet how could he tell them of the horrific death their father had suffered? How could he tell them that he had been caught and mauled by

Deviants, that they had bitten into him like starved bears – not for food but for the sheer, perverse pleasure of wrenching shrieks of agony from his friend. He would not and he suddenly wanted to laugh bitterly – what was the expression? Ah yes – '*he died honourably in battle.*' He *had* died honourably, but questions would surely ensue. They would want to feel the balm of reassurance that he had not suffered, and Rinon would spare them from the cruelty of truth.

Rinon's eyes slipped to the right at the rustle of rich fabrics at his side.

"Rinon," a flat yet commanding voice.

"My King," replied Rinon, Crown Prince of Ea Uaré, eyes lingering on the ruined form of Har'Sidón before turning to his father, who was already staring back at him, expression unreadable but his eyes – his eyes were those of Har'Sidón – dull and blank, unfocussed even though he lived; dead eyes, set in the face of one whose will had faded many years ago, an elf that had shut himself away from the world, even from his own children. Was it for shame? Was it the loss of his queen? His own, inherent weakness or the battle he was slowly losing with Band'orán who was ever driving a wedge between the different races of Ea Uaré.

Rinon despised him for even then, while bitter tears lingered in his own eyes, his father's eyes were as dry as the northern sands. Unfeeling, frigid, lifeless.

Rinon schooled his features with little success, nostrils flaring and eyes glinting. With a curt nod, he turned on his heels and left amidst the saddened stares of the healers, and Thargodén was left alone before the evidence.

His land was at war.

He was a failing king.

Prince Handir sat in the family chambers of the royal suite, high above the bustling courtyard below. A book on Deep Silvan lore sat open on his lap and on any other day, it would have held his interest; but today, his mind found itself elsewhere and so he closed the heavy tome, a little too hard, sending a plume of dust into the afternoon rays of sun. It was a testimony to how little this book had been read in recent times, he mused sadly.

He sighed, his warm, blue eyes turning to the window and focusing on the activity below.

He saw warriors and craftsmen, tutors and healers, statesmen, lords and ladies, all decked in rich finery as they glided over the courtyard—tiny from this height yet close enough to see their predominantly blond hair and pale skin. But Handir's eyes did not focus on any of them, for today his thoughts were for himself and what tomorrow would, inevitably bring.

He had studied long and hard, had excelled in history and strategy, practiced the art of rhetoric and logic until Councillor Aradan had been thoroughly satisfied, for Handir was the king's son and so it was not enough that he be good, the royal councillor had argued. One day, the boy would counsel his own, royal father, their *monarch* no less; he could not afford to be anything less than perfect.

Few royal councillors had made a name for themselves, mused Handir. Not that that was his utmost priority for it was not, yet neither was he adverse to the idea of notoriety; indeed Lord Damiel of Tar'eastór came to his mind. The Alpine had earned fame for his skills of negotiation—what Handir would not do to meet him, to ask him, to observe and to learn from him. It seemed an impossible task, for Tar'eastór was so far away across the Median Mountains, and the road so treacherous—and Handir was no warrior.

He huffed to himself then, for what was he *thinking?* His father would never let him go. The second prince of Ea Uaré had long ago decided it was better to say naught of his dream and thus believe it was possible, rather than ask and have it cruelly quashed under the pretence of keeping him safe.

Aradan had driven him hard enough, he reckoned, and Thargodén had done nothing to stop him, but whether that had been fuelled by the desire for his son to excel, or simply the fruit of indifference, Handir could not say. The fact was that the culmination of his studies would come tomorrow, when he would take the test, and should he pass, he would become Councillor Aradan's apprentice, a man of state.

The thought set his stomach to fluttering and an onerous weight settled in his chest. He was nervous, despite his best attempts to remain aloof.

His eyes returned to the present, and then strayed to his elder brother who stood before the magnificent, full-length window, as rigid as the stone wall beside him. He moved not an inch and it seemed to Handir that he was not real, a painted portrait, a moment frozen in time, until a strand of silver hair danced around his temple and brought him to life.

His hands were clasped tightly behind his straight back for Rinon was always alert, always ready, his head high and his frosty, blue eyes dangerous and forbidding. He rarely smiled, rarely touched anyone in affection. He was as fiery as the desert sun, as cold as the southern glaciers, and just as ruthless.

That rigid, unfeeling face that now stared out over the Evergreen Wood had not always been there and where now it defined who the Crown Prince had become, once that extraordinary face had been kind and soft. Handir still remembered when they had played and laughed and both parents had basked in the love and pride they had for their three children. It was what had held his parents together—their children—Handir reminded himself.

His eyes wandered sideways of their own accord until they latched onto a portrait that hung on the far wall—his mother, the departed queen. Those days of happiness were brutally swept aside one strange day when she had announced her departure to Valley. Rinon and Handir had been adults, and Maeneth only barely past her majority. Still, all three were old enough to read between the lines, to see beyond their mother's lame excuses which they simply had not understood, still did not. It had been the trigger for their great uncle's machinations, his vision of an Alpine-ruled Ea Uaré, where the days of glory in their homeland of Tar'eastór would be lived here too, in foreign lands, despite the native Silvans.

The love the three siblings had once lavished upon their mother turned sour, for how could she leave her *children?* What terrible thing had been done to her that she would turn her back on them in search of her own happiness, away to Valley?

But leave she had and Thargodén had become numb. Band'orán was ecstatic.

The royal children had shouted, then pleaded, begged their father for the truth behind their mother's departure but he would not yield. Their frustration slowly turned to disdain, to rejection and the loss of affection, and only the passing of time had tempered it, putting it into perspective and making it bearable for them at least.

Of course, scandals such as these were never kept secret for long, and sure enough, the three siblings came to hear the rumours—heard them and believed them, for they made sense and their father's silence seemed all the proof they needed.

Their father had erred, had been unfaithful to their mother and she, unable to understand or condone, had simply left. It hurt because her own feelings of betrayal seemed to have been much stronger than the love she had held for her children. It had stung and each had reacted in their own, unique way; Rinon with hatred towards a father that had turned cold, Handir with sorrow and frustration. Maeneth had been sent away to distant relations in Pelagia, home of the Sea Elves.

Handir was lucky for the friendship he shared with Lainon, his ex-bodyguard. The Spirit Warrior had taught him much, had supported him in his times of need when his cold brother would not, and his father cared not, caught as he was in his own web of shame and sorrow.

His thoughts were interrupted, for the king had arrived, and his mind was no longer free to wander.

There was a deep, hollow rumbling in the distance, a sound Thargodén knew well—it was the sound of warriors rushing home, hooves thundering over the ground, spurred on by desperate riders. It would be an incoming missive, or a patrol returning with injured warriors. There were other possibilities – an attack, a battle, another death.

Ea Uaré was gradually falling into full-scale war to maintain its northernmost territories, which were slowly but inexorably being lain to waste by the Sand Lords from Calrazia, pushing southwards into Ea Uaré. As a result, they were driving the Deviants from their abodes on the mountain slopes to the North-east, and into the southern forests. If it hadn't been for the Sand Lords they would have stayed there in their caves, scavenging for food and water for although their mission to the Source had failed and they had become Deviant, Valley always seemed to draw them, keep them in the mountains that bordered Tar'eastór, the ridges and ranges that shielded that place of mystery.

The battleground was no longer referred to as the northern borders but the Xeric Wood or the Crying Lands as the Ari'atór would say, for the battle that raged there was not only one of arrows and blades, but one of sheer will, the utter determination of the Deep Silvan foresters. Their only weapon was their woodcraft, their innate connection with the forest and their unparalleled knowledge of Aria's creation. Brave elves settled purposefully close to the areas in conflict and attended the trees as best they could, bringing saplings with them to repopulate those areas where they had been indiscriminately felled or simply burned carelessly. Some called them pilgrims, while others thought them foolhardy, for they prolonged the inevitable, they said, and taxed the king's warriors for these foresters were no fighters, at least not in the traditional sense.

The Deviants were becoming more numerous, bolder, more ruthless as they were forced out of the mountains, and so, Thargodén had ordered his commander in general, Pan'assár, to muster as many soldiers as he could and assign them to the Eastern and Western quadrants.

To the land in conflict—the North—he would send his most experienced warriors for it was said the Deviants were organising themselves, establishing a seat of power, slowly coming together into some semblance of social order. Thargodén believed it, they all did, although the Alpine purists would not openly recognise it for to deny this truth worked in their favour—using it to discredit the Silvans and their brave stand.

Band'orán. He was a *fool*, a *dangerous* fool.

The noise was louder now and Thargodén's eyes began to make out the figures galloping through the forest on the City Road. It was the Western Patrol he realised and as he strained his eyes, he saw the foremost rider rode double, an elf sitting before him, his body jostled this way and that, helpless in the rider's desperate embrace.

Perhaps it had been Sand Lords, he mused, or Deviants. It was not easy to be close to them he knew, still remembered. Thargodén had killed many in his time as a warrior prince before kingship had utterly changed him. He had hunted them in their caves, even the females and the children. *Dark* memories, things he wanted to forget and yet how was that even possible? How could something as disturbing as Deviants be forgotten? They were rotting bodies with eternal souls and bitter hearts that turned heartless for they were broken and angry, and the face of any elf was enough to send them into a frenzy of hatred and unparalleled violence. It took a strong mind to fight them, to not think too much on what they had once been, of the dream they had shared to never die.

'Strange,' he thought as he looked out over the Evergreen Wood, for such darkness, such cruelty and defilement to be rampant there in the North and yet here beyond the forests of Ea Uaré lay this woodland paradise that was protected with everything they had, even by denying passage to any living thing save for the Silvan Foresters that nurtured it.

Thargodén, Alpine ruler of the Great Forest Belt stood upon the very tip of the mighty overhang, the Great Plateau that jutted out from the carved rock of his fortress kingdom, a platform that seemed almost to hang over the forest canopy, and any who stood upon it were thrust into its wild greenness, as if they floated upon a carpet of the living earth, poised from above to marvel at its wonders.

The overwhelming vastness of the forest rolled away majestically before him and into the horizon, until it softly kissed the snow-covered peaks of the Pelagian Mountains beyond, and a cool breeze gently lifted his silver locks, reverently almost, revealing his sharp, chiselled features, an Alpine silhouette of strength and nobility.

Yet there was no joy upon this singular face, no happiness sparkled in his eyes, no emotion at all save for the blank stare of an ancient Lord, a king of elves who ruled over his subjects and secured their lands but enjoyed none of it for himself, for everything he had been, his very source of motivation, had left—gone from his side.

An eagle's call drew his attention for a moment, his frosty grey eyes finding it as it soared higher upon the warm air. Envy, deep and bitter cut through his icy veil, for even though it was mortal, still, he would have traded his own, immortal existence right there and then, had he been given the choice.

But it was all gone and in one, slow and purposeful blink, the coldness was back in his eyes, the mind behind them sharp and in the present once more for he was no longer alone.

"My Lord," came the flat voice of his Crown Prince, Rinon.

"Speak," was all the king could find within himself to say.

"The Western Patrol is approaching; they have urgent news from the North."

"I will be along shortly."

"My king," continued the Crown Prince, his expression sharpening, lip curling slightly—he was angry. "Captain Darón is dead."

Thargodén's eyes closed and he breathed deeply. Another of his captains gone, one he had known well. "Sand Lords?" he asked quietly.

"Deviants!" hissed the Crown Prince, his jaw working furiously, cold eyes flashing in barely-controlled wrath, eyes that had turned on the king so many times in the past.

The king allowed his eyes to travel over the livid face, one so much like his own, but where Rinon was a fascinating contrast of fire and ice, he was apathy and water, ever running away, endlessly seeking to transcend the borders of its prison, one that had enclosed Thargodén the day he had lost everything, the day *she* had gone.

The following day, the body of Captain Darón was sent off into the evening breeze amidst the sad songs of the Sprit Singers. The citizens flocked to the pyre and mourned the loss of another member of the revered Inner Circle, a servant of Ea Uaré. His family was inconsolable, even when the king approached them and placed an honour stone in the shaking hands of Darón's wife; she would wear it in her hair if she so chose to. Thargodén though, remained aloof and Rinon clenched his jaw at his father's apparent lack of emotion, while Handir was too busy fighting with his own emotions to notice anything at all.

They had done this many times of late, and where Rinon was livid, ready to take up his sword and charge into the fray, Handir analysed and wondered what had to change in the council chambers in order to fight back this escalation, get the Alpine lords back on the same side as the Silvans with regards to how the battle should be fought, a task that was becoming more and more improbable with every failed council meeting.

It was Band'orán, his great uncle, brother of the mighty Or'Talán, first king of Ea Uaré; he was the instigator, the mastermind behind the Alpine purists. While the king, his nephew, stood in the middle. On the one hand, Band'orán called for the Silvan foresters to pull back, closer to the fortress and safety, while on the other, the Silvans refused to leave. Their homes were there, not in the fortress. It was the army's duty to make their lands safe, not pull them back and lose ground, forsake the trees that harboured them – it was absurd; incomprehensible to the mind of a Silvan.

"I have spoken to General Huren and Commander General Pan'assár regarding the early promotion of our better recruits," said Rinon later that day as they sat in the royal chambers at the Fortress.

"And," prompted the king monotonously.

"They agree. They will make an estimate of the numbers attainable and report to me in two days' time. From there, they can be ready to ride out in a week."

Thargodén turned in a rustle of fine cloth, his eyes latching on to the sharp face of his eldest son.

"And the training campaign?" asked Thargodén after a moment.

"Well so far," replied Rinon with what seemed to be genuine interest. "We have received one hundred Silvan boys from the deeper villages; they are half-way through their preliminary training and Lieutenant Lainon is reported to have some promising individuals amongst them."

"Very well. Secure those villages, else we lose the harvest for the entire year," murmured the king calmly.

Rinon sat at the table with his arms folded, thinking that his father would continue, but he remained silent.

"We ride in ten days. I see no difficulty; the groups currently penetrating the North-western border are small and apparently uncoordinated."

"Do not underestimate them—they learn," warned the king quietly.

"I *do* know, my Lord. Rest assured it will be done," replied Rinon. And there it was, that note of irritation and sarcasm, not enough to constitute a lack of respect, but sufficient to remind Thargodén of his son's disdain.

"Thank you, Rinon," he said simply, turning his back on his implacable warrior son who would not forgive him, and then facing the window and the Evergreen Wood once more, for only there did the king find some semblance of peace, a place where he was not judged.

Rinon was a good warrior, a leader and a duteous prince. Yet he was not ready for the throne. He was volatile and Thargodén was unsure of his mind-set with regards to Band'orán. He had fulfilled many of Thargodén's expectations yet still, in all things regarding his father the boy had no heart. But then what had he expected?

He was his father's son.

Fel'annár sat cross-legged amongst the trees of a small copse that lay behind the barracks. Sliding a whetting stone over the sharp edge of his broad sword, he inspected his work carefully before laying it down beside him and taking up his sabre. Sharpening the shorter blade, he faltered as a pang of anxiety washed over him and he scowled, for his own musings had not merited such a reaction, indeed he had been thinking of nothing at all.

It was not the first time such a thing had happened to Fel'annár recently and he wondered at the reason for it. It soon passed though, as suddenly as it had hit him and he shook himself, his fingers twirling his whetting stone obsessively. Perhaps he was just fretting too much about tomorrow. He had learned to avoid attention and it had served him well, until Borhen had forced him to show a little of his skill.

All that would need to change now, for weapons training began tomorrow. They would be put to the test and then put into skill categories. But twenty of the better recruits would be selected by the lieutenants of the ten forest quadrants; these recruits would be promoted to Novice Warrior and sent away to serve; Fel'annár had every intention of being chosen.

He was so young, so inexperienced, in fact he had never even seen an elven warrior fight in battle, had never seen a Sand Lord and much less a live *Deviant!* Another pang of anxiety squeezed his guts at the sudden thought of making a fool of himself. He had held back all this time, hidden his skill in order to survive, to live a normal life and not be singled out. It had got him this far but now, his strategy must change – it was the only way he could get on that list.

It would come at a price, he knew. The questions would start again, the mockery and the disdain, they would laugh at his dreams and his wish to be counted amongst the Silvans. Anonymity had lent him a modicum of peace, and now, notoriety would surely bring him strife, but his goals were more important than his feelings. He had not understood that as a child.

A deep breath and a long, slow stroke of the whetting stone and he peered once more at the edge, the shiny metal above and the reflection of his own eyes. How would he explain? How would they react if he were to use his aerial techniques? Or if he were to use what he had learnt of the Fell Dance? He had dredged it all up from the books he had read and the treatise he had studied as an adolescent. He had tried it and then mixed it all up, and with time came a purge of what worked, what didn't, what might. Indeed, he was untried with it, even on the training field – it was all theory and but cursory practice he had kept to himself.

Lieutenant Turion's face popped into his head and his hand stilled half way down his sabre.

'Why do you hide what you know?'

Fel'annár had wanted to tell him then, that he hid it because it would bring suffering. It would bring mockery and alienate him from his people. All he had ever wanted was to belong and to the mind of a child, that meant being like the rest, even if he looked different.

But he was a child no more; this was a pivotal moment there was no going back on. He would make the sacrifice, expose himself to the mercy of others, free himself of his past. He would hide no more.

Pushing himself to his feet, he slid his blades into the harness on his back and walked back to the barracks, his mind set, his path clear but the dissonance brushed upon his mind once more, leaving him with a lingering sense of foreboding he simply could not shake.

Two hours after dawn of the following day, the sound of thwacking arrows and the steely clang of metal resonated around the training fields. The piercing voices of instructors went up as they organized the recruits, while lieutenants and veteran warriors from every active patrol of Ea Uaré flocked to the side-lines, talking excitedly amongst themselves. They had lost warriors, some of them master archers and swordsmen – they needed replacing and now was the time to do it – only now, those veteran fighters would be replaced with novice warriors. It was surely a sign that something had to change, for should they continue with their current strategies, it was only a matter of time before they were forced back, swept South and to the sea.

The recruits too, were excited, for their grand day had finally come and they would now get to show their abilities, if indeed they had any. Their tutors placed them into skill groups, knowing that the Forest's lieutenants looked on, eager to complete their outbound patrols. Twenty of these boys would see action before the month was through, kill their first Deviant or Sand Lord and the thought was as exhilarating as it was terrifying. They were young and impressionable, still too green to bother worrying about where they would go, only that they *should* go. They all wanted this, and the only way to achieve it was to show the lieutenants what they were capable of.

The Company was no exception and when Fel'annár had told them of his intentions to finally show his skill, Ramien had smirked but Idernon had suggested caution. Fel'annár wondered at the Wise Warrior's reaction for he had expected more encouragement from his friend. Later though, he wondered if it was because Idernon feared being separated—that The Company would be parted even before it had truly begun. Ramien and Idernon were certainly well above the average as recruits, but what about these novice warriors? They had been in weapons training for months, was The Company any better than they were?

His mind focused on the present once more, as the sharp voice of his instructor called his name.

"Fel'annár, take Hanor's place on the archery field. Shoot a precision round, and then a speed round. Understood?"

"Yes Sir!" he answered, smiling as the other Silvan recruits called out their encouragement and the instructor rolled his eyes.

The lieutenants perched on the fences or leant against them, critical eyes and folded arms. Beside them, their Master Archers and Blade Masters counselled them on who to watch more carefully.

There was rivalry aplenty, some of it healthy, but for others it was a matter of pride of the misplaced kind. Some of the Alpine warriors and lieutenants searched the recruits for light hair, disregarding the darker-haired Silvans while others could not be bothered with such nonsense.

Yet it was not only the Alpines that showed their racial preferences—the Silvan veterans did the same, their eyes latching onto the browns and auburns of the Deep Forest where they said the best archers came from. Wagers though, were being placed by Alpines *and* Silvans, for in this one thing at least, they were alike.

Lainon stood with his arms folded, watching as the arrows flew, some true and others atrociously astray, while one ear was turned to the tried and tested warriors standing around him.

" . . . most of them Silvan, except for Borhen and, what's his name?" Jeering began amongst them at the mention of Borhen, albeit these lieutenants were mostly Alpine themselves. Lainon smirked; that trouble maker would be a thorn in the backside of any patrol captain, and they all knew it. Yet what to do with him? for much to Lainon's disgust, he knew the child's lordly father would have seen to it that his son be chosen for early promotion to warrior-hood; it was a foregone conclusion.

"Look at *that*!" gasped one Alpine lieutenant by the name of Sar'pén, his arm straight out in front of him, pointing to one of the five elves currently on the archery field. "Look at his *stance*!" he shouted in disbelief.

"Yes, yes I see it. It is . . . he's *Alpine*," said another in surprise.

'Thwack,' and the arrow sailed true, into the very centre of the target, embedding itself up to the base of its metal tip.

The group of warriors dropped from the fences as one, standing tall now as they craned their necks to get a better look at the elf with the perfect stance.

'Thwack,' another arrow split centre and Fel'annár was already reaching for another projectile. He fired three more, taking careful aim, unaware of the silence that had descended around him. Nobody spoke while he fired and when it was over, one warrior murmured quietly to the rest.

"*That* was precision. Let's see how the boy fires at speed," said Sar'pén, his eyes never leaving the silvery blond recruit he was sure was Alpine. The Silvan warriors however, scowled for although they could not deny the boy's skill, it irked them that the best archer on the field was an Alpine. They enjoyed so few privileges, and to have their status as master archers called to question was nothing short of irritating.

They talked among themselves for a while, before falling into silence as Fel'annár took up his stance once more, his right hand flexing, left shoulder rolling back.

It happened so fast they were left with their mouths slack and their eyes wide, for this—*boy*—this, green child had fired so fast they had barely been able to follow his moves, and as their eyes travelled now to the target, they found five quivering arrows, deeply embedded at dead centre.

Sar'pén turned to the rest, eyes as round as his mouth before bellowing out his claim on the recruit. "He is *mine*!"

The claim was promptly contested by Sar'pén's colleagues who waved their arms and shouted even louder. The Silvan warriors scowled at their commanders as the noise around them exploded into a great din, as they fought between themselves.

"Sar'pén, you lost Abhen, your master swordsman, you already have some of the best archers—you do not need another!" shouted a veteran Silvan, but the Alpine lieutenant was having nothing of it and the argument continued.

Lainon smiled in satisfaction. He had never seen Fel'annár shoot like that, even though he had known the boy had been holding himself back. Fel'annár had been sharp, for he had chosen the best moment to draw attention to himself. He smiled again, but this time not in satisfaction but in fond memory, because truth be told, Fel'annár was so much like he himself as a child. Different, precocious, driven by some inexplicable goal.

The archery concluded and the avid audience all but ran to the next area, where blade work would now begin. The recruits had been organised into five groups of twenty. Each elf was then paired off. The rules were simple; use your blades to defeat your opponent. Those who lost would leave the field and those that won would find others without partners, until there were none left. It was a test of skill with any weapon available, but also one of endurance.

Lainon's eyes found Fel'annár, watching as he was assigned a different group to his two inseparable friends. '*Good*', he thought to himself. All three would have their chances at promotion, it seemed.

The first round lasted forty minutes, at the end of which only one Alpine lad was left standing, panting and sweating as the onlookers exchanged coins and celebrated their winnings.

Fel'annár's group would take the field now, and every single elf watched from the side-lines as the group of boys stood before their respective partners.

With a fierce cry from their instructor, the recruits began their sparring, and Sar'pén and his veteran Alpine archer pushed their way to the front once more, determined to secure the recruit for their own patrol. Beside them, a Silvan warrior was pointing at Fel'annár as he sailed through his first bout.

"That is *The Silvan*," he said to a warrior beside him. Sar'pén scowled at the ridiculous comment, before turning back to the recruits. Shouts and grunts and cheers echoed around them as some were defeated, leaving progressively fewer opponents. Fel'annár won his bouts in mere seconds and was sometimes at a loss as to who else to confront, often having to wait until a recruit won his own bout and then discreetly allowing him some moments to catch his breath.

Lainon knew they were no match for him. He had known he would be good, just as he had on the archery field, but not even the Ari'atór could begin to imagine what would happen in just a few minute's time, could never have predicted just what it was that his friend Turion had found. A gasp from the crowd focused Lainon's mind and his eyes sharpened on Turion's *find* and his latest opponent.

A strapping Silvan lad stood before Fel'annár, an axe in one hand and a broad sword in the other. There was a challenge on his dirt-smudged face and Fel'annár's head cocked to one side. With his long sword in one hand, he slowly reached back over his shoulder and unsheathed a sabre. He stood now, a blade in each hand, and then he smiled at his opponent.

Taking pause, Fel'annár presented both blades, widening his stance and stretching his back leg so far behind him his shin grazed the ground. The short sword was swivelled skilfully back over the blond head and then pointed at the now wide-eyed Silvan. As he was, Fel'annár reminded Lainon of a desert scorpion and suddenly pitied the strapping Silvan lad. As it was, the boy stood puzzled. That quickly changed though, as The Silvan moved forward, but instead of facing his opponent for the attack, he spun around and backed into him, the tip of his long sword touching the tunic of the open-mouthed recruit, just over his heart. He had never even moved.

Mark.

The boy looked down at his own chest, utterly dumbfounded, unable to understand how he had been bested even before he had moved, for all he could see was the crown of Fel'annár's head, and the long, thick plait that kept his hair from obscuring his vision. Fel'annár turned to face the gaping recruit, nodded respectfully, and then moved away, in search of his next opponent.

It was over in minutes, and Fel'annár was left standing alone upon the field.

"That one comes with *ME!*" bellowed Sar'pén yet again, "Alpine, or Silvan or—*whatever!*"

"Nay, I need him in the Eastern quadrant, the terrain . . ."

"No—*I* need him and I will make sure Pan'assár understands . . ."

"*Stop!*" was all Lainon said and he was instantly obeyed.

"None of you can have him," said the Ari'atór slowly, "for you see, he is already spoken for." It was a lie, but Lainon had his own plans—he would simply stretch the truth, so to speak.

"By *who*?" asked Sar'pén angrily.

But before Lainon could answer, the sharp, commanding voice of his friend told them exactly who it was who laid claim to the strange, Silvan warrior.

"By *me*," said the newcomer, taking a step forward, his face stern and commanding.

"Turion!" exclaimed Lainon, to which Turion smiled widely now, offering his forearms that were heartily clasped by his long-time friend.

"We shall see about that," said the irritated warrior standing beside them, and Lainon could not resist one last comment.

"Sar'pén."

"Lainon."

"He *is* Alpine," he began, to which the lieutenant smirked in victory but it quickly vanished when the Ari'atór continued. "And he *is* Silvan," he smiled slyly. There was a mischievous quirk upon his lips and Sar'pén returned it, nodding that he understood exactly what it was that was about to happen.

The battle for The Silvan had begun.

Chapter Five

STRATEGY

"Elves are immortal; time enough to be wise, to be just – time enough to be evil and tyrannical. In love though, we are all alike. Pleasure may be given freely but children are the fruit of an unbreakable bond, the physical manifestation of love that cannot be broken, even through death."
The Silvan Chronicles, Book IV, annex II. Marhené.

Heavy oak doors thumped together, the click of the lock telling Lainon they were finally alone.

"Turion!" he exclaimed, turning to face his old friend with a genuine smile. "It is so strange to see you away from your recruits, here in the *city* no less."

"Yes, well, the circumstances are extraordinary, Lainon," said Turion with an uncharacteristic grin. It was then that Lainon realised what was different about his friend; he was *alive*—for the first time in centuries the Ari'atór could see purpose shining in his shrewd, Alpine eyes.

"Do not tell me you have seriously come to claim your find. What of your work at the training barracks?" asked Lainon somewhat rhetorically, for he well knew he had. There was little else that could have tempted this extraordinary warrior to return to civilization after their years of service together in the North.

"Does that surprise you?" asked the instructor, sitting heavily upon the couch and loosening his collar.

"Yes," said Lainon, and then turned to his friend once more, holding his gaze for a moment before speaking. "And no—we have much to speak of. I cannot tell you how—*opportune* your presence is, my friend."

Turion frowned for a moment and Lainon knew he had picked up on the import of his words; his friend was simply one of the most able judges of character Lainon knew.

"I was right, wasn't I?" asked the Alpine, sitting forward expectantly with his elbows on his knees.

"Yes, yes you were right Turion but," he paused for a moment, seeking how best to infuse his words with the feelings he wished to express. "But you see, I believe you found much more than a Silvan candidate for leadership."

"What do you mean?" asked Turion, his frown deepening. "Perhaps you should fill me a goblet of that wine before you speak, you seem—*unnerved -* if that is at all possible for you Ari'atór," he said with a smirk.

"When I tell you what I suspect – nay what I know," he dropped off as he poured them both a glass of wine. "How long has it been since you last visited our lord King's halls?"

"Not long enough," scoffed Turion, taking a long drink from his goblet. "I loathe the petty politics and gossip—all those ridiculous things that have nothing to do with the important things in life."

Lainon smiled, for Turion was quite the brute, albeit he was Alpine. He spoke plainly, with not a thought for propriety, unless he stood before his commanding officer, of course.

"When you sent him to me, even before I read your letter, it was not the face of some green, Silvan boy I saw, Turion."

"What do you mean—I know he looks like an Alpine, but he's not—not really, it's . . ."

"You don't understand," interrupted Lainon, holding up his palm. "What I mean is, . . ."

A harsh rap on the door interrupted them, and Turion jumped, so immersed had he been in what his friend was about to reveal.

"Come!" called Lainon, annoyance colouring his tone.

A guard entered with a note which he promptly handed to Lainon, before saluting and leaving.

"Gods, Lainon, out with it, what . . ." began Turion, but once more he was silenced.

"A moment," mumbled the Ari as he read. "General Huren has issued the list - the twenty candidates that are to be promoted tomorrow. We must claim our stake and quickly, before someone else beats us to it."

"Lainon, what are you *talking* about!"

"Turion—that boy is from Lan Taria," said Lainon as he rounded on his seated friend. "A half Alpine-Silvan orphan or bastard who was raised by his aunt, Amareth. He is the best warrior I have *ever* seen, even before training. He has bright green eyes—just like his *mother's . . .*" the last word leaving him in a rush of air, a fierce whisper that set Turion's skin crawling as understanding slowly dawned. Turion's eyes widened and sparkled and Lainon knew he still did not fully understand what he was trying to tell him.

"It was not the face of some Silvan recruit, Turion—it was the face of *Or'Talán*, father of Thargodén King. That boy is of royal blood.

He is Thargodén's *son*."

General Huren sat behind his desk, the list of new recruits upon his desk together with a veritable mountain of petitions from a whole host of lieutenants, vigorously expounding their reasons for requesting their choice of warrior. That in itself was not an issue; it was the fact that they all wanted the *same* recruit, the one they were calling *The Silvan*.

'*Who is this boy?*' he asked himself as he rubbed his chin. He had not been present at yesterday's trials, indeed he hardly ever bothered, but this time, it seemed he had missed something of import.

'*What now?*' he wondered. He did not have the time to read through so many missives, so many clever arguments. He was needed at headquarters in a scant few hours and details of tomorrow's promotion ceremony must be completed.

He sighed as he leaned back in his chair, his hand moving to his throbbing forehead and kneading it irritably.

A knock on the door, and Lieutenants Lainon and a strangely pale Turion entered his study. Huren was glad for the interruption, even though it meant he would still be in his office at the midnight hour.

Standing, he returned the salute he was given, before smiling and holding his forearms out.

"I am glad to see you Lainon, and *you*, Turion! What has dragged you out of your beloved country barracks!" he said with a smile.

"Ah! That is the reason we have come to see you, General," replied Turion.

"No, no, do *not* tell me you too have come to claim The *Silvan!* By Ari and Sethá, who *is* this boy? My desk is full of messages and demands and, '*oh, you owe me . . .*' or, '*is it not my turn?*'" he mocked theatrically, before turning back to a now smirking Turion.

"It does not surprise me," smiled Turion. "You did not see him on the field then?" he asked tentatively, already knowing the answer to that, for if he had, this veteran general would not have failed to see the resemblance, even though he himself had not seen it. Turion had been away for too long but this general saw the royal family regularly.

"No, no I did not, so *you* tell me, then. What is so special about him?" asked the general resignedly, gesturing to the two lieutenants to sit.

"I met him at my barracks not a month past. I knew from the moment we first spoke that he would be a fine candidate for leadership."

"He is Silvan, I assume, given his nick name."

"He looks Alpine, Huren, but calls himself a Silvan. The point is that he shows great potential—and I would be the one to show him to the limits of his possibilities—if you will allow it," finished Turion, his eyes fixed on the general, desperately trying to read Huron's first impressions.

"You have been training boys for the last few centuries, have rejected promotion so that you could continue to do so. I do not doubt your educational qualities Turion, but you are all out on recent military affairs."

"I am good, Huren, this you know. You yourself offered me a promotion to captain because you knew I was fit for the position."

"But you refused."

"Yes—because I believe in what I do. Becoming a captain would mean leaving the job I love so much; that is why I refused."

"And now? Should I agree to let you train this—*Silvan*—will you accept the promotion? Think carefully now, for should you agree, you will not be able to return to your former post. We need all the commanders the Forest can yield. There will be no going back, Turion."

Turion looked up sadly, pausing for a moment before nodding. "I understand, and I agree. Calenar is ready to step into my position at the barracks."

"He must be special indeed," said Huren with narrowed eyes, his shrewd mind clearly at work.

"Yes—yes he is," replied the soon-to-be captain carefully.

"Well, I lose a lieutenant, but if he is as good as you seem to think," he began thoughtfully. "Take him for a year and train him—do your best and if you can—bring back a Silvan warrior fit for leadership training."

"One year . . ."

"One year. After that we shall see. Now, however much I appreciate your company Lainon, will you tell me why *you* are here?"

"Because I am going with them," said Lainon simply, to which Huren tipped an eyebrow at the impertinence and muttered something under his breath, before standing, his eyes riveted on his two best lieutenants.

"Yes," he said tiredly, "yes I believe you are."

The barracks were alive, and the soon-to-be novices waited for the dawn and a new beginning, as warriors of Ea Uaré. They would also receive their assignments and now, they speculated on where they would go, who they would serve with, who would command.

Of course, it was the Silvans that lead the festivities, even though most of them were Alpine, indeed tonight, it seemed that discrimination was a far-away thing, for blond heads mixed with the auburns and chestnut hair of the Silvans as they danced and they drunk. The lads of The Company sang a merry tune to the sound of a woodland lyre, much to the delight of the other young recruits who clapped and stomped their feet to the beat of a forest drum that accompanied.

Idernon watched them, a flurry of hope sparking in his mind. Segregation had been present here in the city, but there were almost as many Silvans that returned the ill treatment they received. On the one hand he thought it logical, a defence mechanism; but then, how could the wheel of injustice be stopped? How could the inertia be broken? he wondered. If you give as good as you get you will always *have*—he realised—always have *racism*.

With a deep breath, he raised his eyes from the forest floor and trained them on Fel'annár who was in the middle of a line dance that was fast and furious. There was joy on his face, unmarred by the weight of his mysterious past, uncaring of his troubled childhood.

He smiled, but it was a sad smile because the moment was fleeting and because he knew that the only way to truly heal his friend would be to tell him—tell him who his mother was, who his father was—give him a history and allow him to understand why he had never been allowed to know.

Taking a swig from his bottle of wine, he cast his eyes further afield and to the candle-lit barracks beyond the Silvan revelry. Lainon would be in there with his friend Turion and it suddenly struck Idernon how strange the pair were together. Turion, tough and direct, caring yet unwilling to show it, his face was always straight and his eyes unreadable. Lainon too was straight-faced and Idernon thought it was a trait with leaders—yet the Ari'atór´s eyes were a blazing pool of emotions he did not seem willing to hide, or perhaps he couldn't. Idernon had seen many things there; surprise, respect, hatred, compassion and then, just this evening he had seen something else as the lieutenant watched Fel'annár. He had seen apprehension.

Idernon shook himself mentally and tipped the bottle once more, the liquid sloshing inside. All that was left to know was who they would be assigned to, and where. Idernon's chest suddenly felt heavy, because there was a chance he would be separated from Ramien and Fel'annár, and try as he might, he could not imagine his life without them.

"You are quiet," came Fel'annár's even voice at his side, even though it did not match his messy hair and flushed face.

Idernon glanced in his direction, a rueful smile on his face. "I fret about where we will be sent," he said truthfully.

"As do we all," replied Fel'annár, watching the crowd as he spoke. "Aria forbid we be separated in this first step in our adventure but should it happen, Idernon, should that happen remember this; we are *The Company*! We will always come back to each other."

Idernon turned to meet his friend's confident face and he smiled in genuine joy, his face lighting up so beautifully that Fel'annár chuckled. "Tomorrow is for *us*, to take our vows and become servants to the king. What comes after that we do not know, *cannot* know. Enjoy the *now*, Idernon, claim it for your own."

The Wise Warrior held his friend's gaze for long moments, thinking that just yesterday, their roles would have been reversed and it would be Fel'annár fretting about the possibility of separation and yet here he was, bold and confident, alive and excited and just a little wiser, a little closer to becoming what Idernon had always known he would be.

A leader.

The party had finished, the recruits no longer able to stay awake after the excitement of the day and now, Turion sat with Lainon in his office, a flask of wine between them and the remains of their shared dinner upon the table.

The hearth crackled and hissed, and Lainon drank deeply from his glass, his strange eyes shining a blue deep enough to unnerve any who did not know him.

"What now?" asked Turion, almost to himself. "We cannot tell the king until we have at least an inkling as to how he will react and in this I cannot give counsel. I have been out in the forest for too long."

"Agreed," said Lainon. "And you are right, we must wait. Our king's mind is absent and if it weren't for Aradan, this realm would be on its knees. This is what the people say and I believe it. I would not see Fel'annár's military career over before it has begun because rash decisions are made by a weakened king *and* I do not need to remind you of his elder son's—*singular*—disposition. Rinon is one of a kind. I do not think he will take kindly to what he may perceive as opposition. The boy is already unsure of his father's feelings for him; it is also said he sympathizes with Lord Band'orán and I wonder just how deep in his confidence our crown prince is."

"If we cannot tell the king, neither can we allow Fel'annár to encounter the royal family—they will surely see what you did, Lainon."

"Yes. We would have to tell him before he ever came into contact with the boy and as you say, there is no telling."

"You know our royal family well. What do you think are the most likely outcomes?" asked Turion.

"The king would, perhaps, send him far away so that he does not meet his children. The king's relationship with them is already strained; he will not risk losing them altogether. And then there is the possibility that he would fear for the boy should Band'orán hear of him – which he would," said Lainon.

"You think he would be in danger?" asked Turion, puzzled.

Lainon held his friend's gaze for a while before answering. "I think there is a possibility, yes," he said quietly and Turion was shocked into silence, until another question begged his attention. "Does he even *know*? The king, I mean. Does he know he has an illicit child?" asked Turion.

"Yes, yes he knows. You will remember the scandal with the Silvan lass, the one Or'Talán forbade him to marry?"

"I do. It was with *her* then?"

"Aye. With her, Turion. I can say no more, my friend, only that we must not underestimate the dangers that young Fel'annár may unwittingly find himself in."

Turion nodded slowly, wondering what it was his friend had lived through, for he had been Handir's personal guard at the time, would have seen and heard many things.

"I wonder that he has not yet been told of his resemblance to Or'Talán— his *grandfather*," said Lainon, as if he still could not believe it. "Fifty-one years is a long time to not see a book, meet an elder elf, a veteran warrior."

"Agreed," said Turion, sipping on his wine, blue eyes staring into flickering orange flames.

"We need an accomplice, Turion," began Lainon, leaning forwards in his chair. "This is too big for the two of us; we are warriors, not politicians or advisors. In our haste to do what we perceive as right we may well be sticking our booted feet thigh deep into a pool of quicksand. We need help," concluded Lainon, a hand resting on his chin.

"Who?"

"Handir," said Lainon.

"Prince Handir?" asked Turion, quite unnecessarily.

"He is wise for his years, of even temper and good judgement. It is a risk but ignoring this, Turion, would be a mistake, the consequences of which may prove disastrous for Ea Uaré, and for Fel'annár."

"If Thargodén ever found out you had shared this knowledge with Handir, without his consent, he would banish you," said Turion meaningfully.

"Perhaps, but what is the alternative my friend? That we ignore this thing and let it all spiral out of control until someone tells the king there is some Silvan warrior out there with the face of Or'Talán, his own father? Or worse still Band'orán finds out first and uses it against our king? Had the boy decided to become a forester, none of this would be of any import, but the child wants to be a warrior—a *captain* no less," said Lainon with a fond smile, "he is too good to pass by inadvertently, Turion. The king *will* find out, be it from us, or from those that appreciate Thargodén less."

Silence prevailed for a while as they sat together, each contemplating their options and the strange, volatile situation they now found themselves involuntarily enmeshed in.

"Perhaps," began Turion, "perhaps you are right. Handir can procure us with the information we need to make the best choice. Speak to him, wrench from him an honour-bound oath not to speak of this. We will be patrolling for the next year; far away enough to keep him out of trouble should the worse happen. That should be time enough to better judge our options, with Handir as our source of information and chose the best time to tell them both.

"And what of the boy?" asked Lainon. "What of the comments he is sure to hear?"

"Then we tell him, although admittedly it will unbalance him. He thinks his father dead or banished," said Turion, remembering that first talk he had had with Fel'annár at the village barracks. "Not telling him and leaving him with his questions—I wager that is the short of his entire life thus far—are we to prolong that suffering?" asked Turion. "Until we can guess at the king's reaction I would not tell him, but I will not hold off if logic dictates he should know.

Lainon knew his friend was right. In matters such as these he was always right. The fact remained that now, Lainon needed to find a way to tell Handir he had a brother, not pure Alpine like himself but half Silvan, a child that had not been born to the Queen.

Chapter Six

BROTHERS

"Thargodén, Alpine King of Ea Uaré continued to exist as what Coun-
cillor Aradan once described as 'a shadow of his former splendour'. His
sons, Crown Prince Rinon and Councillor Handir did not speak of
their mother, of her departure to Valley or of the sordid rumours that
had abounded - they had never been addressed and so they had festered,
turning the sons against their kingly father."
The Silvan Chronicles, book III. Marhené

The day dawned painfully slowly, or at least it seemed that way to one
who had not slept at all. The party had been long and Fel'annár had revelled
well into the night, but his joy had turned to quiet respect when a group of
warriors had galloped into the courtyard with three wounded elves. They
had overheard hushed conversation about Deviants attacking the village of
Sen'tarhán, not a week's ride from Lan Taria, killing most of its civilians,
including the babes. There had been blood too, smeared down the sides of
their heaving, sweaty mounts.

Fel'annár's skin had turned to ice. He had always thought Lan Taria safe
and yet he had been wrong. His stomach lurched and a sense of urgency
instilled itself in his chest.

Fel'annár had asked why the wounded had not been tended to in the
forest, to which an Alpine healer had answered him with both humour and
pity, "they need master healers, child." Fel'annár had simply nodded and
then walked away, feeling stupid.

But it was not only the night's tidings that had kept him awake but what
the day would bring with it—Fel'annár would take his biggest step so far

upon the road he had chosen for himself as a child, the path he had prepared for so diligently. He had mercilessly trained his body until it was as strong as it could be. He had read all Lan Taria had to offer on tactics, battles, techniques and armament, on command and protocol—and not once had he resented his obsession. He had simply understood it as an inherent part of himself. It had never been a choice yet even so, it had not been easy.

Turning over and facing his little window, he brushed a finger over the furry leaves of a fern that had grown tall and strong and he was suffused with a sense of calm. He thought of Amareth then.

His message would not have reached her in time, even though he had written no sooner he had been told of his promotion to novice warrior; she would not be there to watch him take his vow—no one would. He breathed deeply; now was not the time for self-pity but pride. Today he would become a novice warrior, a servant of the king. That was his aim, to serve some purpose—to *mean* something—to someone. A frown flickered over his features for he had never thought of it that way before, that his obsession with being a warrior had something to do with feeling worthy. Yet Amareth had loved him as a mother, and he counted many friends in Lan Taria. Nay, it was not for lack of love and it was not for shame for having no father. There *was* something else, something he had never understood, as if a part of himself were missing, a fleeting thought that escaped him—like river rain through open fingers.

Lainon straightened his tunic and breathed deeply. The Ari'atór was nervous and that was not like him at all. Not even during those endless seconds before a battle had he felt this nervous.

It was a testimony to the risk they were taking by speaking with Handir on the matter of the Silvan. Should the prince not like what Lainon had to tell him, he could well run to his father and reveal all. Both he and Turion would surely be punished and banished.

The fact was they had no choice in the matter at all. Logic and sound reasoning had brought Lainon to this very moment, at the doors of Prince Handir's personal office.

Straightening his tunic once more, Lainon knocked upon the hard wood. This was it. There was no turning back now.

"Lainon! So good to see you, brother. You have been busy with the new recruits I hear?" asked Handir, his face alight with genuine surprise, and Lainon's heart sank to his boots.

"Aye, the barracks have been eventful of late, I cannot deny that," he said, allowing a tight smile to ease the stiffness of his features.

"Well, what brings you here? Is there some business to discuss, or are we free to wander outside?" asked Handir with a smile.

Lainon realised just how much his former charge had changed, matured so quickly into what seemed now to be an experienced man of state. It had been ten years since he had no longer been needed as a personal guard and General Huren had reassigned him to his current post. The boy had grown, his mind sharpened, no longer subjugated to the will of his fiery brother or his cold, blank father.

"Both, truth be told, but there is nothing to stop us from speaking outside, indeed I would prefer it," said Lainon. It made sense of course, for what he had to say could not be overheard by anyone, and Turion would make sure they were not spied upon in the woods.

"Then come, we walk and we talk" said Handir. "It has been so long since I enjoyed such a simple moment of brotherly chit-chat."

Lainon was loathe to spoil Handir's joy, for it seemed to the Ari that the boy did not often have such moments. He felt mean and wretched but his hands were tied and the business that had brought him here was too significant, too potentially dangerous to put off—Handir's feelings were secondary, however much it hurt Lainon to admit.

"I hear you passed the grade for councillor—well done," smiled Lainon, watching as the boy's face lit up with pride at his words and his own guilt swelled painfully in his heart. The boy *had* changed, but he was still young, still needy of approval and encouragement, those things his father had become incapable of providing him with.

"I did!" grinned the youngest prince. "I am now, officially, Lord Aradan's apprentice!" he said theatrically, making Lainon smile.

"You deserve it, Handir. You have worked hard, I am proud," he trailed off, his eyes shining. "But come, into the woods with your brother, Councillor, for we have much to discuss!"

And so, with a smile, one rueful and the other a little strained, they both left the fortress, chatting about what they had both missed in their lives. Indeed, an hour had passed and now, they sat quietly upon the banks of a slow stream amidst a shady glade. It was time, thought Lainon to himself, it was time to change the boy's life forever, and however much he tried, he failed to slow his rebellious, thumping heart.

"What is it, Lainon? I can tell there is something you have left unsaid.

I know you are busy with preparations and I do not think you came here just to catch up with me. Are you leaving? Is that what you have come to tell me?" asked the prince quietly. "Are you finally joining your brethren in Valley?"

"No, no, it is not that, Handir, but you are right, there is something of great import I must speak with you about."

"What could you possibly tell me that would matter more to me than that?"

Lainon smiled sadly. This was proving much more difficult than he had imagined.

"Before I tell you, I must place a condition on this conversation, Handir. I need you to make an honour-bound oath to not disclose what I am about to tell you to anyone, not even your king."

Handir frowned deeply and then looked to the ground, his young but avid mind clearly weighing the pros and cons of such an act, for an honour-bound oath was no simple promise. It was something he would die for, before he could disclose the contents. Handir would not accept lightly and Lainon was glad of it.

"I will not betray my king, Lainon, this you know."

"I do know, but consider this. The information must be kept from him for the moment only, until the time is right, and the reasons are purely for his own protection. Does that make sense to you?" asked Lainon.

"Yes," he answered carefully. "But the nature of the information you give me—I may see danger in not telling the king—if that is the case . . ."

"No, no. It is not a matter related to defence, or the enemy. It is not about internal intrigues or anything I believe to be detrimental to the realm, Handir, I would not ask that of you."

"Alright," he said slowly.

"Handir, trust me. I take full responsibility for my actions. I ask only that you help me, help *us*. I have the king's best interests at heart, I swear."

"I know you are a Kingsman, Lainon. My father holds you in high esteem. I do trust you. You have my honour-bound oath to not speak of what you are about to disclose to any other than to you."

Lainon bowed his head in respect for the trust the young prince placed in him, and he had meant what he said. The responsibility would be his alone to bear.

"Handir, you have a brother."

The prince laughed. "Do I? He's more of a frozen *stalagmite* if you . . ."

"Handir," interrupted Lainon, before pausing, making sure the prince was listening before he spoke once more. "Handir, you have a *Silvan* brother— one you have never met."

Lainon's explanation was met with blank silence, but there was nothing more he could say to make the prince understand. Indeed, he *had* understood, only the information had been so utterly shocking to him he had yet to react.

"Handir."

"What do you mean I have a Silvan brother? that is not . . ."

"You share the same father," said Lainon, willing the boy to understand.

The prince was silent for a moment and when he did speak, it was to ask a question Lainon had not expected. "Does he know? Does my father know?"

Lainon closed his eyes for a moment, for what to say? It was complicated and it had never been his intention to create an even greater rift between Thargodén and his children.

"He knew only of his conception."

"He *knew*," repeated Handir flatly and Lainon could read the growing coldness in his young charge's eyes.

"I doubt he knew of the child's fate, Handir. It is a complex story, one you should hear from your father."

"He *will* tell me," continued Handir, his voice still, unnervingly monotonous. "He will tell me or he will lose me."

"Handir," said Lainon, touching the boy's forearm to anchor him, to draw his attention back to wherever it had strayed. "Listen carefully, my friend, for what I have to tell you is of the utmost importance," he began, watching Handir's face carefully for signs that he was listening and understanding.

"Handir."

"Yes."

"Your brother—your brother is young, a fledgling warrior—the best I have ever seen. I tell you this because I do not want him to suffer the consequences of this information falling into the wrong hands, or falling into the right ones at the wrong time. He does not deserve to see his dreams dashed—he is at no fault."

Handir's head whipped to Lainon and the Ari'atór resisted the urge to step backwards, for in the prince's sky blue eyes there was a fire that burned so brightly it reminded him—of Fel'annár.

"And you tell me this—now—because?"

"Because until one month ago, he lived in his village, in the Deep Forest with all that remains of his family. Now, as he becomes a novice warrior he has—drawn attention to himself. I know it is a simple matter of time before your father and your siblings hear of him, and when you see him, there will be no doubts in your minds. I seek only to protect the king, protect you, Handir, for well you know there are those in Ea Uaré that would use these circumstances to their own ends, their own greed for power."

Lainon's slanted eyes continued to study Handir's face. The fire had abated somewhat, and his stare had turned to the side, a sure sign that he was, finally, reasoning out the barrage of information Lainon had hit him with.

"What do you suggest we do, Lainon," said the prince, a hint of sadness now tingeing his words.

"I need you, Handir, to keep me informed of any references, of the slightest hint, joke, comment or otherwise, regarding the one they call The Silvan. We must correctly judge the time to tell the king of what we have found in the forest. He cannot be left to find out for himself and yet we cannot risk an adverse reaction, for the boy's sake."

Handir looked at Lainon once more and the fire was back. "I have no care for my father's feelings, Lainon, he leaves me—indifferent," he stressed, before turning his back on his former guard.

"I do not believe you mean that, Handir."

The prince spun on his heel, so suddenly Lainon stepped backwards as the fine cloth of the boy's robes fanned around him, his dark blond hair falling back into place moments later but his face, his handsome, serene face was now twisted into a snarl Lainon had never seen him wear.

"Oh, but I *do*, Lieutenant Lainon. I do mean what I say. He is responsible for the departure of my mother! He pierced her soul, ripped it apart so badly she abandoned her *children*. He forsook her and his own legitimate children for the sake of some Silvan *slut*, with whom he *dared* conceive a child," roared the red-faced prince.

"Handir," called Lainon, holding up a hand to stop the tirade that now flew furiously from the prince's mouth.

"*That* is why he never explained anything to us, for *shame*," he spat, "for shame and *cowardice* for he would surely know we could never condone such an act—he gave her a *child*!"

Lainon wisely waited for the storm to blow over before attempting to speak once more and when he did, it was calm and slow.

"Handir, I ask only that you consider this. We do not know the circumstances, we cannot know until the king decides to speak of it and well I know he never has. I have known your father since before he was king, still a crown prince, your own age. Do not judge him rashly, Handir. You are the wisest of your siblings, the most capable of rational thought—do not let your heart run away with your mind."

Handir turned slowly so that his back was to Lainon once more.

"The heart always wins over short distances, Lainon. It will not let the mind curb its passion."

He needed time, that was what Handir was telling him and yet they did not have it.

"Leave me, Lainon."

"Handir, you cannot . . ."

"You have wrenched from me an honour-bound oath. I will say nothing for the moment," said the prince tiredly.

"Will you . . ."

"Yes—I will inform you should I hear anything that may alert my fa..., my *king* or Rinon."

Lainon bowed to Handir's back, his heart heavy now with the onus he placed on the prince's young shoulders. He wanted to console him, but Handir's emotions were a broiling, whirling cauldron of hate, incomprehension, confusion and hurt and Lainon would do well to leave him be now, to find his equilibrium, if indeed that were at all possible.

"And Lainon."

"My Prince."

"It is good to see you. I *missed* you," he said quietly.

Lainon smiled at the prince, his heart breaking for the boy because in that one sentence he had shown the colour of his life, the colour of loneliness.

Lainon had silently left and Handir felt his entire body sag, a testimony to just how much his former guard's words had affected him. He felt tired, exhausted almost and so he slowly lowered himself to the ground and sat, alone in the glade, alone and numb, shocked to the core at what Lainon had told him.

'. . . *You have a Silvan brother—one you have never met . . .*'

He wanted to think, to analyse but he could not, for his thoughts flew this way and that, with no order, only chaos and his heart throbbed mercilessly, locked in a strange battle with his mounting anger—at his father, his mother.

'. . . *a brother . . .*'

Lainon was surely mistaken, his mind screamed, but the information the Ari'atór had given him had been more than enough it seemed. If Lainon believed it, Handir could not gainsay him and yet—surely, surely it was *impossible . . .*

But it wasn't, and in his heart, he knew the truth of it.

'*A Silvan brother.*'

'*A fledgling warrior. The best I have ever seen.*'

His eyes filled with tears until they became too heavy to contain. *That* was why their mother left, he realised suddenly, for the conclusion had simply and quite naturally, clicked into place.

That is why she could not stay—it had not been a simple case of infidelity; a *child* had been conceived. It had not been a one-night affair, it had been a matter of the *heart*. All those years of suffering, of not understanding why she had abandoned them, thinking she had left them only because their father had committed adultery, for selfish *pride*. It had not been like that at *all*—she had left because their father had loved another woman, had *loved* her enough to give her a child.

He could not say how he felt about anything right now. Would he have done the same in the queen's position? Would he have left them all behind to escape the pain? Could he have forgiven and forgotten for the sake of his children? And could he ever forgive his Silvan brother for driving his mother away? For tearing his family apart? As he had said to Lainon, the heart wins over short distances and he wondered if *his* could ever tackle his overwhelming sense of betrayal.

Chapter Seven

CHANGING TIDES

"The Alpine warriors of Tar'eastór created a code that, once undertaken, could not be broken. The Warrior's Code was an oath not all elves could embrace for it came at a high price. A life for the safety and protection of king and land. Unconditional service unto death.
Warriors were revered and they in turn revered those they protected. There was little that could overshadow the love and devotion of the people for their glorious warriors."
The Silvan Chronicles, book II. Marhené.

Why Fel'annár had cast his eyes over the group of on-looking parents, sweethearts and siblings as he took his vow he could not explain, for there was no one there for *him*; no father, no mother, no aunt or siblings. And yet he *had* spotted the face of a young Alpine lord in fine robes who had been standing towards the back. His hair was of dark gold and his skin white and smooth. But it was not his colouring that had caught Fel'annár's attention. It was the vague similarity in their features, that and the way the lord had looked upon him. Perhaps he too, was surprised and there was no wonder, for Fel'annár's features were regarded as unique and although this enigmatic lord did not have his own, admittedly strange green eyes, his face was familiar all the same.

He had shaken himself mentally, turning to re-join his fellow novices, smiling at them as he moved to stand beside them, but try as he might, he had not been able to resist one last glance at the crowd, only to find young lord gone.

Well he *was* half Alpine himself and was only now encountering more elves of that race. His features had always been a cause for comment and yet now, despite his unique eyes, Fel'annár fit better with the Alpines here in the city than he did with the Silvan people. He was not sure he liked that thought and he wondered if, perhaps, he would be allowed to wear his leather bracelets with his uniform. He mentally snorted at himself for the childish idea but his left hand moved up to touch the braided leather around his right wrist, the band Amareth had given him upon his coming of age.

"Fel'annár."

"Um?" he responded distractedly, turning to meet the face of Idernon who now sat beside him.

"Briefing is upon us."

Fel'annár took a moment to gather himself with a deep breath. He had been sitting here for too long and his muscles ached. His head too, was a thumping reminder of the night's revelry.

"The time is come then," said Fel'annár.

"Aye," answered Idernon, eyes landing on Ramien beside him as he stood. "Our time together may be short, my friends, for there are only twenty novices for many quadrants."

"The Company will be disbanded then, broken before it truly begins," said Ramien forlornly, unfolding his legs and joining Idernon, a sad smile stretching his lips. Reaching down, he offered his hand to Fel'annár who took it with a vigorous slap.

"Never that, brother," said Fel'annár, hoisting himself up. "The Company can *never* be disbanded for it is a bond of love and respect; that cannot be changed, nobody can change that and if we are indeed to be separated, we will continue to learn and evolve and when the time comes, when we are all three competent, seasoned warriors, we shall come together once more and be *great*," he stressed, his eyes alight with the conviction that his words were true. "You will see. When I am able, I will find you and we shall ride together—for our king and our forest, for our *people*," he smiled, his eyes fixing first upon Ramien and then on Idernon.

"You truly are a leader of elves, Fel'annár," said Idernon. "I have always known this and I tell you truly now, whatever I achieve in the years to come, *you*—will always be my Captain," he almost whispered, his eyes bright with the emotion that had captured him, coloured his features and his words and made his eyes shine overly bright.

"And mine," said Ramien. "It is our destiny," he smiled, glancing at Idernon to confirm he was not alone in this. "We choose *you,* and I swear all I do now, will be to make myself worthy."

"I do not deserve such fine words, brothers," he chuckled, even though his own eyes were bright. "I have yet to prove my mettle in battle. I am only a novice and you speak to me as a captain!" he laughed, but it was a nervous laugh, one Fel'annár used to diffuse the solemnity of the moment; but Idernon had not finished.

"Nay—say not useless words, Fel'annár. There is nothing to prove, only to learn. You do not realise your potential yet, but I – *we* - we do. From the outside, things become clearer sometimes. I see your skill as a fighter, your heart as a protector. I see your senses, stronger than any other I have seen. You will be a leader, Hwind'atór. Of that we have no doubt."

There was no resisting Idernon's heart-felt words and suddenly, all the bitterness of his early years, the recurrent self-pity made way for nascent belief—belief that he could truly do this; walk the path of a novice and become the warrior, the *leader* he was destined to be.

Hours later, Turion watched the novice from afar as he performed his strange exercises, the ones the boy had invented for himself. It was beautiful to behold and the newly invested captain found himself mesmerised, even though it was not the first time he had seen it. The slow perfection of the movements, the effort behind every lunge, every arc of the long sword and swipe of the shorter sabre in his other hand; it was a treatise on power and precision.

Round and round he moved, his blades in slow but continuous movement, slicing and arcing, jabbing and swivelling in his hands, pointing one way and then the other as his body moved to accommodate them—*strange,* realised Turion. It was normally the other way around; the body moved and the blade accompanied but in this style, the blade, the *weapon,* was the vehicle and the body adapted to whatever movements were necessary.

Turion cocked his head to the side, assessing the virtues of the concept, watching the clever moves as they were performed at perhaps only a fourth of the speed with which he would need to do so in battle. It strengthened the muscles, he realised, perfected the move. The boy was good—he was very good.

He remembered then that one of the other recruits had called him Hwind'atór, the Whirling Warrior. He understood now, for the child was, quite literally dancing with the blades; a whirling surge of pure, measured power that would not easily be vanquished upon the battlefield. The thought that Fel'annár was still a novice suddenly struck him as utterly absurd and he shook his head in a subconscious attempt to free himself of the ridiculous notion for the warrior he observed knew far more than any novice, any warrior Turion had ever met.

Movement to his left alerted him to Lainon's presence beside him but he did not turn to look.

"I have read of the warriors of ancient Tar'eastór when still it had been called Ga'lenár. They trained in a similar manner—it is so foreign to our own methods and yet there is much merit in what he does," said Lainon, his slanted eyes now anchored on the novice as he swivelled upon his heels and then flipped backwards.

"Yes, it is in the War Tomes, book two I believe. I have read it," murmured the captain.

Lainon smiled at his friend. "How did he take the news of his assignment?" he asked.

"His face was an open book, Lainon. He looked so young as he tried to process his impending separation with his friends. They have always been together it seems, his only family so to speak."

"Strange, is it not, for to look upon him now, there is nothing boyish or innocent in his movements. He is strangely—*threatening* and yet, paradoxically—*vulnerable*."

Turion turned his surprised eyes to his friend. "Yes," he said in disbelief, "yes that is *exactly* it, Lainon. We have much work to do. We must teach him war craft, we must harden his mind, and we must lead him to closure where his family is concerned; prepare him for the truth he must soon hear, from us."

"He will make a good captain," murmured Lainon.

"Lainon," answered Turion a little too quickly, now looking squarely at his Ari lieutenant, the light of some weighty truth shining in his eyes.

"If I am right and we train him well, he will be more than a *captain*, my friend," he said carefully, waiting for his friend's reaction before continuing.

"There is something about him, what made me leave the village barracks. I cannot put it into words—except this. The boy inspires loyalty—*my* loyalty," he whispered, the shadow of incomprehension lurking beneath Turion's stern features, an expression Lainon now shared; but he too, was lost for the words and so he sat, shoulder to shoulder with his captain and friend, and turned his eyes back to the Whirling Warrior—and smiled.

Lainon still remembered the strange song he had heard when Fel'annár had arrived at the city barracks. It had been a song of proclamation he had thought at the time, unable to understand what that meant, and Turion's strange words were one more piece of the puzzle Lainon had set out to solve.

"You are quiet this morning, brother. Has that Silvan representative riled your Alpine blood?" asked Rinon ironically as he lounged upon the ample seating before the hearth of their family chambers.

"No," replied Handir distractedly, and when he offered no further information, Rinon turned to face him.

"Well?

A deep sigh preceded Handir's words. "I am busy, Rinon."

"You have not but a moment to share in brotherly conversation?"

"Since when do *you*, indulge in brotherly conversation Rinon? What is it you *want?*" asked Handir with a flick of his wrist.

"I see I will have to change tactics," said Rinon with a snort, before sitting up and leaning forward. "After this morning's council meeting you spoke to that Forest Dweller privately; what did he want?"

"Good morning," came the voice of the king as he glided into the room and moved to pour himself a glass of apple juice. It had been an intense morning in the council chambers.

Both brothers stood and bowed before sitting once more, Handir's eyes trained on those of the crown prince, but the king was already answering Rinon's question.

"He is concerned Rinon, 'tis all. You heard the reports from the North-west just as we did. They fear that by the time our warriors arrive that our crops will be lost. He seeks assurances and he is not getting them."

"What assurance does he think we can give him? We fight, is that not enough? We have lost a third of the North-western quadrant in but two seasons. Does he think more meat for the desert scimitars is easy to come by? Nay, we need a change in tactics if we are to win this war."

Handir's look of disgust was seconded by a hardening of the king's features, though it was fleeting.

"Rinon, I do not believe that is what he thinks. What I believe he truly seeks is the knowledge that here, in the heart of the city, the Silvan villagers are esteemed by the Alpine well enough to feel for the plight of the Silvan people. He seeks to observe, to understand, to know that all that can possibly be done is *being* done. He wishes to assure his anxious people that the Alpine people are protecting them as best they can, and believe me, it is in our interest that he return to the forest and says it is so."

The king listened silently but Rinon huffed impatiently. "They seek our protection in a land that is not safe. They refuse to fall back and let our warriors deal with it—they are in the way, meddling in the affairs of the military and they are too mule-headed to step down and admit it."

"Rinon," said Handir, raising his voice for the first time as he stood and approached his brother. "You speak of the Silvans as if they have no right to be protected in their own homes—you forget – that they are *Silvan*; their trees cannot be left alone to fend for themselves, they are just as much a part of their lives as the sun, the water and the earth – you cannot separate a Silvan from the forests, Rinon, you cannot ask them to forsake their sentinels. You asked me what Erthoron wanted because you do not possess that information. Are you now to tell me you in fact *know* his motives for seeking private council with me? That all he wants is more troops and to otherwise hinder our efforts to push back the enemy? It is absurd."

"You are overly naïve, Handir," said Rinon, rising to his feet so that he could look at his brother on equal terms. "You do not see how he tries to manipulate you into sending more troops sooner, more supplies, more boons when what he should be doing is evacuating the area. He plays on your inexperience and you see it not."

Handir held the ice-cold eyes of his brother, his own warmer blue eyes steady and confident. "You confuse naivety with objectivity, brother. 'Tis not always necessary to have an immediate opinion—sometimes one must wait and observe—you would do well to try for you speak of our *citizens*, be they Alpine or Silvan; do not presume the Silvans to be without their reasons –

just because you do not understand them does not mean they are not there. Do not succumb to ignorance but more than this, do not *show* them your ignorance."

The king raised an eyebrow, his keen eyes moving from Handir to Rinon and still, he remained silent.

"Clever words, Councillor. And that is all they are. Keen is your mind but you are still so young, have never seen battle and likely never will. You cannot see the sacrifice of our warriors, all you see are the demands of the foresters and the political implications. You do not understand what it costs to protect those villages, those crops," he said as he moved closer to his brother. "Heed your own words, brother. Be objective and consider at least the possibility that you are being *played*."

"I never discarded it, Rinon; I said only that you cannot presume that is, indeed, the case. I certainly do not. But now listen to me. Do not underestimate the political implications. Should Erthoron go home and claim we have not listened to the Silvan people, I do not need to remind you that they are in the majority. Tread carefully for they believe they are right to stay and defend the trees, just as you and our army believe you are right to demand they leave them behind. Something must change."

They stared levelly at each other for a moment, before Rinon nodded and moved away, his eyes meeting those of his father before leaving the room.

"I fear Rinon moves ever closer to Lord Band'orán and our cousin Barathon," said Handir, almost as if he spoke to himself. "With every day that passes I sense a growing—*disdain*—towards the Silvans. It is misplaced, unfounded, and *dangerous*."

"Handir," said the King, speaking for the first time since he had entered the room. His voice although soft, was loud enough to draw the prince's attention and pull him out of his inner musings.

"My King," he answered, the hint of a question in his tone.

"Watch him, Handir. Anchor him if you can. This rift between the Silvan people and our military rulings must not be allowed to grow for the Silvans already feel they are treated as inferiors by the Alpine majority here in the city."

"And they would be *right*," said Handir.

"Yes," said the king carefully. "Alas that is a growing reality, but what we forget is that out there," he pointed to the Great Forest, "out there, *they* are the majority—and we cannot live without the forest, Handir, we cannot live without the Silvan natives of this land. If the Silvans revolt, we may have civil war on our hands."

Handir listened to his father with growing concern, for although they were of like mind on this point, Handir had not realised just how volatile the situation was.

"You think it a possibility?" he asked.

"Yes, yes I do. If this slow but persistent scepticism persists, Handir; if those Alpine barons under Lord Band'orán are allowed to continue with their subtle poisoning, sooner or later, with the right guidance, the Silvans will turn on us."

Handir's eyes were wide, his avid mind a whirlwind of information. "I will do all I can, but our uncle's influence at council is considerable."

"I know, but we have Aradan, Handir—and we have *you*," he smiled most uncharacteristically and for a moment, Handir felt grateful for his father's words, grateful and utterly shocked.

"Father. If you know all this, why do you not come back? Come back to your people, show them the strength you once possessed, surely still do?"

The king's sad smile took Handir back and he braced himself for the king's answer. But it did not come and the sparkle in Handir's eyes died.

"You did well," sad the king before turning, and leaving in silence.

It took a moment for Handir to process the words of praise, but instead of enjoying the moment, it simply confused him, and he suddenly realised why; he did not know how to react. He should be angry with his father, for creating a child with a Silvan woman, for triggering his mother's departure to Valley, for hiding the truth from them for all this time.

He spent the rest of that day pondering the question, for his father was an enigma. If he had, indeed, reached out in his own, mercurial way, then Handir would take his hand and try at least, to understand him, understand why he had done—whatever it was he had done.

He realised then, that the mystery and the scandal, the gossip and the hearsay surrounding the departure of their mother was, at least partially, the product of ignorance. He had not the information necessary to understand, and if he could not understand, why had he judged his father negatively? Was that not what his own brother, Rinon, had done with the Silvans? the very same attitude Handir had reprimanded him for?

His mind reminded him of his immediate dilemma—a decision had to be taken. Would he try to glean the truth from his father, the story of the queen's departure, of his involvement with the Silvan woman, the reasons that had prompted him to create a child - or would he desist? But then—had that choice not been taken away from him just yesterday? Had Lainon not shattered any hope of a status quo in which the royal family would continue to live its life of stilted communication?

He had no choice, he knew that now. He had a brother, one that was oblivious to his royal heritage. He could not begin to imagine the shock of it, and the consequences it could bring should the Alpine purists hear of it and use it against the king. It would be an irresistible temptation for Band'orán to discredit Thargodén and indirectly promote his own claim to the throne, something he had been doing for many years without success. Something like this would be a heavy blow to the king's credibility—Handir could not allow his great uncle to find out.

He visibly shivered, feeling his own conviction bolstered. Handir was no coward, even though he was not a warrior. He too, had a dream, one of unity for this colourful and diverse society that had somehow lost its way, lost the harmony that had once existed in his distant memories.

Chapter Eight

INTO THE FOREST

"Immortal souls love immortally."
The Silvan Chronicles, Book I. Marhené

Deep in the north-western reaches of Ea Uaré, it was dark, even though it was not yet evening. There was a shadowy half-light that cast a greyish blue tinge to everything, making the forest seem unreal, like a vision from a vivid dream. It was treacherous too for the forest floor was nothing but a twisted, heaving knot of tree roots. It would be all too easy to get a boot stuck amongst them and twist an ankle, or worse. It was surprisingly hard to navigate and by the time the trees had thinned somewhat and Turion called for camp to be set up, the Western patrol heaved a sigh of relief as they set about their respective duties. Lainon though, had requested Fel'annár join him at a hearth Fer'dán was still nurturing.

"You know how Deviants come to be - you have heard the stories, I am sure. But heed me, Fel'annár. Do not overestimate your ability to fight them. This battle is not only one of bows and blades but of the *mind*," emphasised Lainon, his eyes firmly anchored on Fel'annár, willing his novice to understand the importance of his words and not discard them as the product of an overprotective mentor.

Fel'annár simply nodded as he continued to listen avidly to the wise words of the Ari'atór Lainon, for none could possibly know more than a Spirit Warrior about the Deviants.

"The younger Deviants from the mountains are misshaped but not clumsy, do not be fooled. They can be surprisingly fast—and whatever you do, do not let them speak to you for they will unbalance you with their filthy words and then take advantage of your inattention."

"Are all mountain Deviants like this? Or does it depend on which range they are from?" asked Fel'annár with a frown of concentration on his brow.

"They are all the same. Now, it is the *cave* Deviants that you need to watch for. They are larger, more powerful, and somewhat more intelligent. Their skill with blades is more sophisticated, but they will also use bows, clubs, scimitars and sling shots which they are surprisingly good at wielding."

"What is the ratio of mountain Deviants to cave Deviants, Lieutenant?"

"A good question. Our scouts know there is a veritable army of mountain Deviants to but a handful of cave specimens but that does not mean there are few of them. Cave Deviants are frequently seen in bands of usually between ten and thirty at most, whereas mountain Deviants normally move in larger numbers. We also know that they seem to be organizing themselves; there is a pattern to their movements of late and some of our commanders claim they have established a hierarchy of sorts."

"Is there any truth to the stories of larger Deviants, and of the wild wolves that often accompany them?" asked Fel'annár, his eyes a little too wide as he waited for Lainon's answer with bated breath.

"Yes, there is some truth in it. The more northerly patrols have reported strangely large individuals and hairy, stinking wolves, three times the size of their forest cousins. That is all we have for the moment as sightings have been rare, but they do exist."

"Lieutenant, Captain Turion is looking for you," said a warrior, briefly taking his fist to his heart in salute at his superior.

"Thank you, Angon," said Lainon as he rose from his sitting position. "Fel'annár, accompany Angon to gather firewood and procure meat if there is any to be had; you are under his command."

"Yes, Sir," said Fel'annár with a salute as Lainon walked away and he was left alone with Angon, a veteran Silvan warrior he had yet to speak with, despite the distance they had travelled together.

"Come," said Angon curtly as he led the way into the forest. "So, you are one of the early promotion novices—the one they call The Silvan?" he asked as he began to gather firewood.

"Yes," said Fel'annár, stifling the smirk that threatened to blossom on his otherwise blank features.

"*I* am Silvan—*you* do not *look* Silvan," said the warrior.

"That is precisely the—*joke* I suppose," answered Fel'annár somewhat sourly.

"It is not funny," said Angon simply, bending once more to pick up a piece of dry kindling.

Fel'annár, wisely, said nothing, for he was unsure of this warrior's intentions.

"You are clearly *Alpine*—what have you done to deserve the name of The *Silvan*?" he said, his manner finally showing clearly in the colour of his words. Sarcasm, mockery.

Fel'annár anticipated his own adverse reaction and quelled it ruthlessly, taking his time before answering.

"I have lived and loved in my forest home," he began steadily. "I am a novice because I wish to serve my *Silvan* kin," he emphasised before continuing. "I am here to learn so that I may protect my *people*—my mother's people." His tone had risen steadily until his final words rang strong and heart-felt, and Angon was left staring at the young novice, at a loss for words it seemed, until he finally looked down, and when his eyes met Fel'annár's once more, there was a smile in them that did not quite reach his mouth.

"Well boy, you are not easily cowed and that is a *Silvan* trait." There was no apology and no more words were shared, other than a curt, "come," and they were away again, in search of food for the patrol.

An hour later, they had returned to camp with a string of rabbits, but Fel'annár had not been invited to join the troop—*again*—and so, as was his custom, he sat alone, some distance away from them, checking the fletching of his arrows as if it did not bother him at all. It had been this way since they had set out, and although he could not say he was surprised, it rankled him nonetheless. He had heard the stories of course, was not ignorant of the fact that novices were not easily accepted by the warriors. They considered them a hindrance, albeit they understood their need to learn in the field, and in this case, Fel'annár had been promoted earlier than was usual. They would think him cocky and in need of a lesson and he could not say he did not understand—he *was* a liability.

"You, *Silvan*," shouted a warrior, apparently of Alpine origin who sat before the early evening fire together with the rest of the patrol, save for Lainon and Turion, who sat a little further away at their own fire.

Fel'annár looked over his shoulder at them, struggling but succeeding in keeping his face blank and unconcerned.

"Bring water from the stream for our tea," said the warrior, his comrades chuckling at their friend's antics.

"Yes, Sir," said Fel'annár patiently for he knew what they did. They were surely testing him and he would not fall to their bait—he had already endured Angon's test and so, picking up a pail, Fel'annár started towards the stream, but he was rudely hailed once more.

"Use this," said the warrior, watching as Fel'annár trotted back and picked up the smaller bucket the warrior handed him..

Back from the stream, he handed the bucket to the warrior, who, taking it, proceeded to turn it upside down, emptying it completely upon the ground before handing it back to their mortified novice.

"You did not rinse it out—clean it first and then fill it for our tea."

"Yes, Sir," was all Fel'annár allowed himself as he once more took the bucket and did as he was told, clenching his jaw to suppress his mounting anger.

This time the bucket was accepted and the warrior brewed tea as Fel'annár sat alone once more, and Turion and Lainon watched from afar with keen eyes.

Not that he had expected it, but he was disappointed when the tea was made and he was not offered a mug of it. It was cold and his hands were numb, and with no fire to warm them. Resigned, he continued to whittle new shafts for his stash of arrows, until another voice hailed him once more.

"Silvan. Skin these rabbits—we are hungry—make haste."

Rising, he took the offered rabbits and set to work, carefully skinning them, and even returning to the stream to rinse them.

Taking the prepared rabbits, the warrior set to cooking them, and once again, Fel'annár was excluded from their meal. They ate with relish, indeed it seemed to Fel'annár that they purposefully exaggerated their slurping and their crunching, loudly sucking on their juicy fingers as they relished the wood barbecued meat. His own mouth watered and his stomach growled like a starved cat, although luckily, he was too far away for them to hear it. A small mercy, he thought sourly.

It finally came to a head when one warrior began to talk of child warriors who thought themselves special. Of inexperienced novices that were nothing but a thorn in their backsides. Of how they were all the same at the end of the day, that with his first Deviant kill, he would lose his lunch, just like everyone else.

Now Fel'annár knew for a fact that that would never happen, he would not allow it. He was well-prepared for that moment and although he could not deny a pang of apprehension at the mere thought, he was sure enough of himself to handle it.

And so, it continued well into the night, until it was time for his watch and he sat forlornly upon a boulder, hungry and thirsty, his senses stretching out to the forest, albeit with one eye upon the sleeping warriors huddled together, their cosy fire crackling softly. He wondered when he would finally become a part of their group for he missed the camaraderie, and Idernon and Ramien came to mind, their companionship and their support—perhaps he was not as strong as he thought he was.

Light footsteps told Fel'annár that Turion was approaching. He did not take his eyes from the fore though, and simply acknowledged his commanding officer with a softly spoken "Sir."

"I found this sitting by the fire, unaccounted for. I thought you may be interested," he said, a tinny clink alerting Fel'annár to the fact that Turion had left an object at his side.

Looking down, he saw a single leg of rabbit and a mug of water. With a glance at Turion that was more a request for permission, the captain nodded and then watched as the young novice's hand shot out and grabbed the tiny morsel of meat, taking it to his mouth and sucking, his eyes rolling backwards and then closing in what could only be described as ecstasy.

With a soft chuckle, Turion waited until the admittedly frugal meal was devoured and when only the bone was left on the plate and the water drained, the novice wiped his greasy lips and then smiled at his captain.

"You have done well with the warriors, Fel'annár. It would have been all too easy to lose your temper and complain to me, or Lainon. It is what they were waiting for you to do—testing your loyalty as a warrior."

"I understand, Captain. It has not been so bad, save perhaps for the lack of warmth and a friendly smile. I can handle that, Sir."

Turion smiled ironically. "What about the blankets? The swaps in guard duty? Missing arrows? Empty canteens? You do not mention these things and that speaks in your favour, except perhaps in that you underestimate my powers of observation."

Fel'annár smiled in defeat for it was all true, in fact his life had been passing uncomfortable for the entire trip out. He had expected to be put to the test, but perhaps not quite in this way. "I knew that you knew of some of their—antics—and I believe that you kept out of it purposefully; it is necessary, perhaps, that a commander allow his warriors to organise themselves—to an extent . . ." he trailed off, his face looking at Turion for confirmation that he had not overstepped some unspoken boundary for he wanted to know.

Turion sat looking at the novice for a while, and Fel'annár fidgeted, wishing he had just stuck his boot in his flapping mouth. Luckily though, the captain had not taken offence at his words and instead, had read his intentions for what they were—curiosity.

"Very good," he smiled softly. "But a word of advice. It is not a test of endurance, but one of reaction. If you continue the way you are, it will not stop. *You*, must stop it, and the only way to do it is to *tell* them something," he finished, his eyes twinkling in challenge. Fel'annár's eyes watched carefully, his mind considering his captain's words. '*Tell them something*'. Tell them *what*? he asked himself, but Turion was already on his feet and with a nod, he walked back to the camp.

When dawn brought with it another day, the warriors found a pail of fresh water already boiling on their rekindled fire, and chestnuts crackling over the hot coals. Twelve freshly prepared trout fillets lay upon a clean rock, not a bone to be seen, and the warriors of the Western patrol glanced over at the young novice with renewed respect. The boy sat sharpening his sabre, apparently uninterested, and Angon smiled.

From afar, Turion elbowed Lainon beside him, smiling to himself in satisfaction. '*Well done*,' he thought. The boy had understood him for his message to the warriors was clear. He respected them, in spite of the difficulties they threw at him.

Now, all that remained to be seen was how the warriors would react.

How many times Handir had found himself in this very same situation during the past few days he could no longer count, and always, the outcome had been the same—indecision, doubt, fear.

This time he sat upon a stone bench, away from the bustling crowds of his father's court for he needed to think—he needed to concentrate and decide on a tactic that would get him the information he needed without earning his father's wrath.

But then, he scoffed, how does one go about asking one's father about how he cheated on his wife, one's mother, especially when said father was a *king*? It was absurd, for if you added to that that said king was the son of the mighty Or'Talán, well he may as well douse himself with pig fat and set a torch to it.

The first step, supposed Handir, would be to find a way of bringing up the subject without sounding combative, a way of making his father comfortable enough to talk about it. It was a monumental task Handir was not at all convinced would work; in fact he was sure he would fail for there was a deep secret confined in the depths of his father's heart. Aradan, perhaps, would be better equipped for the task.

Aradan, the king's most loyal councillor was indeed deep in the king's confidence and Handir suddenly wondered if it wouldn't be wiser to confide in his mentor, spilling the problem in all its glory and then wait with bated breath at the words of wisdom Aradan would surely have.

There was a risk though, and that was the elf's staunch loyalty to the king. It could well lead him to tell the king of the Silvan child and he could not risk that. But what if he simply asked about the circumstances surrounding the queen's departure? What if he left out the fact that Handir knew he had a brother, that his father's secret child had been made known to him?

Yes, it was finally coming together; he had made progress and now, all he had to do was wait for the right moment to approach his mentor. But one thing he *did* know; it needed to be soon, very soon for the risk of the boy's identity becoming known was too great.

As it turned out, Handir did not have to wait long, and after the next council meeting, Handir had seen his chance for what it was. Aradan was in a good mood, the day was yet young, and the king had not requested his presence. Bolstering his resolve, he trotted up to his mentor and took up his pace, stuffing his hands into his ample sleeves as he was wont to do when walking and thinking at the same time.

"Lord Aradan."

"Councillor Handir," he replied perkily enough, and Handir was encouraged.

"I have need of your counsel," he said innocently, too much it seemed, for Aradan stopped short and turned to his young apprentice.

"What is it?" he asked in genuine concern.

"It is a *private* matter, my Lord, of some import. I would not burden you with it but I know not who else to turn to."

Aradan studied the boy's face before slowly nodding. "Alright, you have my full attention."

"Thank you, my Lord," he said. *So far so good* he thought. "I know you are more than aware of my family's—*communication* issues."

"Handir, do not use those euphemisms with me. While I am pleased you remember your lessons, we speak now as friends, I dare say. As such they are misplaced. Speak freely and for the sake of Ari, *plainly.*"

"Lord Aradan, if I may. I must first ask that you consider this conversation a private issue and, as such, to be spoken of only between ourselves."

"Handir, I cannot promise that," said Aradan with a warning glance. "Should you disclose something I feel of relevance to the king, I will not withhold it from him. But this, of course, you already knew," he murmured, searching his prince's soft blue eyes for the answers to his unspoken questions.

"I do know, Aradan. But my dilemma is this: family conflict is leading to an ever-growing rift between myself and the Crown Prince, indeed with my own father. I know you are sympathetic to the Silvan cause, as I myself am, and that you dislike the ideas that Lord Band'orán is promoting. I consider it my duty to remedy this and the only way forward that I can see, is to break the barrier of silence on the matter of the queen's departure. Only then will I be able to work with my father and brother to return this kingdom to what it once was, reverse the downward spiral into conflict and perhaps, even treason."

Aradan stared disbelievingly at his young charge, before letting out an overdue breath. "After all this time—is this not a little—out of the blue? You cannot think me so naive as to presume I would not read between the lines—that there is a *reason* for doing this now?"

"Nay, I respect you, Aradan, this you know. I would never underestimate you. I simply wish to promote my theory and gain your confidence. I will speak to my father on the same question I wish to ask you. Does that help me to earn your discretion?"

"It may," said Aradan as he began to walk once more.

It had to be enough, decided Handir, but that did nothing to quell his trepidation.

"Alright," he said slowly and Aradan glanced at the boy worriedly. "I need to understand the circumstances surrounding my father's—*indiscretion.*"

Silence.

"I understand if you are under oath, Aradan. I wish simply for any information you can offer, even if it is a simple impression. I know you were already deep in my father's confidence at the time. I know you know what happened."

Silence.

Handir looked down, his confidence failing rapidly. Aradan was not talking.

"Aradan, this is important. It is not a whim, it is of the utmost significance to this kingdom that I understand him so that I can defend him."

"Defend him from *what?*" asked Aradan curtly.

"From those who would seek to discredit him."

"And who would do that?"

"Now it is *you* who underestimates me, Aradan. If you do not wish to speak of it do not, but do not turn the questioning upon me when well you know of whom I speak."

Silence.

It was not working; his plan had failed. Either he conceded something, or he would desist.

"Aradan, would it help if I told you what you truly want to know—the wherefore of my sudden conviction to know the truth?"

"Yes—it would make all the difference, Handir," said Aradan slowly, his eyes searching the second prince with a depth that unnerved him.

"And yet we come full circle, for to do so I must have your promise."

Silence.

"I cannot give it," said the Chief Councillor tightly. "Yet I will concede this one thing."

Handir stopped abruptly and turned to his mentor, his face now unguarded and open, young and vulnerable, but he cared not for in some unconscious way, Handir knew Aradan was about to reveal something of import.

"It was not some careless whim, Handir. It was not a moment of weakness that sent your mother away from her children, away from the only elf she had ever loved," said Aradan softly, a cloud of crushing grief almost visibly surging from his bright eyes.

"What then?" Handir whispered, his own eyes filling with unshed tears of empathy. "What was it that could achieve such a thing?" he pleaded.

Aradan's face softened before he slowly enunciated the words he knew his young charge could never have imagined.

"It was *love*, Handir. He loved a Silvan woman with eyes the colour of summer moss. He loved her as much as he respected your mother."

The tears in Handir's soft blue eyes finally brimmed and then slowly escaped and the prince looked away in shock. His father had not loved his mother, he had loved another he could not have . . . he had loved the woman that gave birth to the Silvan.

"Handir," called Aradan softly, but there was no answer, for the prince was lost in emotional chaos, half-hearted denial, disbelief, anger, incomprehension.

"I will leave you to your thoughts," was all he said before striding away, flailing in his own sea of tumultuous memories he did not care to relive.

But there was a question there too, one Aradan now needed an answer to, and which Handir had not wanted to disclose, not unless Aradan gave his word not to speak of it.

It was a dilemma, even for one such as Aradan.

Chapter Nine

FIRST CONTACT

"Love cannot be surpassed for it is all-encompassing to an elf. Life itself can be choked by her the whiles, for is it not better to face the void in love, unaware, than to face eternity without it, in painful lucidity?"
On Elven Nature. Calro.

Angon disappeared into the trees. The other warriors tracked silently behind Turion at the fore, and before Lainon at the rear.

Fel'annár was in the middle, feeling somewhat indignant at being treated like a weakling, a helpless twit unable to fend for himself. He had been told that, should there be a confrontation, he was to climb into the trees and offer cover with his bow. Fer'dán, an Alpine warrior was to accompany him—as if he were a *child!* he scoffed angrily. He had tracked back home with Idernon and Ramien, albeit that had been for rabbit and other small game. Here, though, they searched for signs of *Deviants*, and suddenly, the mere comparison, and his own, callow stupidity made him chuckle out loud, garnering the other warriors' disapproving gazes.

Fighting the blush that threatened to flood his face, he disciplined his mind as best he could, banning his inner dialogue from distracting him with a deep breath and a purposeful blink of the eye, and soon enough, he realised that the forest had quietened and the warriors moved differently. Their bodies were tightly coiled, their steps purposeful and quiet, eyes fixed on the path ahead, peripheral vision straining to take in as much visual information as they could. This was the closest Fel'annár had been to the enemy and his attention threatened to falter once more – excitement, apprehension.

He took another deep breath, but the fight to stop his own thoughts from manifesting themselves became harder with every step he took. His mind searched for protocols, strategies Turion would enforce, techniques he would use with his bow. His mounting distraction became apparent when he missed Turion's silent signal to ascend.

He was the last to scamper up the bark of the nearest tree and take up his position near Fer'dán, who glared at him in reproof. Fel'annár decided he deserved it as he straightened his ruffled cloak and once more, cursed his puerile ways.

Still a novice, he realised ruefully, yet determined to prove himself. He bore the stern, non-verbal reprimands and prepared his bow, watching Fer'dán as he did so, yet always with an eye on Turion.

Bird call from their scout had Fer'dán drawing on his short bow and Fel'annár did likewise. This was it then, he realised. He was going into battle with Deviants for the first time, albeit from the safety of the trees.

The enemy could be heard now and a soft breeze brought with it their scent. Fel'annár scrunched his nose up in disgust, for the smell was pungent—so much so it made his eyes water, impairing his vision. Swiping at them impatiently with his sleeve he rapidly took up his draw once more, unaware of the smirk that Fer'dán had allowed to escape, for the boy had unwittingly smudged his cheek with dirt.

"Steady, boy. Do not take to the ground unless you are ordered to. Take out the archers first if there are any, and if there are none, take out those in the fanciest clothes," instructed the veteran warrior calmly, as if they prepared for a summer picnic.

"Aye, Fer'dán," said Fel'annár a little too tightly—he was nervous, and he was irritated—at himself.

"Aim for the chest or neck."

'*Chest or neck*,' repeated Fel'annár to himself in surprise, surely the eye or the neck; he did not understand and made a note to ask Lainon later.

Another call—imminent contact—they were coming and he was ready. His breathing doubled to keep up with his thumping heart, his eyes as wide as they could be and his mouth slack and open.

The fine hairs at the nape of his neck prickled painfully and his sight narrowed to where he knew the enemy would appear. He was ready, he said to himself again, in spite of his writhing stomach.

"Steady, boy," came another warning from Fer'dán but Fel'annár heard it as if from a distance.

A guttural roar, more terrible than Fel'annár could ever have predicted, echoed around the glade and painfully in his ears, and the very sound of it was enough to shock him so that for a moment he could not move. It had been the sound of an animal, not a mortal, the sound of a wounded beast and Fel'annár found himself wondering why he had not expected that. Yet the battle was already underway, and Fer'dán, seemingly unaffected by the unnatural bellow, released his second arrow. Jolted out of his stunned paralysis, Fel'annár drew and then released, his keen eye following his own projectile until it embedded itself in the eye of a mountain Deviant who shrieked and then fell to the floor, mercifully dead.

Fel'annár smiled despite the cold sweat that had beaded on his forehead, and then drew once more, letting loose another, green-fletched arrow, his smile wider as he watched his second victim fall, its eye pierced.

The group had been small and the archers had not been needed upon the ground, and so, with no more mountain Deviants left alive, a satisfied novice followed Fer'dán to the ground.

"Clean up—Angon, see to it," barked Lainon, as Fel'annár watched in awe of his Ari'atór mentor whom he was observing in battle for the first time.

But the dark lieutenant suddenly whirled on his heels and came face to face with a startled Fel'annár.

"What are you *smiling* at!" he hissed, taking the young novice completely by surprise, his piercing blue eyes glinting like ancient steel under the desert sun.

The other warriors, including Turion, had gone deathly silent as they watched their lieutenant face their young novice.

"I do not understand," said Fel'annár, his worry and incomprehension written clearly on his open face. He thought he had done well; he had not missed a single shot.

"If a warrior bids you aim for the chest, you *comply!*" he shouted mercilessly.

Fel'annár made to open his mouth and defend himself, but could not quite manage to get his thoughts together, for the lieutenant's face was a dreadful sight.

"You are a *novice*, boy. You are not yet qualified to make tactical decisions. This will not happen again," he finally said, a little more calmly, before he spun on his heels and went to oversee the clean-up, the heavy air around them seeming to part before the Spirit Warrior, aware perhaps, of his anger and the terror he had masked as ire.

A friendly hand squeezed Fel'annár's shoulder, making him jump. It was Angon who simply walked past him. He smiled timidly before another hand landed in the same place, silent and strong and it was not long before all seven warriors had offered their silent support. Fel'annár had erred because he had disobeyed Fer'dán, yet he still failed to understand why it was so important to aim for the chest, where the damage may well not be fatal—why not go for a sure kill? It was beyond his ken and he resolved to ask Lainon about it—later of course, for the Ari'atór had been fierce in his wrath and Fel'annár had no intention whatsoever of crossing him again until he had calmed down.

Blowing out noisily, he slung his bow over his shoulder and followed the warriors, for there was dirty work to be done. The thought of touching the stinking bodies of the Deviants admittedly turned his stomach for they were a gruesome sight. He had prepared himself as best he could and had seen the drawings, read the descriptions, yet their unholy screams had taken him completely by surprise—nay they had *terrified* him and he swore he would not be taken unawares again.

They had gathered the half-rotten bodies and then dug open graves so that the birds could feed on them. Burning them was not an option here in the thick of the forest, yet neither could they leave the carcasses to pollute the ground.

They set up camp a fair distance away, and Fel'annár was invited to sit with the troop and its commanders for the first time. They talked quietly as was always the case after a skirmish and he was glad of it, for he did not wish to spoil the moment with some infantile comment, preferring instead to listen and speak as little as possible.

He was good at that—not drawing attention to himself.

Lainon watched him from across the fire, the orange flames that danced before him reflecting in his slanted eyes and lighting them up like a mountain puma hunting under a moonless night. The boy was worried, in spite of appearances, but he had respectfully held his peace, waiting perhaps for this very moment when Lainon would explain to him why he had shouted at him before the entire patrol.

Yet it was not Lainon who spoke but Turion.

"You are confused and that is understandable," he began, waiting for the rest of the warriors to quieten. "I will tell you why you deserved that down-braiding," he said matter-of-factly as Lainon nodded, staring into the flames as he listened.

"In battle, it is often the case that the archer's aim is not at its full potential. The excitement of the fight, exhaustion, poor light, an injured companion; there are many variables. It is the work of a good archer to guarantee a hit, whether it kills or simply maims. That way you never waste an arrow. If you take a difficult shot you may lose that arrow—your results will be poor and your companions on the ground will suffer the consequences."

Fel'annár listened carefully before opening his mouth to ask the question that was screaming to be freed, but Turion stopped him with his hand.

"Wait, and listen. I saw your marks and I know you did not waste arrows, but it was simply circumstance that allowed you to snipe, rather than to confront in battle. Had you been on the ground and firing your bow, would you have been able to make those shots?" asked the captain rhetorically.

Lainon turned to face the novice, daring him to gainsay the captain, and to his absolute shock—he did.

"Yes," he said a little too quietly, before looking around at his companions in silent apology. "Under the correct circumstances, I know I could make the same shots. I believe I have learned a lesson, but I also trust my instinct in this. If I know my circumstances permit, I therefore know I can make the shot. Had I been tired, perturbed in some way, injured, I understand the need to take a guaranteed aim, rather than one that may send my arrow astray. But that was not the case. I was safely perched in a tree, fresh and alert—I believe it was a good tactic and yet I did indeed disregard Fer'dán's guidance and for that I know I deserved your ire, Lieutenant. I will make sure that does not happen again."

Both commanders stared at the young novice, still processing the boy's bold words with blank faces and fiery eyes.

"How can you be so sure, Fel'annár? You have never engaged in battle before, you do not yet know how you will react. Your words are based on faith. It is the duty of the commander to ensure his warriors' safety—never trust to faith in that, Fel'annár."

Fel'annár held Turion's steady gaze before dipping his head in silent acknowledgement. "I understand, Captain," he said softly.

"You should also be aware that you *were* nervous, Fel'annár – we could all see that, even if you could not," said Lainon. There was a warning in his eyes and Fel'annár would not gainsay him. He was right. His tendency to downplay his own emotions, to disregard them as unimportant had been honed over years of defending himself, of telling himself that he was alright. Again, all he could do was nod, this time more slowly. He thought perhaps, that he had learned a valuable lesson.

"Good. Now, that said, I must congratulate you on a magnificent aim— you have earned the respect of my patrol, and *that,* is no easy feat," said Turion with a smile, all the seriousness and the severity gone from his tone and his expression, and Lainon was surprised to see the hint of a blush on Fel'annár's beautiful face.

Such contrasts warred within this one, mused the Ari'atór. So mature and intelligent, so naive and unsure, so solemn and disciplined, and yet so confident and—*feral.*

"And Fel'annár," added Turion as an afterthought. "Do something with that unruly hair of yours!"

The patrol chuckled in mirth, but in relief too, the tense atmosphere suddenly dissipating and Fel'annár said no more. He simply sat, listened, and learned; of warfare, and of himself.

The early morning breeze felt crisp, and it was just what Aradan needed to clear his mind of the dreams that had plagued him all night, from which he had awoken with a start, his heart pounding erratically and his soul heavy with crushing pity and shared grief.

Unwittingly, Prince Handir had opened a door long shut, one he had bolted and chained lest the demons behind escape. It was useless though, for they had slipped through to his consciousness like a sluggish, poisonous haze, lingering hauntingly, unwilling to leave him be.

There was no mystery though, for he knew why that was. There had been something in Handir's eyes, something the prince admitted to withholding, something which would only be revealed should Aradan promise not to speak of it. In good conscience he could not, for the boy offered no guarantees as to the nature of the information and yet—and yet he *had* to know. His considerable intuition told him it was important, hence the dreams.

Thargodén had been his friend for many centuries, still was, despite the dramatic change that had taken place in him after the queen left. The people attributed it to grief at the loss of his wife, but Aradan knew better. It was not the loss of his wife, it was the loss of his *love*. He felt the desperate urge to make Handir understand, force him to see his father as he had once been, show him that what had happened to Thargodén could have happened to anyone.

It had always felt so wrong that the king's own children should treat him with such frigid disregard. He did not deserve it and yet, when Aradan forced himself to see it from the perspective of the royal children, he could do naught but to understand their bitter resentment. As far as they were concerned, their father had gone with some Silvan woman of no import and had earned the wrath of his queen, who promptly and silently left for Valley, her children to remain without the slightest of explanations other than that she could not stay. Their father, when repeatedly asked why she had done such a thing, had simply turned away, disregarding their need to understand. And so it had festered until the king was left with two princes and one princess who were little more than strangers to him.

With a heavy breath, Aradan rose and began his short trek back to the fortress. It was decided. He would take a risk and give Handir his promise. If there was some way, any way at all that justice could be done and Thargodén could, at least, regain one of his sons, then Aradan would see it done.

Lunchtime, and Aradan watched the king as he pecked at the midday meal, his face indifferent, as if he had surrendered his will and simply moved with the errant tides. Rinon sat to his right, eating heartily, his face completely straight and emotionless, his movements abrupt.

To his left, sat Handir, graceful and dignified, but there was a faraway look in the boy's eye and Aradan knew he pondered his dilemma, still shocked perhaps at the morsel of information Aradan had not been able to keep from him.

"Have the new patrols reached their destinations, Rinon?" asked Handir in an obvious attempt at making the meal at least bearable and reduce the possibilities of a poor digestion.

"Aye. Our captains have already reported. They are in position and already fighting back small pockets of the enemy—they fare well it seems," said the crown prince, always eager to talk of all things military.

"It was a good idea to promote the novices, Rinon. Perhaps now the Silvan foresters will be satisfied with the extra defences we have sent them."

"They will *never* be satisfied, yet well they should be," said Rinon as he skewered a piece of roasted meat too harshly, sending a nerve-grating screech of metal on metal straight into Aradan's brain.

"Incidentally," added the crown prince, his voice muffled by the food in his mouth. "Doralei speaks of a novice with the best aim he has yet seen. He shows much promise."

Handir froze for a moment, before schooling his features and looking at his brother for the first time. "An Alpine?" he asked lightly, too lightly, and Aradan recognised that recurrent trait in his young apprentice's voice.

"A half-breed it seems, but they call him The Silvan. I will make a point of watching out for him when they return."

Handir simply nodded, but it was too late. Aradan had seen his surprise and was now irreversibly intrigued. He would sate his curiosity later, when he had Handir alone. And so it was that after the meal, Aradan invited the young prince to his study. Handir had simply nodded, thinking no more of it other than Aradan's ongoing training, but when they arrived and the chief councillor offered him a glass of wine, he knew this conversation was not one of tutor and apprentice. With his hopes raised, he accepted the glass and sat before a long window that looked out over the beauty of the hidden Evergreen Wood, trying with all his might to look calm and collected.

"I have been thinking, Handir. Thinking and debating and I believe your self-appointed quest to be a good one. Tell me why you are doing this now, for you have my promise of discretion—I will say nothing to your father."

Handir was shocked at the change and suddenly found himself debating the wisdom of confiding in Aradan. It was a moment that could not be undone – once he told Aradan what he knew, it would no longer be in his hands, he would lose control, but when he thought once more of the alternatives, he knew it was the right decision.

"Why the sudden change, Aradan? Yesterday you were adamant about not giving your oath. What has changed in but one day?"

Aradan held Handir's eyes and the prince found himself suddenly drawn into their grey wisdom. First, he had seen that familiar, blank expression that any good advisor learned to wear; but as he observed more closely, fell deeper into it, he saw sadness—and grief. He was telling the truth; this change of mind was genuine, whatever had triggered it.

"This has gone on for too long, Handir. The suffering he has endured has changed your father so that he is unrecognizable, but a shrivelled shell of his former self. All that is left is his inherent strength, his will to continue leading his people—the king remains, but the elf, the elf is withering inside."

Handir had never thought of it like that. His father had always been cool, sparing in his affection, strict in his attention to detail, although he remembered Rinon telling him many years ago that he remembered his father had not always been thus.

Drinking from his glass, he steadied himself before turning his eyes back from the forest and training them on the councillor once more. His nerves must have betrayed him though, because Aradan frowned deeply, apparently reading his emotions as clearly as if Handir himself had written them down and shown him.

"I have much to learn from you in masking myself, Aradan," said the prince in understanding, "but this—this is—it is too close to home, too transcendental."

"We are not in the council chambers now, Handir. We speak as friends. I will not judge you for that."

"Lainon came to me recently," he blurted, and then measured himself before continuing. "As you know, he has been collaborating in the novice project."

"Go on," said Aradan encouragingly.

"Well, he—found something—*someone*," he said, glancing uncertainly at his tutor.

Aradan's frown deepened and Handir steeled himself, pressing on.

"Aradan it seems—it seems Father had another son, with a woman that was not my mother."

Aradan swayed backwards as if to avoid a blow, his eyes wide and gleaming as they searched those of his young charge, yet no words left his slack mouth; even so, Handir thought he could read them all in that moment.

"He is younger than I, but old enough to be a recruit, and good enough to be chosen as one of the early promotion novices. He is currently serving his apprenticeship with Lainon and Turion in the North-western patrol."

There, he had said it—it was over and a wave of utter relief washed over him, his tense muscles relaxing for the first time in days and leaving him weak and shaky.

And yet the silence continued and Handir now observed his tutor closely. His eyes had dropped to the side, shock still rendering him silent but he could still see his distress, his turmoil and yet—there was no confusion at all.

"You may ask," pressed Handir, "how Lainon would know such a thing, indeed I did. I attended the vow ceremony and I saw him, Aradan, I saw him from afar—there can be no mistake."

"How can you be so sure?" whispered Aradan.

"Because his face is his credential—he is the very image of my grandfather, Or'Talán."

"Lássira, what have you done," whispered Aradan, as if he spoke into the wind.

Handir started at the comment, and a suspicion began to form in his mind and as it did, his head cocked to one side, words rolling off his tongue without his permission.

"You knew . . ."

"That there was a child? Yes. But Handir—he is supposed to be beyond Valley—with his mother in the Unknown Lands."

"Gods," whispered Handir, shocked at the unexpected turn the conversation was taking.

Aradan sprang to his feet in a flurry of robes, raking his hand over his blond hair in agitation, and then reaching for the wine bottle. Sitting clumsily, he topped their glasses and took a deep breath, glancing up at the prince in concern.

"Make yourself comfortable Handir, for there is a long, long tale to be told, one it is time for you to hear."

Chapter Ten

LÁSSIRA

*"It is a king or queen's duty to ensure the continuity of their noble line
and provide offspring which may rule, should their progenitor pass into
the Source. A spouse must be noble, and of acceptable lineage to the
Ruling Council."*
The History of Ea Uaré. Calro.

"*Move!* Angon, Lainon, with *me!* Fer'dán, Vor'en, Fel'annár, *up!*" came
the urgent voice of command. Silence and stealth were no longer necessary,
for the enemy was almost upon them.

The two archers scampered up the tree, dislodging dry husks from the
bark and sending them flying as their heavy boots propelled them high into
the boughs. Meanwhile, their companions drew their swords and waited on
the ground. It was not a long wait, and soon enough, the first cave Deviants
Fel'annár had ever seen came crashing forwards, their massive black scimitars
drawn as they bore down upon the elves with a mighty howl that sent a
spear of utter dread down Fel'annár's spine—he would never get used to that
keening wail, he thought.

Fer'dán had already fired an arrow, its twang alerting the novice to the
fact that he had sat there paralysed for too long—*again*. Drawing, he shot
once, twice, three times, each one killing one of the wretched, rotten souls
with an arrow through the eye.

There were Deviants beneath the tree now and Fel'annár knew there was
no angle for the shot and so, he began to target other, larger areas of their
bodies. Their strength though, was unfathomable as they bore down on the

elves below. He understood now – there was no time to aim, only to shoot as many arrows as he could and defend the swordsmen as best he could.

His arrows were now hitting shoulders and thighs, occasionally the neck, but all of them were incapacitating enough to allow his companions the upper hand. However, the once human abominations kept coming, their number greater than they had originally and the moment Fel'annár had awaited with trepidation finally came.

"*Fel'annár! Fer'dán!*" bellowed Turion through the chaos.

This was it, and with a sideways glance and a determined nod at his fellow archer, they both shouldered their bows and jumped to the forest floor, swords already drawn.

Fel'annár faced a one-eyed Deviant with a hideous slit down the centre of its head, and had just enough time to wonder if that was its brain he could see oozing out of one side. It smiled, showing its yellow, decaying teeth and black tongue. Fel'annár screwed his face up in queasy disgust for its breath smelt of all things putrid, and as its slithery tongue came out to lick its cracked lips, it was all Fel'annár could do to stop the rising bile at the back of his throat from spewing out of his slack mouth.

With a dodge to the right, he brought his sword around and found the liver, lunging into it as he had been taught. The Deviant squealed like a spring pig, before pitching forward, dead.

Swivelling on his heels he faced his next opponent, a Deviant that was so tall it looked down on him with a vicious smile, its gloved hand shooting out to throttle him, a strange clicking sound coming from its throat - not fast enough though, for Fel'annár had drawn his sabre in his left hand and sliced at the black limb, severing it completely and then following it with his eyes as it flew to one side.

He almost panicked when the Deviant made no noise at all, as if the loss of its hand meant nothing—and it did not. He needed to distance himself from it and the only way was to flip backwards. When he landed, he took advantage of the surprised beast and sliced through its stubbed forearm, the second chunk of foetid limb falling to the ground with a thud. Fel'annár's head shot from the useless flesh and then back to the Deviant and still, it bore down on him and the novice's eyes bulged in disbelief.

Bringing his sword up to protect himself from the black scimitar, his arms shuddered painfully under the sheer power behind the blow—he had to gain more distance. Swivelling on his heels, he side-twisted, and then turned once more, his sword gaining impetus until it found its mark and cut across the beast's neck, watching in morbid fascination as the sharp edge opened skin and muscle, and then grated over the bone at the back. Its hideous head tipped backwards and dangled for a moment on leathery skin, before toppling to the floor with a ripping sound, closely followed by the frozen body that crashed to the ground in a cloud of dirt.

A cheer went up and Fel'annár startled, only to find his kill had been the last. The seasoned warriors of the North-western patrol had been watching him.

He felt his face flush as he went to clean the muck from his sword, more shaken than he ever imagined he would be. He was aware that his companions moved towards him and when he turned to face them, unsure of what they would say, Angon held up his right hand, the head of the dead Deviant firmly secured in his gloved fist by its long, ropy hair. Fel'annár stared at it for a moment in abject horror, the thick, dark blood dripping from it, its face forever frozen in twisted agony. It all came back to him, the squishing of flesh and blood, the grating sound of steel over bone and the ripping of skin. It was too much and he dropped to his hands and knees and emptied his stomach pitifully.

The warriors roared in laughter, slapping their thighs and each other's shoulders as coins were exchanged, their howls of mirth never stopping, even when Lainon made his way through with a bladder of water, a wry smile on his face.

"Here," he said in exasperation, slapping the novice on his back. "Drink!" he said, before adding, "You did well, Silvan." With that, the lieutenant turned towards the men and smiled mischievously, for both Lainon and Angon had just earned a few coins.

Fel'annár had indeed, lost his lunch.

"So, this—Lássira—he met her *before* he met our mother?"

"Oh yes, many years before. It was a public affair, looked upon with indifference for the most part, for she was not of noble blood and that was of no concern to anyone, so long as they did not marry. Our society, back then when your father was still a prince, was much more liberal than it is today.

Their relationship was seen as an informal dalliance the prince afforded himself and Or'Talán made sure that was the way it remained, in spite of the truth."

"That they loved each other, but could not marry," anticipated Handir.

"Yes—yet even if Or'Talán *had* bent the rules, something he was often wont to do, he could not. His own hands were tied for the Alpine nobles would never have condoned it. Had there been a clear Silvan leader at the time, had there been political equality it may even have been a convenient marriage, to bring together our multi-cultural society and I even tried that tactic with Or'Talán. To no avail though, for the Silvans had little say in matters of state, and the Alpines would have their way or veto the heir to the throne. This, Or'Talán would not accept and so he forbade their marriage."

"Even then, the rift had begun then?" asked Handir sadly.

"Oh yes, even then. Now, Thargodén was devastated at the news, and Lássira—Lássira was heart-broken. They had both known it was a lost cause from the start, but they had clung to hope as lovers often do. The certainty of their doom was a cruel blow that Lássira struggled to deal with."

"What do you mean?" asked Handir in mounting trepidation.

"She—began to fade, Handir. The knowledge that she could never belong to the only elf she had ever loved was tearing at her immortal soul. She became delicate, her health often failing and Thargodén was beside himself with worry. You see, although it had been forbidden for him to marry, he had vowed to take care of Lássira for all the days of his life, even if his father forced him to marry another, which we all knew he would, indeed within the week, your mother had been presented as the queen to be."

"And they were married?"

"Yes, they were married, but Thargodén could not hide the truth from your mother."

"And she took the Last Road?"

"What? NO! No. She was not naive, Handir. She knew their marriage was one of convenience, she knew Thargodén held no love for her . . . I *am* sorry," added Aradan as he saw the deep hurt on his young apprentice's face.

"The point is that they continued to see each other, secretly, for many, many years. Meanwhile, the queen duteously bore two sons and one daughter and Thargodén came to respect your mother very much. But you see," he said, leaning forward now as his hand went to his chin, "she did not only respect him, but came to *love* him. She loved him so much she bore his children and became the perfect queen. She bore his infidelity with quiet dignity; all she asked was that he be discreet and not humiliate her."

Aradan took a steadying breath, glancing at Handir to judge his mood before moving to the final part of the tale.

"Gods," whispered Handir as he rubbed at his face. "They were found out then?"

"No. Thargodén was nothing if not cautious, for by then his father was long gone, dead at the Battle Under the Sun. He was king now. Besides, his respect for his wife would not allow him to compromise her in that way. No, it was Lássira. She was slipping, slipping into grief so far it frightened her. With each day they saw each other, deep in the forest, she was paler, weaker, frailer of health and spirit; she was dwindling and they both knew it.

Thargodén, with a heavy heart, bid her take the Last Road – away to Valley. He pleaded day in, day out for her to save herself but she could not leave him, even if she *was* doomed to meet with him under these secret, somewhat sordid circumstances. Thargodén toiled relentlessly with the problem, indeed I was there, every bit a part of his suffering.

"The child."

"Yes—the child. That was to be the solution. They would create a child so that a part of Thargodén would always be with her, get her safely to Valley, a safe passage if you will, her last life line. And so, soon enough, the news came to us in secret that she was with child. She would begin her journey to Valley and give birth to the child there, in the Unknown Lands."

"They conceived a child for the wrong reasons," muttered Handir.

"No, Handir—you underestimate the terrible loss of love—to love that one soul mate and confront the finality of their death is a terrible thing, and conceiving a child seemed an acceptable way of avoiding that tragedy. You must look at this in perspective."

"And you thought that is what happened? That she would be waiting for him beyond Valley with her child, *their* child?"

"Yes, that is what I thought, Handir, as does Thargodén. That his son is here, tells me that she never crossed and so she is either alive and no longer fading, or she succumbed before she could cross."

Handir sat, allowing Aradan's last words to sink in. And then a question popped into his mind.

"Aradan—how did Mother find out? I mean that is what must have happened, she found out a child had been created."

"Yes, she found out, although we never knew how that came to be."

"But who would benefit from such a thing? The purists would simply let it be, for an Alpine king and queen sat on the throne; it would not be in their interest, surely?"

"Apparently not, but who is to say there were not—*personal*—interests? That someone from that faction wished to take the throne for themselves?"

Handir started, before he blurted out, "Band'orán? Nay he would not be so bold!"

"Your great uncle would not force the issue, no, but if he saw an opportunity to allow things to simply—spiral—he may well have taken it. Unfortunately, we have no way of discerning the truth Handir, only that someone else knew, and saw fit to tell the queen."

"So, you know nothing of this boy then?" asked Handir.

"Nothing."

There was an awful silence for a while, before Aradan's soft voice broke it. "What, what is he like, Handir?"

"He is . . . difficult to describe, Aradan; that and I only saw him from a distance; but I will tell you this much. He is quite simply—*beautiful*. I do not know what his mother looked like, but she must have been stunning. His eyes . . ."

"Are the colour of summer moss?" said Aradan gently.

Handir stared at Aradan, before nodding. "Yes, just that, Aradan.

Minutes passed in silence, before Aradan spoke once more.

"I am glad you told me, Handir. And I can see why Lainon came to you with this. The situation is potentially volatile at the least," said the councillor, back to business now.

"I know, Aradan. Lainon was aware of all this, I assume?"

"Oh yes. He was your guardian, of course. He ran many errands for Thargodén. He knew Lássira."

"What worries me the most, Aradan, is that this boy is, in Lainon's words, the best novice warrior he has ever seen. That and his extraordinary looks will draw attention to him. All it will take is a veteran to see his face and declare him Or'Talán reborn. So far, he has lived in his village, deep in the heart of Uaré but now, in the king's militia . . . it is surely only a question of time before someone asks the wrong questions."

"Yes, and there is no telling how the king will react, first to the question of whether Lássira lives or not, and secondly, what he will do with the boy. And then there is Rinon."

"Rinon would see him as a threat. Another brother, a bastard, Silvan brother. I cannot see him accepting that at all. Maeneth, however, would probably be overjoyed!" snorted Handir, his lovely sister's face floating in his mind's eye.

"There is one more thing," said Handir, deep in thought. "The boy has a nick name; they call him *The Silvan*, the one Rinon mentioned at lunch. My brother has taken it upon himself to seek the boy out when they ride in—we cannot allow it, Aradan."

"Nay. You must write to Lainon and warn him. What did Lainon suggest, by the way?"

"He wanted me to keep him informed of any talk, of any suspicions that may arise. He knows he will have to tell the boy soon enough but he needs to know that he will not be jeopardising his charge, or indeed the king, by doing so. I sense in him a desire to protect the child, Aradan, almost as if he were a younger brother."

"This is, *convoluted*, Handir, the ramifications are endless and we must not take rash decisions. We must sit for a while and digest what we have learned, observe those around us and above all, we must listen—listen to every bit of news that comes from the field. The slightest indication that rumour is starting is when the king must be told, before he hears it from someone else and thus, the boy must also be told, and when that happens, I suggest he not be here. We must get him assigned somewhere abroad, so that he is not caught in the storm that will surely be unleashed."

"That makes sense, yes," mumbled Handir. It was then that his face changed from one of deep thought to dawning realization. "You know, I could always ask my father once more about the possibility of traveling to Tar'eastór as part of my apprenticeship with Lord Damiel." He turned to Aradan as if he had just solved a great puzzle, the hint of a smile upon his lips.

Aradan smiled back, nodding slowly as he did so. "That would be interesting, yes. You would need a patrol to accompany you."

"It is perfect, Aradan," said Handir, his eyes no longer dull but sparkling with excitement. "I prepare the king and then precipitate my journey when the need to act becomes paramount."

"Alright," said Aradan as he stood. "We wait and we listen; you meanwhile, will speak to the king and remind him of your desire to travel, I will put in a word for you. When the time comes, your journey must be made—only then will I tell the king, and *Lainon* will tell the boy he has a family."

Chapter Eleven

AWAKENING

"Aria is not a Creator but the executing hand of Creation. She is the essence of this world, the power that moves air and water, moves stars and people's hearts. Aria is energy – the soul of this world."
On Elven Nature. Calro.

The enemy lurked close by and the warriors remained alert as they sat around a small fire, drinking tea and sharing muted conversation, most of it revolving around Fel'annár. The novice had become an integral part of their circle and with acceptance came confidence—and then the questions came. How old was the average Deviant? Why was their skin green around the joints? Could the physicians not invent some sort of cream to block the stench? And what was that funny clicking sound?

The warriors did not mind though, for they had rarely worked with a novice who took so much interest in his training, who asked such poignant questions with eyes shining in curiosity and respect. He was also a source of endless entertainment for the veteran warriors, for there was a freshness about him. He was yet untainted by his experiences in the field, still trusting and open, and yet they all concurred in that he had greatly changed over the weeks they had served together. Still, he *had* vomited with his first close-up kill, something they still chuckled about for the poor boy had been unlucky, his first Deviant unwilling to go elegantly to its death.

And yet there was one thing they were not aware of at all, unless one looked closely enough, as Turion did. He had worked with these warriors before, albeit many years ago. He remembered their dour, curt ways and yet now, weeks into their patrol, they too had changed. Their eyes seemed lighter, they smiled and even made jokes, most at Fel'annár's expense.

Turning his attention back to the conversation, Turion heard Fel'annár enquiring as to the wisdom or otherwise of shedding one's boots at bedtime. There were chuckles and some knee-slapping as Angon attempted to explain why he, as a Silvan warrior, would personally never do such an unwise thing. Turion snorted and Lainon smiled and the others huddled round for the explanation, but Fel'annár's attentive gaze suddenly faltered and he leaned back, as if he had heard something he had not expected.

"Boy!" joked Angon— "I am imparting great wisdom here; the least you can do is pay attention," he said in mock irritation, but it had been enough to draw everyone's attention to the now completely blank stare of their novice.

"Hwindo . . ."

Nothing.

"Fel'annár!" hissed Lainon, waving a hand before the unseeing eyes.

"What is *wrong* with him?" asked Angon, perplexed.

"I do not know," answered Lainon with a frown, sharing a worried glance with Turion.

"Fel'annár?" tried the captain softly, and then started when the boy finally spoke.

"Something is wrong," he mumbled, his lips hardly moving at all.

"*What*, what is wrong?" prompted Lainon in mounting trepidation.

Turion, meanwhile, let out the caw of a blackbird to request a status report from the warriors on duty. After a prolonged silence, the guard's answering call resounded in the otherwise deathly silence—*all was well*, he said.

Turion turned back to Fel'annár, who seemed to be coming back to himself, his eyes blinking repeatedly as if they stung him.

"Something is wrong," he repeated, shaking his head from side to side.

"Fer'dán reports nothing, Fel'annár," said Lainon.

Fel'annár slowly held his hand up before his own face, horrified now to see it visibly shaking before he repeated, "Something is wrong."

Angon could stand it no longer and stood, his hand upon the pommel of his sword, for his finer hairs were standing to attention and his skin crawled painfully—there had been something in the boy's voice, in his conviction he simply could not ignore.

Turion called back to Fer'dán and they all waited, their breath caught in their throat lest the simple rush of air mask his answer. This time, it took longer than it should have, but when it did reach them, it was an alert warning. That meant one of two things; that there was a threat still far enough away to give them time to prepare, or—that Fer'dán was unsure.

"Break camp. We move now, prepare your weapons," said Turion urgently, turning once more to a slowly rising Fel'annár, still, apparently not completely back to his usual self.

The boy stood before the grey, waning light of a darkening forest, and of a sudden his long hair and strange green eyes seemed brighter than they ever had. He was a vision to behold in that moment, for some pent-up power seemed to surge through him and to the surface, not quite breaking free. If Turion had looked behind him he would have realised he was not alone in his impression. He startled then, as Fel'annár spoke once more, his voice unsteady, vulnerable.

"What is wrong with me?" he whispered as his eyes suddenly focused and a cold shiver ran down the length of the captain's spine.

"Nothing," he lied. "Come, we break camp—we are leaving," he said curtly, waiting for the boy to move before jogging to the fore and leading them out. There would be time enough to broach the subject—later. For now, Turion trusted his instincts. They would move to higher, safer ground before resting for the night. Such deep silence spoke of Sand Lords, not deviants – their enemy was shrewd and cunning, not mindless and impulsive.

The patrol began their cautious trek through the wood, their senses on full alert. Whatever it was that had happened to their novice, it had frightened them all, leaving them with the uncertainty of whether the boy was right, that there *was* danger; after all, Fer'dán had not been sure and it had been that fact alone that had finally set them to moving once more.

Their eyes swivelled from one tree to the other, up and then down as the light became dimmer and dimmer and the forest seemed to close in around them, tower over them, purposefully intimidating them. They were seasoned warriors but there was something about this night that unnerved them all, especially Fel'annár, who remained silent and withdrawn, occasionally checking his own hand which still shook despite the fact that he had managed to calm himself somewhat.

Lainon cast worried glances at him, and Turion turned back to check his patrol more than he usually would.

The hoot of an owl stopped them all dead in their tracks—Fer'dán signalled a proximity warning.

"*Positions*," hissed Turion, watching as each warrior took up his designated place, Fel'annár climbing the nearest tree, slower than he usually did. The captain resolved to keep a close eye on the boy for he did not seem to be himself as yet. Distraction and his first battle with Sand Lords could be a recipe for disaster, he knew. Lainon would be thinking the same, no doubt.

All too soon, the soft clinking sound of foreign metal invaded the unnatural silence and the warriors were thrust into a silent, frantic conversation of hand signals and bird calls, conveying orders from the ground to the trees and vice versa. Position, numbers, weaponry . . .

The cry of an eagle preceded Fer'dán's shadow as he finally joined the patrol.

"Sand Lords—at least twenty-five . . ."

Fel'annár tried to avoid the calculating stares of his fellow warriors but he felt them burning holes into him all the same. He had been right, something indeed had been off, but how had he known? What strange malady had taken him that it had set his head to thumping, his vision swimming and his hand shaking? Anxiety took hold of him for a moment and his breathing became erratic. '*Stop*,' he scolded himself; '*Stop lest you make a fool of yourself,*' he repeated silently. Closing his eyes, he remembered his own invented exercises to centre himself before training. They had failed him on his first encounter with Deviants but he wasn't giving up. Applying the technique now on the threshold of his second battle would be a challenge at the least, but try he did. Closing his eyes, he collected himself, forgot the lingering anxiety of the strange turn he had taken and breathed deeply. In his mind, there were only Sand Lords now. His hands did not shake, there was no anxiety, only the enemy and his weapons. His heart beat was steady, muscles ready to wield his weapons. The pressure at the back of his neck no longer hurt. Opening his eyes, he calmly watched from the trees as the first, cloaked warriors showed themselves and he shot, a shriek alerting the other trespassers to his dangerous presence, and with another arrow, another fell to the ground in a heap of fine cloth and metal.

Elven shouts mixed with the clipped cries of the cloaked invaders and where once there had been ominous silence, now the cacophony of battle reverberated in Fel'annár's ears. Strangely though, his emotions were not affected. He was aware only of his muscles as they flexed and relaxed, pulled and rolled, and when he was called to the ground his eyes sought only the enemy, his flashing blades carefully calibrating, his limbs executing his moves to perfection.

The sounds of battle soon dimmed and the whoosh of his blades became louder, the beat of his heart ever present as it ticked strangely steadily, even when he pierced the bellies of his foes and severed their armoured legs. His eyes now registered not only his foes before him, but his companions around him.

An effortless change from blades to bow and he had drawn and killed a Sand Lord that bore down on Angon, only to swivel sideways and shoot once more at another that threatened to slice into Fer'dán with a scimitar.

His body calmly informed him that he should bend backwards and draw his swords once more and effortlessly, they were back in his hands—long sword and sabre—and he whirled them around before stabbing forwards, into the eye of a great, lumbering warrior.

Silence now, save for his own movements—his heart and his breath but he did not feel his body at all—was only aware that it moved, calm and coordinated, and his eyes saw everything; strange though, he mused, that there was a green and purple tinge to everything—as if he was looking through painted glass.

Everything seemed to move so slowly, everything except his blades in both hands, that whirled and swirled and hummed around him in a strange, rhythmic song that did not distract him at all, rather it centred him even more.

It was suddenly that his body came back to him, heavy once more, and he realised he had stopped moving. He blinked once, twice, the strange colours slowly dissipating, only to reveal Lainon and the North-western patrol standing silently before him, and on their faces, was what Fel'annár could only later describe as—consternation.

Fel'annár woke with the first timid rays of autumn sun, hardly having slept at all. Nodding at the duty guard who stood silently, he moved to the side of their camp and sat cross-legged, alone. He needed to think, to straighten out the turmoil in his mind because after the events of the previous evening, he was, quite simply—scared. Yet more than even this, he sensed the warriors averted gazes and their quiet avoidance.

Slowing his breathing and closing his eyes, he desperately searched for a plausible answer to what had happened. It had all started with pressure at the back of his neck that had him thinking he had a headache, but the pain was not a familiar one. And then, quite suddenly, an overwhelming wave of pure anxiety had slammed into him, almost stealing his breath with the force of it. He remembered trying to pinpoint the source of it but he could not. It had been too sudden, too strong. None of his own, childish worries could ever warrant what he had felt and he knew it—it had come from without, not from within.

He remembered almost panicking, and then words rolling from his errant mouth.

Something is wrong.

He heard the words as if someone else had spoken them and he shivered, the anxiety still tearing through him mercilessly. He wanted to cry.

Something is wrong.

He had repeated it, and was aware that he was frightening his companions, but he had lost control and it *terrified* him.

He had heard their bird calls, faintly in the background, but Fel'annár already knew.

Something is wrong.

He felt light, as if he floated upon a cloud, and yet at the same time strangely heavy, his chest weighing down his otherwise floating body—it was *absurd.*

He opened his eyes in exasperation, hearing now as the camp came to life. He should carry out his duties but his mind was still a swirling, heaving mess of disjointed memories and impressions. There was no more time though, and so he slowly rose and walked back to his companions.

Water boiled over a fire and Fel'annár shot an apologetic glance at Fer'dán, who simply nodded solemnly, watching as the novice sat—not quite able to meet his gaze.

A mug of tea was placed in his hand and he looked down stupidly at it, before looking up into the frank stare of Lainon, who gestured to him that he should drink it.

He took it numbly to his lips and drank slowly, his mind turning inwards again, still aware enough to know he was being watched.

"I am sorry, brothers," he said quietly, his eyes firmly fixed upon his mug in shame.

Silence followed his words, before Angon spoke.

"What? You are *sorry?*"

"Angon," said Turion, holding his hand up for silence, and then jerking his head to the side.

As one, the warriors rose and left the circle of fire, leaving Turion, Lainon and Fel'annár alone.

"I have shamed myself, Captain. In the one thing I wanted most in this world and I have failed," whispered Fel'annár, still unable to lift his eyes from his mug, the urge to cry in utter frustration angering him for the weakness he thought it implied.

"Fel'annár. Have you no recollection of what happened last night?" asked Turion. "Can you not remember the battle?"

"I remember—I remember feelings and sensations. I remember hearing my own heartbeat, I remember fighting but not the details. I remember my failing eyesight and hearing, I remember terrible weight and dizzying lightness," he trailed off, aware that his tone had been steadily rising. He scowled deeply, his eyes finally rising to meet Turion's worried eyes.

"It does not make sense," he said slowly, his eyes pleading with the captain for an explanation.

"No," began Turion carefully. "From that perspective, it does not. But listen to me, Fel'annár, and take good note as you always do."

The novice nodded dumbly, his face the very picture of abject misery. "From *our* perspective," he emphasised, "from where *we* stood, you have not shamed yourself, child."

Turion watched as Fel'annár stared at him uncomprehendingly.

"Fel'annár, what we saw last night was a warrior the likes of which most of us have never seen—most, except *me.*"

Fel'annár's expression changed to shocked puzzlement, his head cocking to one side.

"Child, there is little I or anyone else can teach you about the martial arts. You fought as the mighty warriors of old, like Gor'sadén himself, and the Gods confound me for I tell you I know not where you have learned to fight the way you do. You did not shame yourself, Fel'annár—*Hwind'atór*—you saved the day."

Fel'annár's eyes were round, utter shock leaving him stupefied and unable to formulate a single sentence.

"Now, after what I have said, I will tell you *this*", continued Turion. "You seem to have a—*gift*—Fel'annár. I know not the nature of it and I believe you are completely unaware of it—but you *do* have it. Whatever it is, it seems to be manifesting itself for the first time for I sense your anxiety, your fear."

"Yes, *yes*," he said eagerly, hoping that Turion would cast some light on it, ease his fraught mind.

"Patience then, Hwind'atór. Let us watch and wait and discover this thing together. Do not be frightened, for I believe that what happened to you yesterday is a good thing."

A desperate, somewhat strangled groan escaped the novice, for it hadn't felt good at all and he said as much. "I cannot fathom it. I was not myself and yet I was. It was as if my body—acted of its own accord—as if I had no—*control*—over what I did, saw or heard."

"Can you be more precise, Fel'annár? Can you remember any details?" asked Lainon, leaning forward in anticipation.

Fel'annár took a few moments to think. "I remember my, my eyesight was strange—there were blue, green and purple edges to everything. I remember my muscles, the way they flexed and relaxed, which ones moved my weapons, my eyes. I could hear little more than my own heartbeat, my own breathing, everything else was—muted—even the screams and the shrieks."

Lainon and Turion shared a puzzled stare before the captain continued with his questioning.

"Alright. I think we have a start. At least one thing seems certain, Hwind'atór. You are most intuitive, for you felt the presence of the enemy long before any of us did. This may or may not be connected with what happened to you in battle. If it happens again, you must try to control it, and for that you can count on us but do not hide it."

"I won't," he said after a moment. "I am still confused but—you have helped me to calm myself at least."

"Good," said Turion with a reassuring smile.

"Just—just one more thing, Captain."

"Yes, what is it?" asked Turion as he rose to leave.

"Why are you calling me Hwind'atór?"

The captain smiled before glancing at his lieutenant and then back to the young boy standing expectantly before him, looking a little less pale than he had been before.

"Because after what I saw last night, I cannot help but call you thusly for it is true—you *are* the Whirling Warrior," he said, a cheeky grin on his usually stern features. "Your friends have named you well."

Fel'annár's eyebrows rose to his hairline and he turned to face Lainon in silent question.

But the Ari'atór simply smiled, nodded, and went about his business, leaving behind a flummoxed, yet strangely relieved novice warrior. He had not shamed himself, and his captain had compared him to the greatest warrior alive: Gor'sadén of Tar'eastór.

Chapter Twelve

THE PATH AHEAD

"To the East, Tar'eastór stands proudly atop the mighty Median Mountains, home of the great Alpine elves who write lore, and are the best sword masters, or so they say. They are versed in the healing arts and prone to logic and the art of rhetoric. They are all these things and yet no one would claim they are humble, for that would be deceitful. These elves are great warriors, leaders; glorious in battle."
The Silvan Chronicles. Book III. Marhené

Lainon

I have much news to share with you, promising news for the most part, all with which you must be kept abreast.

After much thought upon the matter, I have confided in Aradan and he is now fully aware of the situation. He, in turn, has told me the story of Lássira, a story I know you were aware of, and were not at liberty to discuss with me.

I now also understand the question that must be asked, for if The Silvan is here, where is his mother?

Aradan and I are now working closely together. He wishes only that Thargodén may redeem himself at least with me, that somehow my father can become the elf he apparently used to be, the one I cannot remember having met. As for myself what do I seek? Perhaps to understand—my father, my mother, how I should feel about having a half-brother—who can say, for I certainly cannot.

The only worrying development so far is a comment that Prince Rinon made at table not a week past. Word has come to him of the exceptional military skills of The Silvan, and he has vowed to keep an eye out for him when he returns to the city. This cannot happen, of course, for it is as you say; his resemblance to my

Lord Grandfather is uncanny. To this end I have devised a plan, one I believe may be suitable to all.

I have previously told my father of my interest in tutoring in Tar'eastór under the venerable Lord Damiel. I plan to remind him of it, and then execute my journey when need dictates we reveal this secret. We would somehow ensure that The Silvan is part of the entourage. This is when Lainon must speak to the boy, and Aradan will do likewise with the king.

It will not be easy to coordinate, and Rinon is likely to precipitate things—we want neither my father nor the Silvan lad finding out the hard way.

How goes the patrol? Send news and your thoughts on our plans.

Handir.

Lainon folded the parchment and then burned it over the fire. Their plan was bold but he was strangely glad that Aradan was in with them. He had worked closely with the advisor for many years while guarding the king's second son. He was a good elf, a friend to the king and although of Alpine origin, was not sympathetic to Band'orán's notions of Alpine domination. Lainon would confer with Turion and write his reply as soon as he was able, yet what to say? That Handir had a half-brother with some strange power? That he had fought like a devil possessed and scared the very wits out of their most veteran warriors? Nay, he would say nothing for it was not yet relevant. He scoffed to himself then, for how could something so transcendental be '*irrelevant.*' The idea was absurd, but it was too much to reveal as yet—the players were unaware of their roles and until that changed, it would do no good to complicate matters beyond what they already were.

Raking his eyes over the patrol, Lainon lingered for a while on an apparently serene novice who now spoke timidly with the troop. He knew the warriors were still wary of the boy—unable to explain in any coherent way what they had seen. Some turned to talk of spirits and possession and although they did not really believe that, the seed of doubt had been planted. Lainon knew the time had come to veer towards the North. It was time to show Fel'annár, or Hwind'atór as they were now calling him, that not all battles were fought with blades.

"Was there something else, Aradan?" asked the king, his voice listless, tired.

"Yes, my Lord. I wish to discuss the possibility of Prince Handir tutoring with Lord Damiel of Tar'eastór for six months. I know he has already put the idea to you, but I wish to add my voice to the project. He will do well, I am sure."

"Is it necessary? He already seems to be excelling under your own guidance," said the king as he moved to stand before the full-length window of his study, his eyes once more on the Evergreen Wood, as if he were addicted to it, unable to wrench himself away from it for any significant amount of time.

"He is, indeed. But Tar'eastór will pose new challenges for him. It will prepare him well for moments of crisis, and there is no one better than Lord Damiel in this.

The king snorted. "Indeed, I have been on the receiving end of his negotiating skills—he is clever, shrewd and most learned."

"Add to that," continued Aradan, "the political benefits of renewing talks with the Alpine Lands; I think there are many good reasons to send Handir. He will represent us well, renew our alliance with the elves of the Median Mountains, meet with your cousins."

"It would be a good test for him," said the king, his voice still monotonous.

"Aye," smiled Aradan. "I would suggest waiting for a few more months, perhaps until after the year-end festival. If you accede to the idea, I must make haste and write to King Vorn'asté, so that suitable preparations can be made for our prince."

There was a long silence as the king considered the possibility of Handir leaving for an extended stay. Of the two brothers, he was the only one that was, at least, courteous with him. And yet Thargodén had lost all hope of ever redeeming himself in his sons' eyes; too much time had passed without the slightest hint of affection. But then, he scoffed, why would they? Had he given them any cause to be affectionate towards him? Had he so much as touched them in all this time? Had a kind word or an encouraging nod? Nay—he had done nothing, he realised bitterly. What was the point? They would never forgive him his trespass—the terrible sin of loving one he had never been allowed to have. It was a useless idea and he knew it. Only hope would make that possible, and Thargodén had none.

With a heavy heart, he simply nodded at his councillor and friend. Aye, he would allow the boy to travel. He may be incapable of mending the rift with his children, but he could make the boy happy, in this one thing at least.

"With one condition. I want a company of fifty with him; Handir is no warrior."

"I will see to it of course. A messenger will leave for Tar'eastór tomorrow. Do you wish to send any further correspondence, my Lord?"

"I will send a message for Vorn'asté, of course. If Handir is to stay in his house, I would have his personal assurances on the matter. I should also send along something for our cousins, as you say," he added, a trace of disapproval flitting over his otherwise blank face.

"A wise move, my Lord," said Aradan with an arch of the eyebrow, for Thargodén was not partial at all to his cousins in Tar'eastór, and Aradan could not say he disagreed. They were Alpine, had never approved of Or 'Talan's move on Ea Uaré. They found it distasteful, not because he would effectively be colonising those lands, but because he would live amongst its natives.

"Thank you Aradan," he said, the hint of tiredness back once more. The advisor cursed the Gods for his friend's misery, for no one had deserved it less than this Alpine king who sacrificed so much for Ea Uaré. Indeed, every breath he took was an act of bravery, of service, for if it were not for The Great Forest and The Evergreen Wood, this extraordinary elf would have faded to nothing centuries ago.

And so, despite his success in assuring Handir's trip, he left with a familiar weight on his chest, and no small measure of contained frustration. This king was surrounded by family, family that seemingly cared not at all for him, that showed no emotion, had not the slightest consideration for his well-being. Others, he mused, had no family and had suffered for it all their lives.

'Do not fail me, Handir,' he begged. 'Bring the light back to this family, to our king.'

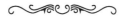

Handir

So far, all goes well. There have been some issues that will need addressing, but nothing regarding the boy's identity. For you, however, there may soon be. I calculate another few months in the field. After that we will return home and the boy will become a warrior, albeit he will not be expecting it so soon.

Regarding Rinon, it is, indeed, a problem. Perhaps we could orchestrate things so that the boy will not be deprived of the moment he has been waiting for all his life. If we could celebrate a vow ceremony while your brother Rinon is abroad, I would be most appreciative of the effort Handir. I know this is something that should not concern you. I ask only as a personal favour to me; he deserves it. I would not have Fel'annár sacrifice that which he has worked so hard to achieve.

Lainon

Finishing the letter, Handir looked up to the heavens for a moment and then tossed the parchment into the fireplace in his rooms.

"Well?" asked Aradan impatiently.

"*Fel'annár . . .*"

Aradan's eyebrows rose in surprise. "What of it? You would speak of plants — *now?*"

"Not 'it' but '*he*'. It is the novice's name."

"Ah—a Silvan name indeed," he commented lightly, but his eyes watched Handir. The prince had not wanted to know his name, he thought. He would think, perhaps, that by simply knowing it, the boy became real, that he could no longer pretend he was inconsequential.

"Lainon asks that we find a way to celebrate a vow ceremony without running the risk of Rinon seeking out the Silvan."

"Surely that can wait," snorted Aradan. "There are more important things at stake here than one's *pride.*"

"No Aradan. Not for a warrior, and before you try to refute that," he said, one hand raised towards the councillor, "it is not a question of pride—it is a necessity—one the king insists on. I could not care less myself, but Lainon seems adamant. He asks it of me as a *favour.*"

"He has involved himself personally with this boy—hasn't he?" asked Aradan thoughtfully as he sipped on his wine.

"Yes," said Handir as he swirled his own wine slowly. "Perhaps too much. The possibilities of this project failing are high—I do not want Lainon hurt. His reasons are noble, though, even if they do not fully coincide with mine."

Aradan stared at Handir's profile. His face was apparently placid, relaxed, but his eyes were far away and even the king's Chief Councillor could not rightly say what he was thinking on.

The truth was that Handir struggled with the thought of Lainon protecting this—Fel'annár as a brother would. To him he represented the departure of his mother, the separation of his family. Why would Handir even be expected to care about the boy at all.

'*Because he is unaware of it all—he does not know,*' his logical mind told him.

Even so, Handir had no feelings for him at all. The boy was a necessary player in this game but he would not be part of the future; he was not why Handir was doing this now. He was doing it for the good of the kingdom, for his father and his siblings—for himself.

And then Lainon's face floated before his mind's eye once more and as it did, a memory came to him quite suddenly, accompanied as so often happens, by a smell—of nut pastries hot from the oven and the scent of sweet honeysuckle. He saw his father's smiling face and heard his mother's joyous laughter. He remembered a rough table top that seemed to run the entire length of the room—the kitchen he realised. He sat on someone's knees and heard the voice of his elder brother as he bounced Handir up and down, his own laughter joining that of their mother's.

Wide-eyed, Handir was shocked at the intensity of the memory, so much so that a tear came to his eye and he swiped at it impatiently. He had been wrong; those memories of happier times when his family had been together, when his father had still been vibrant and strong—he had not forgotten, he had simply stopped remembering.

"I have already told you, there is little more we can teach you with your weapons, but where we are headed now, it is the *mind* that will keep you alive, Hwind'atór."

Fel'annár walked between Turion and Lainon at the end of the line. They had been travelling on foot for a week now, and with every step they took, the trees seemed to be wilting under the weight of something that could not be seen. Sunlight filtered through the high boughs of foliage, playing strange shadow games on the ground. Why that should bother him was beyond him.

"Evil is not just the twisted face of a Deviant, or the dark machinations of some obscure Sand Lord. It is a deep, crushing sorrow that penetrates the body and arrests your mind, your soul. Your task as a warrior in the North will be to control your body and block that sensation, protect yourself against it so that you may protect others, think clearly when they cannot."

Turion glanced at their young charge from the corner of his eye. He listened intently as he always did, a faint bruise still shadowing his left cheek, fruit of a nasty blow he had taken some days ago when he slipped on a patch of fresh resin and fallen hard. The boy had been indignant, claiming he had never fallen in a tree, and Lainon had to explain to him that here, not all trees were willing to host elves in their boughs. Fel'annár had been horrified and since then, had bombarded them with incessant questions as to why that would be.

"I have heard the stories, Turion, I know what they say. They flock to Valley for good reasons, for valid reasons, for how can one passively accept his fated death? How can you sit by idly and allow it to occur when there is a chance to change it?"

"Aye, and therein lies the tragedy of it, Fel'annár. They were once good people who never meant harm to anyone. But when their bodies begin to fail and yet they cannot die, the horror—the sheer terror of it, is enough to pervert them. Those only recently returned from Valley are not so dangerous; you can tell them apart for although they fight, they are not so skilled, not so aggressive, as if they still had doubts as to what they do. The older Deviants have no such doubts, and neither should you, Fel'annár. If you falter, if you think too much, they will kill our mothers and our fathers, our children—they will raze our world to the ground."

Fel'annár nodded. He had not thought about it that way at all. He had simply killed Deviants as he would a mindless monster. And they were. The trick was, indeed, to not think about what they had been like before they had been turned, something he supposed he would, inevitably end up doing.

"How does a warrior guard himself against that? To not think on their origins?" he asked.

"Not all of them can. I have known many excellent warriors who cannot serve in the North. After but months, they return to the city and the healing wards, their minds in turmoil and their souls darkened and in tatters. It takes them months to regain their spirit and serve once more. Our commanders do not recruit just any warrior for these areas; they recruit only those who are stronger of mind and will."

"Can one train to endure it? I mean, if you succumb at first, can you learn to block it? To guard your heart?"

"Yes. In fact, that is the way of it. Everyone suffers at first, until you learn to pinpoint its effects—that is when you can block it. Don't go in there thinking you can guard yourself from the start Fel'annár. That will not happen."

Turion watched the novice as he spoke, noting his wide eyes staring straight ahead, his Adam's apple bobbing visibly.

The poor boy was nervous—they all were at this point in their training, but somehow Turion had almost thought Fel'annár would be impervious to it—he was not, and that was a comforting thought somehow.

Turion had spoken with Lainon about the strange events during their skirmish with the Sand Lords and they had both agreed to keep a close eye on the boy. They needed more information on the nature of his—gift—if that was, indeed what it was. Once they were better informed, they could find a way to help him with it. However, Lainon at one point implied that it was the Spirit that affected their young charge. It was a strange thing to say, for Lainon was Ari'atór, albeit he had not taken his vows, but it did lend him the advantage in all things related to Ari, and as such, Turion would not discard his words.

"Fel'annár," called Lainon from his other side. "Your hair has escaped again. See to it that you secure it from your face before our next confrontation."

A lovely blush blossomed on his bruised face as he turned to the Ari'atór. "I confess I do not know what to do."

Lainon's eyebrows rose, and Turion rather thought he saw an idea dawn on his lieutenant's face.

"Well, there is one way. It is a little—*exotic*—but it could work. We Ari'atór have hair of a different texture to that of the other elven races as you know, and while you are not Ari'atór, your hair is thicker than any Alpine or Silvan I know. Our warrior braids could work, I think. I could show you when we make camp later."

Fel'annár's sceptical eyes shot to the strange, thick twists that stood high upon Lainon's crown. "I will be a sight! An Alpine Silvan with the hair of an Ari'atór!"

"Popular with your lovers, boy!" jested the lieutenant in a rare show of emotion and Fel'annár chuckled while Angon and Fer'dán snorted behind them. Soon enough, the two warriors had shared the story with their companions, and by twilight, as they set up their camp, Lainon, their mercurial Ari'atór, was braiding Fel'annár's hair in a way none of them had ever seen on an elf that was not Ari.

Thick twists had been worked from front to back, from his hairline and then down his back, sitting atop the straight, unbraided hair beneath, both layers falling almost to the small of his back and when Lainon had finished and the boy turned, the troop hooted and cheered, cat calls echoing around them. Fel'annár blushed and stood, bowing theatrically first to Lainon, and then to his feisty audience.

"How do I look?!" he shouted merrily, no hint of his earlier anxiety. For the next half an hour, the warriors fooled around, swaying their hips and 'ooing' and 'aaring', linking each other's arms and *skipping*—and Fel'annár, Green Sun, was always in the middle of it, laughing and flicking at their hair in return.

Lainon and Turion watched from their nascent campfire and smiled. "He is an extraordinary boy, Lainon. I wish the best for him."

"I know," said Lainon, turning to face his captain and friend. "You told me back at the barracks that here is something about him that inspires loyalty; it is why you left your beloved training fields; it is why I, too, am here."

Turion held his friend's gaze for a moment. Something important was happening, and they two would have a part in it. It was almost as if they had been appointed this task—appointed by who, though, Turion could not say and yet he felt it, in the deepest recesses of his mind he knew neither of them had ever had the slightest choice in the matter. And then, he thought, that even if he *had* had a say in it, he would still have chosen this path. The boy had wormed his way beneath Turion's thickened, warrior hide, into his heart, had worked a strange, arcane magic that had captivated him from the very start.

They raised their mugs and clinked them together, before sipping on the hot tea, enjoying the entertainment, for tonight, the forest was at peace.

Chapter Thirteen

HE IS OURS

"To be a Silvan elf is to feel the Spirit, Aria, for it brushes against our souls — comes from the trees and is like air — life-giving. You cannot separate a Silvan from his woodland home for to do so is to leave him bereft of that touch, take away his joy and leave him lost, adrift in unknown waters."
On Elven Nature. Calro

The next morning, the patrol kitted out in their heaviest gear and set out stealthily through the forest, towards the North-west and one of the denser areas of the forest. Had they continued due North they would have reached the Xeric Woods in a week, but as it was, Turion had no plans to take the patrol there and so they set a brisk pace towards their next stop, Sen'oléi, a village where they were to gain information on the enemy's movements and establish whether its inhabitants needed help in the way of provisions or infrastructure. Being relatively close to the dry forest — the northern Xeric Wood, these Silvan foresters held great insight into how the enemy moved, and that was what Turion now sought.

It would be the first time in months that the patrol would encounter civilians, and the thought was a good one, for there would be hot food and comfortable beds. There might even be a day of rest in which they could bathe, wash their clothing and care more extensively for their weapons.

Fel'annár's hair was a success, for he was able to gather up the thick top braids and tie them at the back of his head. It was perfect and Lainon had joked that it pulled at his eyes, making him look like an Ari'atór.

Turion confessed to being absurdly confused, for Lainon never joked. He was severe and curt, enigmatic yet fierce, frightening even, yet when he was around The Silvan, the Spirit Warrior smiled and made witty comments, and thought of other things that were not death and despair. Turion liked this side of his friend.

After two days, the patrol emerged from the dense trees and into a glade, where some sunlight still managed to filter through the high boughs. They had been smelling the wood smoke for many hours now, and the Silvan members of the troop began to reminisce on their own homes, so similar to the village they now entered.

Fel'annár lifted his head and relished the timid warmth of the early winter sun on his face, smiling before opening his eyes and looking around the settlement. The Silvan foresters stopped to watch as the warriors walked single file towards the village hall, a large wooden construction which sat on one side of the clearing. Gathering closer, the villagers patted the lads upon the back and called out warm welcomes. The lasses though, were whispering and when Fel'annár passed them and winked saucily at them, they broke out into giggles. Angon poked their novice in the ribs while Fer'dán flicked at his hair, making the girls laugh even harder.

Children too, scampered around the warriors as they marched by, brushing their hands over worked leather and woollen cloaks, and when one of the more daring imps reached for a sword scabbard or a quiver, they were batted away with a good-natured scowl. The children screamed and squealed until their mothers scolded them and ushered them away with apologetic smiles.

Fel'annár felt a pang of nostalgia, for although much darker and enclosed, this village brought to mind his own forest home of Lan Taria. He understood this society, indeed they were the very reason he had chosen to do what he now did and of a sudden he could not wait to take his vows and be counted amongst the king's warriors as an equal rather than a novice.

As a Silvan settlement, there would be a Village Leader, a Spirit Herder and a Master Forester; these three figures were the leaders of their people and their starting point would be to find them. Erthoron, Golloron and Thavron popped into Fel'annár's mind and he smiled at the thought of them.

Soon, they arrived at the wooden hall where two tall elves stood waiting. Turion stepped forward and placed his fist over his heart.

"Well met. I am Captain Turion of the Western Patrol, and this is my Lieutenant, Lainon. We have come to ensure your safety and assess your defences."

"Well met, Captain. I am Lorthil, leader of these people, and this is Narosén, our Spirit Herder. Be you welcome brothers."

The entire patrol bowed to the two Silvan leaders, and then Lainon looked sideways at Narosén, his fellow Ari'atór, the Spirit Herder and bowed solemnly. Narosén returned it, his eyes just as blue and weighty as Lainon's. Yet where Lainon wore the simple uniform of a lieutenant, Narosén was clad in long, black robes; his hair, equally black, was full of tokens, beads and stones, feathers and vines and braids of every length and thickness. It all lay in a jumbled mass upon his head and then streamed down his back and past his rump.

Once inside the village hall, they were led to a long table that sat before a large hearth that had only recently been lit. They had been expected, and now, three younger elves set bread and water on the tables, smiling at the staring warriors as they passed.

"Will you sit, warriors, and share a meal with us?" asked Lorthil, gesturing to the tables. The warriors' eyes had gone round and their stomachs rumbled loudly, the promise of food—*hot* food—at a *table* with fresh bread made their eyes misty and their mouths water.

"We would be honoured, Lorthil," said Turion as he turned and nodded to the warriors, the hint of a smirk on his otherwise rigid features.

An Alpine warrior reached for the bread, but Angon's hand shot out to stop him, bidding him wait. Sure enough, a soft voice lifted against the silence.

"Aria, we thank you for the bounties of the forest. May we take sustenance from them, and replenish these lands, nurture your creation and praise thy name."

With a smile, Narosén lifted his head and smiled, the sign any well-educated Silvan knew meant the meal could begin. Abashed, the Alpine warrior smiled ruefully as he reached once more for the bread, slower this time, offering it to Angon first, before tearing off a piece for himself and stuffing it into his mouth so that it bulged, and Fel'annár giggled.

Muted conversation broke out as the warriors ate and the leaders spoke of their plans for the day. Fel'annár, eager to learn, had only one ear on his companions, and the other on Turion and his procedure, tucking away all his words and nuances. He might one day find himself in this very situation, as a captain he reminded himself.

"Tell us of the enemy, Lorthil. What of them?" asked Turion.

"We lost three elves in the fields a week past now. It was not a coordinated attack but a pack of scavengers. However, the enemy is pressing in—we can all feel it—there is something coming this way but we are unable to identify exactly what."

Turion scowled as he turned to the Spirit Herder. "What say your omens, Narosén?" he asked respectfully. The captain was Alpine, but he was well-versed in the culture and rites of the Silvan people and their Ari Spirit Herders.

"They speak of many things of late," said Narosén softly so that only Turion and Lainon could hear. "They speak of a dark wave of festering evil—something approaches, gnaws at the forest for the trees whisper."

"What do they say?" asked Turion.

"We know only that they fight their own battle, Captain, on a plane we cannot perceive. But the more sensitive of our folk speak of resistance, a desperate fight our woodland sentinels seem to have taken up."

"It sounds dire," said Lainon. As an Ari himself, he understood these people's superstitions, believed them and even felt them, to a point.

"Yes, but there are whispers of something else—it may be of no import, but they speak of—of an awakening."

A strange tingling washed over the captain, turning his skin too sensitive and he glanced at Lainon with a scowl; but the Ari'atór was not looking at him but at Fel'annár—watching as the boy ate, seemingly oblivious and Turion wondered at that. He had not missed Narosén's veiled glance at their novice, the gleaming blue eyes overly bright, and in them was the spark of something Turion could not place, even though he knew it was important.

An awakening, Narosén had said, and Turion, sceptical Alpine that he was, believed every word the Spirit Herder had said.

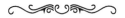

They slept well, as if they floated upon a cloud of silk and feathers, although the truth was not quite so luxurious. It was a matter of perspective, of course, but the fact was that they lay well into the morning upon pallets of leaves and blankets, soft and warm, their bellies full and their minds filled with memories of home. Fel'annár had awoken to the sound of his own mouth working as if he ate—the aromas of spring pea soup almost perceptible upon his salivating taste buds, the image of it slowly dissipating in his waking mind.

Now, after a refreshing dip in the nearby river, Fel'annár lounged back against a tree, listening to his companions talk quietly of mothers and fathers, of sweethearts and lovers, of nut cakes and venison pie. For him, it had always been Amareth's pea soup, and a dreamy smile was back on his face.

Rising slowly, he murmured to his companions, "I am going for a walk," to which Angon replied, "Stay within the perimeter, Hwindo."

Fel'annár nodded and strolled away, walking slowly and allowing his mind to wander, for it was safe to do so here.

He thought of his performance as a novice, of what he had learned, of that which haunted him now—the strange malady that had taken him not so long ago. He thought of Turion and Lainon, of their lessons and guidance, and he thought of Amareth, of Idernon and Ramien whom he missed and wondered where they would be. All he knew was that they, at least, had been stationed together, to the Eastern patrol. Perhaps they would walk upon snow, he mused, for they would be close to the eastern mountains that marked the end of Ea Uaré and the land of Tar'eastór.

He stopped suddenly and trained his eyes on the sight that stood before him. There, a mighty oak towered over him, its branches so thick and long they bent to the ground and upon its brown bark, patches of vivid green moss covered the mighty limbs like a soft, woollen blanket. The sheer size and beauty of this magnificent specimen stole Fel'annár's breath; never had he seen such a thing in all his years. His eyes filled with awe and a rush of emotion he could not quite place. Before he could move towards it though, a soft voice startled him.

"'Tis awe inspiring, is it not?" asked Narosén, who appeared at Fel'annár's shoulder silently, making the boy flinch.

"It is . . . *majestic,*" whispered the novice, his mouth barely moving, his eyes fixed on the massive expanse of its branches and leaves, eyes alight in Silvan wonder.

Narosén, however, was watching the young warrior carefully, his own, deep blue eyes anchored firmly on the strange green irises of the half-Alpine boy.

"'Tis strange to come across an Alpine who admires a tree the way you do, child."

Fel'annár scowled, ripping his eyes momentarily from the tree to the Spirit Herder beside him.

"I am *Silvan*," was all he said.

"You do not look Silvan," came the all too familiar retort which always managed to exasperate Fel'annár. Calming his irritation, he explained as briefly as he could so that he would be left once more to admire the oak before him.

"I am both, Sir, but my heart lies in the forest, with my people."

"A Silvan at heart then, if not in blood."

"In blood too, Narosén," said Fel'annár somewhat curtly.

"I do not mean to offend, only to comprehend, warrior. I—I have been observing you for some time now. You are restless and in your wandering, you have come here, to this tree—why?" asked Narosén softly, his eyes gleaming and his head tilting slightly to one side, as if he laboured to understand something.

"I did not come to the tree, Narosén, I simply came across it."

"That is a matter of perspective, I suppose," said the Spirit Herder with a smile. "Come, join me?" He held up a skin with what Fel'annár could only hope was wine. He was not on duty and would be permitted to drink, in moderation of course, so he gave Narosén a tight smile and nodded, following him under the boughs of the oak until they sat near its base.

Accepting the skin with both hands and a respectful nod, he took a long draught, savouring the rich, woody aroma that warmed his chest, before handing it back and watching as his strange companion drank.

"Why do you watch me?" asked Fel'annár in genuine curiosity.

"I am not sure, eh, what should I call you?" asked Narosén with a frown.

"I have many names," said Fel'annár with a smile. "Hwind'atór, The Silvan, Fel'annár . . . you may choose," he said with a smile as he drank once more.

"The Silvan?" came the surprised question.

"Yes, I know—I do not *look* Silvan as you have already pointed out. I inherited my father's face and colouring, yet my eyes are those of my Silvan mother. It is more a question of the soul, Narosén. I feel Silvan, they are my people, the ones I wish to protect . . ." he finished, his thoughts turning inwards.

"Then Silvan you are, of that there can be no doubt. I knew from the way you admired our sentinel," he said lightly, but Narosén's eyes betrayed him, for there was a deep, almost hungry expression in them.

"Sentinel?" asked Fel'annár, his eyes riveted on Narosén.

"The more sensitive members of our society say this tree is our guardian, the one that looks over us in this part of the Great Forest."

"What do you mean by *sensitive*?" asked Fel'annár, his right hand smoothing over the mossy ground beside his legs.

"There are those who can feel the trees, that feel their emotions. They can sense their moods, feel their joy, suffer their *fear*," he whispered finally, blue eyes wide and almost aflame as they sank into Fel'annár's. "Even the king has a measure of it, they say – strange for an Alpine though it is."

Fel'annár was mesmerised and yet not quite sure of how to interpret Narosén's words. It was then that his mind rushed to show him Lan Taria, a young child with a penchant for sleeping with his windows wide open, a chubby hand brushing over a green leaf, a tiny window beside *his* bed at the barracks that had turned all the colours of the forest, strangely foreign emotions when a young recruit sat beneath the bows of a willow, a hand brushing over the roots of a tree; again, and again.

Narosén's eyes were trained on Fel'annár's hand, watching in fascination as one, long finger reached out and brushed over a root and the young warrior froze, as if struck.

"Fel'annár?" whispered the Spirit Herder, his voice echoing strangely around them. "Child, do not be afraid . . ."

Fel'annár heard, as if from far away, but he could not answer and the colours were back, that green and purple halo appeared once more, surrounded everything but when he looked at the sentinel now, it shined a dazzling white blue, transparent. Something moved inside it, the sap pumping up and down the trunk, pulsing into the branches and into leaves, a living life force of pure, liquid light.

He had not breathed for some time. Finally, he sucked in a laboured breath, standing shakily upon legs that threatened to give way. Narosén followed suit, his eyes never leaving those of the boy.

"Do not be afraid," said the Spirit Herder again, awe-struck as he watched a white-blue light reflected in the boy's eyes, as if he stood before the naked sun and yet there was nothing there, only the old oak.

"What . . ."

"It is a *good* thing, Silvan. Feel it, let it in . . . Aria has blessed you. Would that I could see what you do."

His mind was filled with emotions and sensations, of sureties and doubts, of something arcane he could not fathom and it was suddenly too much, and with a cry, he fell to the forest floor, only his strong arms keeping him from falling flat on his own face.

Narosén was beside him in a flash, his own face alight in wonder and awe, the strange blue light now dwindling in his own eyes. He spared a glance into the brush to his right, where an elf stood watching, and Narosén nodded at him, and then watched as Lorthil returned it, before melting away into the darkness of the forest.

"*Now* I understand," murmured the Spirit Herder, his face shining with wonder. "There is hope, hope for the Silvan people." He smiled then, before looking down upon the beautiful child that sat on the ground beside him, scared and confused. His long hand reached out and smoothed down the strange locks of blond and silver, before his fingers traced the outline of his large green eyes and then ran down the side of his smooth, rosy cheek.

"Fel'annár of Ea Uaré," he whispered, watching as the singular face turned to meet his gaze, deep confusion swirling in its depths.

"You, are *ours*!" announced Narosén solemnly.

Chapter Fourteen

DELIVERANCE

"All elves feel the Spirit, but the Silvan people more acutely. Some though, can even understand it, interpret it.
These elves are the Listeners."
On Elven Nature. Calro.

The next day, Fel'annár did not awake with the delicious memory of Amareth's pea soup on his tongue, but to feelings of deep dread, the acrid smell of burning wood and Lainon's urgent voice, barking out orders as he pulled on his outer leather vest and tightened his vambraces. Lainon's blue-black hair was still loose and it flew around his shoulders, agitated yet controlled, like oil in water, his thick Ari twists audibly banging against the reinforced leather of his pauldrons.

"UP! Kit out *now!* There is fire to the North. We move in five minutes!

Fel'annár sprang out of bed in nothing but his breeches, eyes searching for his boots and then remembering Angon's oath to never sleep without them. Pulling them on, he slipped into his white linen shirt and then the sleeveless leather vest, securing the clasps with one hand and reaching for his vambraces with the other. Buckling them on he slipped his blades harness over his back and then his quiver. Reaching back, he tied the heavy upper locks to the back of his head as he jogged out into the clearing, standing in line with the rest of the Western Patrol. His head thumped painfully, and he realised he must have been breathing the heavy smoke even in his sleep.

Deftly stringing his bow, he slipped it back in its quiver over his head – he was ready. It was a cold winter morning but no clouds greyed the sky. Instead, a thin blanket of smoke loomed over them threateningly, slowly descending and stinging their eyes. They stood together with Lainon and watched as their captain spoke with Lorthil, the village leader, their words hushed and urgent.

Elves ran here and there, not chaotically but with purpose, calm and measured. Some carried supplies to the Village Hall while others collected food, or herded children into the open glade, lining them up and counting them. It was a testimony to the life these people led, for the forest was spectacular in its beauty—the colours and textures, the smells and sounds, the simplicity that came with living off the land; yet the price they paid in return for such a privilege was this—the constant threat of fire, of attack, the insecurity that was inherent to these parts of Ea Uaré. The city dwellers called them stubborn, selfish for putting themselves at risk for it meant deploying more warriors to defend them, but the Silvans argued that the army existed for this very reason—to defend their nation. Where else would they be sent? Fel'annár tried to imagine these people living in the city but he could not. They were two different worlds, two completely different mind-sets.

Turion turned his back on Lorthil and addressed the patrol and although his face was inscrutable, his words were tinged with urgency and worry.

"This is what we know. There is fire to the North, and the breeze is pushing it westwards, towards the foresters' outpost. I need water pumped from the river this way through their irrigation pipes," pointed the captain, "so that Lorthil can oversee the villagers and take preventive measures while the rest of us travel to the source and douse the flames if we can. Fel'annár, Fer'dán, you are in charge of ensuring these people get the water they need to protect themselves should the flames reach them; the rest of you, *move out!*" he ordered, swivelling upon his heels and leading them into the darkening grey curtain of ever-thickening smoke.

Fel'annár frowned deeply, feelings of inadequacy assailing him once more, turning only briefly as Fer'dán's heavy hand rested on his shoulder for a split second before he ran off towards the river.

Turion was either protecting him, or was still unsure of his worth. There was a third option too, one he did not want to consider, but it had pushed its way to the fore and would not be ignored. What if Turion thought him an invalid, cursed with some strange illness that rendered him useless to his patrol? What did it take, he wondered, to be accepted as an equal? To prove his mettle? He utterly ignored the fact that Fer'dán too, had been sent to the pumps and he was a tried, veteran warrior.

Reaching the pump, Fer'dán opened the lock as Fel'annár began to work the mechanism, watching as the water slowly gained momentum and the liquid began to flow down the pipes that had been skilfully engineered, straight into the heart of the village where the Silvans gathered it in pails and began to wet the ground, the foliage and the trees surrounding the settlement.

After ten minutes of furious pumping, Fer'dán took over as Fel'annár watched the water, ensuring the pipes aligned adequately. His arms burned with fatigue, but not enough to stop his errant mind from returning to the strange events of the day before. They harrowed him, and Narosén's words came back to him.

'*Do not be afraid..*'

"Fel'annár!"

Fer'dán's sudden yell jolted him and his head whipped to his companion. "The wind is changing."

Fel'annár scowled, and then looked around the glade, his heart dropping to his boots and leaving him feeling strangely light. His nose prickled uncomfortably and smoke collected at the back of his throat, leaving a bitter taste in his mouth. The situation had become urgent, for the flames were now approaching Sen'oléi. Anxiety slammed into him with a force that almost made him stumble where he stood, the strange dissonant harmony he had first heard that morning flaring painfully at his temples. That sensation was back, realised Fel'annár, the feeling that whatever caused his dread did not come from himself but somewhere else.

'*It is a good thing . . . embrace it . . .*'

His brow furrowed even more, and he wondered if Narosén had been right. Perhaps if he just relaxed, stopped fighting it—perhaps if he moved *with* it and not against it—whatever *it* was . . .

Fer'dán scowled at his companion as he pumped, and then visibly flinched when Fel'annár whirled around to face him. There was a strange light in his companion's eye, he would later say, something that compelled him to obey, even though *he* was the senior warrior.

"Fer'dán, continue pumping while I go to the Hall. I will return in ten minutes!" he shouted. Fer'dán simply nodded and Fel'annár was away, sprinting parallel to the water pipes.

His long legs pumped hard and his chest laboured to provide his muscles with the air they required. He was not even sure why he had so suddenly left his companion, but he had decided to go with his instincts and this is what they had screamed at him to do.

Inside the glade now, he slowed his pace, his mind registering the growing chaos for the people of Sen'oléi no longer seemed calm and organised, but in a state of mounting anxiety. They had formed a line and were now passing buckets at great speed towards the tree line, wetting everything they could. A small crowd had gathered to one side and it was there that Fel'annár found Lorthil and Narosén.

"Lorthil—what else can we do? What are your priorities?"

"We are all accounted for, save for three. The last to arrive tells us the flames are but twenty minutes away on foot. I dare not risk sending a rescue party," shouted the village leader, a hint of desperation in his voice, for he knew the patrol had gone to the source of the flames—they would not be able to help those who had strayed on the path home.

One woman struggled in the arms of two men, who only just managed to hold her back as she screamed and writhed in their clutches, kicking out in a desperate attempt to free herself.

"No!! No!! My *children!!*"

The villagers behind the struggling trio covered their quivering mouths, clearly at a loss as to what they should do. The flames were fast approaching and if they did not get all hands to work now, their settlement would be engulfed.

"You can't leave them there! *Pleeeease!!*" screamed the desperate woman. A mother's tormented wail, her face twisted in disbelief and terror. It was her *eyes* though, that Fel'annár could not escape from, for something inside them sent a violent shiver down his spine. What a terrible sight, a lovely face so utterly transformed by suffering. It struck him that he had never seen such an atrocious thing, not even from the Deviants. His own eyes welled, not in pity but in horror, and then he looked to Lorthil who was now having to shout over the din of the encroaching flames.

"It's too dangerous! Eloran will keep them safe—by Aria, can you not see—stop, *Alféna!*

"What is their route?" yelled Fel'annár. "From where do they emerge? Is there a *path?*" he yelled.

"Yes—there, do you see it?" gestured the leader and then coughed and spluttered. Fel'annár followed Lorthil's eyes and barely made out the small path that led into the forest, now almost completely hidden by the darkening smoke.

"Can you send someone to relieve my companion at the pump?" "Yes!" shouted Lorthil, and then grabbed at Fel'annár's vambrace with surprising strength. "You do not know the way . . ." he said quietly, his mouth close to his ear, his tone pleading. There was a message beneath his words and Fel'annár searched the ancient elf's eyes. But there was no time to ponder the question for the noise was now a roar and the elves around them began to shout louder, their desperation finally showing for this was as close as any fire had ever come; they needed all the hands they could find.

"Fel'annár—you cannot go—I *forbid* it!" shouted the leader, his face stern and his eyes flashing but it was not enough—Afléna's plight, her *eyes* were all he could see now and his ears were filled with a strange wailing, the sound snaking around his soul and choking it.

Alféna ceased her struggle, and her wide, trembling eyes anchored themselves on Fel'annár, watching his every move, as if she dared him to fail her.

"Alféna," shouted Fel'annár, taking her by the shoulders and forcing her to pay close attention. "Eloran—your son?"

"Yes!"

"And he is with two other children?"

"Yes!! My three-year-old twins, Eloran is still young. *Please*," she ground out now, her voice but a painful, scratching echo of what it had been not minutes before. Her hands came up to clutch at his leather tunic, crumpling it in her desperate, clasping hands. "*Please*," she whispered. Her eyes seemed to grow larger then brighter, and her face all but faded away. All that she was, all her despair was concentrated behind the honey-coloured orbs that screamed at him, compelled him so that he could not ignore her, could not fail her.

"Fel'annár," warned Lorthil one more time, but there was defeat in his tone—he knew he had lost.

"I must try," shouted Fel'annár urgently, his hand resting on the leader's sleeve. "If you cannot stop the flames, lead your people to the South-east; it is relatively clear of the enemy; we will find you," he yelled over the din, before nodding and turning one last time to Alféna.

"I will find them—help your people to save this place," he said, his own voice strangely unfamiliar to him, and then he dashed away, into the smoky haze until he was lost from sight, the tendrils of smoke swirling furiously behind him in waning circles and then disappearing.

Lorthil watched after him with anger and respect. He himself had never been a warrior but he did merit himself with the skill of recognising one. That did not douse his anxiety though, for nothing could happen to this one.

"To the pumps! Protect these trees! Foresters—you are in charge!" screamed Lorthil, once more the strong leader of Sen'oléi. Alféna's eyes stared for a while longer at the spot where she knew the path to be, the path that could no longer be seen. Strange, green eyes came to her mind's eye.

'*I will find them,*' he had said, and as Alféna turned to help her people, she realized that she believed him.

Smoke burned his eyes, forcing tears to stream down his face, leaving streaks of stark white against his grey face. Wiping at his reddened eyes in irritation, he continued to track through the dense foliage, his ears straining to pick up the slightest hint of Alféna's children. The good news was that he had not yet encountered the flames, but the smoke was a serious hindrance. He would pay the price later.

The heat became ever more oppressive. Sweat poured down his neck and back. The trunks before him were but looming shadows of grey and black— there was no colour at all and the hiss and crackle of flames began to grow louder. The ground beneath his boots was hot and soon enough, pockets of fire could be seen here and there.

Casting his eyes upwards, he could see furious flames just off to the West. He guessed the patrol would be right there, hacking away at the forest, clearing the dry wood away from the flames. '*Eloran, where are you, boy?*' he asked as he stumbled on, unsure of how long he could keep going before he too, was forced to seek refuge.

Reaching back, he pulled hard on the hood of his cloak and ripped it away from the collar. Tying it around his nose and mouth he pressed on, eyes streaming and lungs heaving.

Hissing wood became the crackle of burning timber and the heat became almost unbearable, as choking clouds of smoke stole his breath and he coughed until his throat stung painfully. A mighty whoosh to his left had him staggering out of the way as a tree suddenly burst into flames and the wailing in his head became a shrill scream. He covered his ears as if to block the sound but it was no good and for the first time, he wondered if Lorthil had been right, that he should never have disobeyed his order—perhaps good leadership was exactly this—deciding the better of two evils, even when you knew your decision would cost lives.

The sound was driving him to insanity but it unexpectedly stopped, just as his eyes anchored on a large oak. Even the hissing and crackling and the roar of encroaching flames was dampened to nothing and he knew he had found them.

His lungs heaved and he coughed violently, the fit doubling him over for a moment. Straightening, he strode towards the tree, and without the slightest hesitation, he scampered up the bark until his hand latched onto the first branch and he swung himself up, ignoring the painful heat as it singed his hands. Higher he moved, calling out for the children, eyes searching wildly about him.

It was half way up the tree that he finally heard the desperate shouts of a young elf. A child, but not so young.

"Eloran?!" shouted Fel'annár as he made his way up. "*Eloran!*" he yelled again and soon enough, he had his answer.

"Here!" came the strangled cry of frightened youth.

"Eloran! Guide me to you!!"

"Over here! Please, over *here!*"

With one, final spurt of energy, Fel'annár hoisted himself up another branch until he finally made out the hazy figure of a boy, lying flat along a wide branch, his arm outstretched towards a thinner branch that bent dangerously under the weight of two tiny children.

Fel'annár's heart ached. He could see them now, and although his eyes burned he could not blink. They cowered together upon their precarious perch, joined in a desperate embrace, short, chubby fingers grappling with the fabric of their bright, Silvan tunics, frozen in utter fear.

He had no rope and even if he had, he doubted the children would let go of each other to catch hold of it. "Eloran," he shouted as he approached, so as not to startle the boy.

"*Help* them!" wailed the boy. "I can't reach them and they won't move!"

Fel'annár's eyes analysed the situation. They were, indeed, paralysed and even should they move, the branch would surely break, and should Eloran or himself try to approach them, the weight would be too much.

The possibility that he would not be able to save them began to grow in his mind, but the pleading eyes of Alféna came back to him and he could not—he could not turn back for he was a warrior of Ea Uaré—he would die trying with Aria as his witness.

The boy began to cry, his outstretched arm slowly returning to his side and for the first time he looked back, over his shoulders. Large, watery eyes anchored on Fel'annár and agony pierced his heart at the expression he saw there.

Purple and green began to tinge the outer parts of his vision and Eloran's face changed from grief—to *fright* and he shuffled away from the branch, pressing his back to the bark of the tree. Fel'annár scowled but he had no more time to think, for the colours began to invade his sight and he saw nothing but blue and green and all the colours of the forest, where just moments before all had been shadowed.

He saw the pulse of brilliant blue sap as it pumped through the trunk and the branches, into each and every twig. He saw the brightness of the children's souls, watched in fascination as the liquid life of the tree pulsed once, twice, and then of a sudden the branch which was too weak to hold him seemed to become fatter, wider, stronger, the light within the brown skin becoming so powerful it almost blinded him. He reached out to touch it in fascination, watching as it sparkled on contact with his skin and he wondered. Gingerly, he stepped down onto the branch, feeling it strong and steady, and although he did not understand it at the time, did not hear the desperate yells of Eloran, he knew he would not fall, that he could place his weight on it and that he would not plummet to his death.

Fel'annár moved slowly along the branch, desperately trying to block the logical part of his mind that screamed at him to jump away. He was soon crouching before the two children who remained firmly clasped in each other's arms, their eyes scrunched shut. If he called to them now they would not heed him and if he touched them they could lose their balance and fall. He must be quick, give them no time to react.

With startling speed, Fel'annár reached out with both hands and grabbed the children by the collar of their tunics, pulling them back towards the thick, central trunk where Eloran still sat rigid and wide-eyed. Panicking, the children reached out desperately for the trunk, their brother, anything within their reach, but Fel'annár could not allow it, for they would not let go and so he bid them cling to him, one to his chest and the other to his back.

He had been quick and it had been enough, and they wrapped their short, booted legs around his chest and back, their arms locking around him in a painful embrace.

"Hold on," he shouted. "Don't let go—you will not fall, I promise," he said, with a confidence he did not feel. "Eloran—*move!*" he yelled, for the boy was rooted to the spot and Fel'annár frowned—was he not happy his siblings were off the branch? There was no time to ponder the question for plumes of billowing smoke were all around them, and Eloran spluttered and choked, finally moving his back from the bark and following Fel'annár. They burned their hands and scraped their skin and they coughed until they wretched and finally, they were upon the ground—a wall of fire looming over them from the West.

"*Run!*" screamed Fel'annár, but no sooner had he said it than he realised they could not—it was all they could do to stagger away, away from the wall of destruction and choking fumes as the flames devoured the wood around them, engulfing it, destroying what was once beautiful and Fel'annár's heart broke for the tragedy of it.

The wailing in his mind stopped, leaving a ringing silence in its wake—as if something had died.

When the smoke finally became thinner and their backs could no longer feel the burning heat, Fel'annár's mind began to work through his predicament. He needed to continue eastwards and if he was lucky, he would find water, for that was the only thing that would save the young ones now.

It was a simple calculation, he mused. Find water now, wherever it takes you, and should you walk into the enemy, then your death will be just as certain as if you had not tried at all.

The people of Sen'oléi battled the fire for many hours. Now, they were exhausted and sat in stunned, grieving silence. It had been enough to save their settlement, but they had lost three children, and their eyes were drawn to the figure of Alféna, who would not stop to take rest. Instead she collected the pails, filled skins of water and organized food to be prepared. Her gaze was often drawn to the forest path but her face remained completely blank, as if she had banished all emotion, preparing herself, perhaps, for what might emerge from the smoke – or perhaps what would not.

The Western Patrol returned to the knowledge that Fel'annár, their novice, had gone after the children, disobeying Lorthil's express orders. Fer'dán had said only that the novice had acted strangely, and that he had taken off suddenly, without the slightest of explanations.

They were black and burned, red-eyed and spluttering and they staggered towards the river, throwing themselves upon the bank where Lainon and Turion's trained eyes raked over their warriors.

Some of the villagers were there in a moment with cloths and bowls and other provisions they had anticipated needing and soon enough, those with some knowledge of the healing arts were sitting with the warriors and seeing to their needs.

Two had burned their forearms badly and another had twisted his knee and as for the rest, they coughed and spat out grey phlegm, and then lay back on the cool grass as they sought to calm themselves.

Angon removed his gloves with a grimace, and then inspected his reddened hands. Pulling his boots off, he scowled at the burns he found there and then dragged himself to the bank, gasping as he lowered his feet into the cold water.

Fer'dán was soon beside him, looking over in sympathy at his friend's burned skin.

"Was it intentional?" he asked simply.

"Aye. We found evidence of Sand Lords. Even now they will probably be reaping the rewards of their vile deed and pillaging the water source nearby."

Fer'dán's nostrils flared at Angon's words, for any hope he had been clutching to that perhaps Fel'annár had made it out of the flames and to water and safety, had suddenly been dashed.

Nearby, Turion sat in nothing but his breeches and boots, despite the cold weather. His bare chest was red and painful to the touch, and the mere brush of clothing would surely be excruciating. Lainon sat in a similar fashion, his under-shirt open, black and ripped, revealing a nasty scratch across his ribs. His strange, dark face seemed black now for he had not bothered to wash himself and the whites of his eyes stood out starkly, setting off his deep, blue eyes. Yet there was no sparkle in them now for they were dull and unmoving and a perpetual frown marred is forehead.

"Perhaps he escaped the flames, Lainon. Perhaps he lost his way and is waiting for the smoke to dissipate."

Lainon turned to Turion, seeing his own reflexion mirrored on his captain's face.

"Who can say," replied the Ari quietly but it was flat and lifeless, and Turion knew he despaired. "Look at us, Turion. We barely made it out of there—*together*. He is alone and has been inside that place of death for far too long. No one could have escaped that, not alone.

"But he is not any one, Lainon. We have seen strange things of late and I think that if anyone could, perhaps pull off such a thing—it would be him."

But Lainon did not answer and so, they simply sat, their thoughts turned inwards, to the strange child, the skilled warrior, the joyful soul that had touched them all, to the *fool* that disobeyed Lorthil's orders and dashed away on some hero's mission he could never fulfil save in his own imagination.

Muted footfalls heralded the arrival of Lorthil and Narosén and together they sat, depositing two large baskets on the ground beside them. Inside were skins of what they assumed would be water.

"Do you mind if we join you?" asked Lorthil quietly, holding out one of the bottles to the captain.

Turion simply nodded tiredly and then coughed, before drinking from the bottle and closing his eyes. "Honey?" he asked, surprised.

"Nectar, yes—it will soothe your throats and calm your cough," he said as he watched Lainon help himself. Soon, the skins were being distributed amongst the troop, and Turion watched them before turning back to the village leaders.

Turion's voice, when he spoke, was loud and his tone curt. "Why were those young children out in the wood? Surely you could see the potential danger? Forest fires are not new to you."

Lorthil frowned and looked to the ground before answering. "Children often accompany their elders into the fields. Thus, they learn and become productive members of our society. Should we cease to take them, what a great victory for the enemy that would be, do you not think?"

"And an even greater one to have claimed their lives," stressed the captain.

"You do not understand," said Narosén from the other side. "You are not Silvan. It is our way, one which sustains our society so that this land may prosper, so that you Alpine can feast at your kingly tables."

Turion's nostrils flared at the acetic words. "Not all the Alpine are as you imagine them to be, Spirit Herder," he said shortly, looking away then, a clear message to the Silvan mystic that he did not wish to speak on the subject any longer.

Narosén let out a long breath, before raking his own long hand through his dark locks. "I am sorry. This is not the time for petty argument."

Turion turned back to the Ari, nodding his agreement before turning away again, but he stopped halfway, for the Spirit Herder was speaking again, albeit softly, as if to himself.

"They may not be lost, Captain. I cannot be sure, but there is a song on the breeze, a song of guidance.

Turion was not a religious elf and although he respected the Silvans and their superstitious ways, he simply could not bring himself to believe.

Chapter Fifteen

FANFARE

*"The northern lands of Calrazia are a sea of sand where nothing seems
to grow and the sun knows no rival. All we know of its inhabitants
are their warriors; Sand Lords we call them, for although cloaked and
hooded in black, their gauntlets and armour are finely wrought, their
vambraces graced with gems that sparkle as brightly as their honey eyes.
But it is not a good light; it is dark and forbidding,
the promise of infinite cruelty laid bare for the enemy to see."*
The Silvan Chronicles, Book III. Marhené.

One full cycle of the sun and still, Turion sat alone, away from the warriors, and Lainon understood him well. The Alpine was proud to a fault and did not want to be in anyone's company whilst he mourned what now seemed to be the certain loss of their novice, for with every passing moment, mourn he did.

Alféna had finally allowed herself to sit, her face no longer cold and detached, eyes fixed on the smoky path ahead. Someone had draped a blanket around her shoulders and had left food and water at her side. But she had not moved at all and so she sat, and she waited, and she broke their hearts.

Lainon however, had yet to believe that Fel'annár had perished, and while Turion slowly descended into silent despair, Lainon surfaced from its murky depths. It had been Narosén's words, he thought, for Lainon was Ari too, understood the Spirit Herder better than most for their perception of the world was different, and yet it was not something he could readily explain. But then, even had Narosén remained silent, he had somehow concluded that it was all together absurd, incomprehensible that the boy could perish, after all they had been through, after all the careful planning. They were on the brink of carrying it all off, the hope of restoring a strong and powerful king upon the throne so very close.

So absorbed was the Ari in his own inner turmoil that he visibly flinched when Fer'dán abruptly rose from the ground, standing tall, his body as tight as his bow string, his head tilted upwards as if he listened. But Lainon had no time to wonder, for the early afternoon silence was suddenly shattered as a cry from a distant guard cleaved the grieving silence.

The sound echoed eerily around the glade and for a moment all seemed to freeze, nothing seemed to move at all until the echo dissipated and understanding dawned upon them.

Someone approached.

Seconds later, the insistent call of a sparrow hawk had the elves slowly rising to their feet, and as a brambling joined the sparrow hawk's song, the villagers and the warriors of the Western patrol lifted their faces to the soft breeze. Hair of dark brown and auburn, dark blond and black lifted softly as the wind played with the silky strands, as if it teased them or perhaps it soothed them.

The sparrow hawk and the brambling made way for others to join their melody and a chaffinch, a house martin and a siskin joined the harmony, adding deeper tones and trills. The Silvan foresters smiled into the weak winter sun and then lifted their own bird calls to join the woodland orchestra— woodpecker and spotted flycatcher, warbler and jay . . . it was frantic and it was utterly beautiful, and tears pooled in their eyes for bird and elf were rejoicing in song—this was not the approach of an enemy, it was a welcome, a solemn hail, in the purest of Silvan ways.

Placing one booted foot before the other, slow and tentative at first, Lainon inched forward, his body leaning from one side to the other, as if the movement would help him to discover the identity of what approached from the thick forest belt ahead.

The symphony suddenly ended and the thick, tense silence was back, warriors and villagers left standing amidst the echo of their ancient melody.

From the mist of the trees, an outline became visible, a form slowly defining itself. A warrior burdened both front and back and beside him, a shorter figure, hunched over and covered head to foot in a cloak that was too long for him.

There was no mistaking the tall, powerful warrior that was their novice and Lainon was striding now, his long legs propelling him so fast he broke into a run, bounding forwards, one word flying from his lips, a hoarse cry of utter relief that rent the air and set their skin to prickling.

"Fel'annár!"

An overwhelming sense of gratefulness infused Lainon and he smiled as he ran. 'Aria be praised, not dead, not dead!' he rejoiced.

"Hwindo!" shouted the warriors. "Hwind'atór!" they cried as their fists punched the air above them, sending the lingering smoke spiralling away and then running after their lieutenant.

The villagers too, moved forward although more cautiously at first, and even Alféna slowly stood, her eyes focusing once more on the world around her.

"Eloran?" she called softly, her eyes still blank but as she slowly began to walk with the villagers, her voice rose and her eyes leapt to life as she realised her son was staggering towards her, barely held up by the warrior at his side.

"Eloran?! she called, still unsure of what she knew was true but dare not believe and then she was running, and then sprinting as she shouted the names of her children, arms held out before her. It was enough for the spell to be broken and they all rushed forward, hair streaming behind them like standards on a dawn of victory.

Lainon skidded to a halt, his leather skirts still fanning around his trembling knees, only to hesitate as his eyes registered what it was that stood before him, not because he did not recognise the young novice, the fledgling warrior or the orphaned child whose mother had died, the boy who was yet to meet his father. A surge of pure emotion travelled the length of Lainon's body and then lodged itself at the back of his throat and his eyes pooled at what his mind was beginning to recognise. Glancing sideways for a brief instant, he found Narosén staring straight right back at him, as if he too, was seeing something he had never seen before—as if he understood.

The children had been wrapped in cloths, their faces almost completely covered except for their red-rimmed eyes that nevertheless sparked with life. Alféna shrieked as she pushed roughly through the gathered crowd and engulfed Eloran in a bone-crushing embrace. He hugged her back timidly, too tired to make the effort and a healer stepped forward and promptly hoisted the boy into his arms and away to the Village Hall. Alféna watched them, and then turned to Fel'annár slowly, her eyes following the clever harness the warrior had fashioned to carry her children. They sat huddled inside, their heads poking over the top, hair and skin completely grey but *alive.*

Tears streamed down her face and she wrenched her eyes from her children to the warrior who simply stood and stared back at her. Her eyes danced over his dusty face and one, shaking hand reached out to cup his filthy cheek.

"I knew you would come back."

Fel'annár did not react though, and Alféna joined Lainon's attempts to loosen the cloth harness which had been tied so tight that it took their best efforts to loosen the knots. Eventually though, they came away and the children were freed and with one, last lingering gaze upon their saviour, Alféna and the children were gone.

Freed now of his burden, Fel'annár sank to his knees and bowed his head in utter exhaustion, his once glorious mane of silver blond hair flopping heavily over his chest and covering part of his face. Lainon sank down next to him, his eyes moving to Fel'annár's burnt hands, his ripped tunic and ruined shirt below. Turion was removing his weapons harness and quiver, noticing he had no arrows left, but still, the novice did not move at all.

"Fel'annár?" called Turion as he worked.

Fel'annár lifted his gaze, as if his head weighed a thousand boulders, his red-rimmed eyes moving slowly, as if they had stuck to his eyelids and his breathing too shallow, too fast. The healer was back and knelt before the barely responsive warrior, peering into his eyes.

"Fel'annár—can you hear me?" he asked. The novice opened his mouth to answer, but all that came out was a painful rasping sound that rapidly turned into a fit of dry coughing that sent him to his hands and knees in misery.

Gesturing for the warriors to bring him in, Fel'annár lifted his hand and then grasped the captain's tunic as if it were a lifeline. With a quiet rush of air, his urgent words were just loud enough for Turion to hear.

"Sand Lords, fifty, from the North-eastern river marching South-west. Half a day . . ."

Turion's eyes bulged as he realised just what lay that way—Sen'uár—and then a terrible light came into them. His mind made up in an instant, he whirled around to meet Lainon and the warriors.

"Kit up, we move in thirty minutes."

Lainon's head whipped to the captain, and then to Fel'annár and the healer.

"Do what you can, my friend," said Turion to the healer. "Make him ready to fight for the odds are dire . . . we have no *choice*," he whispered.

Angon, Fer'dán and the Silvan healer had half dragged Fel'annár to the river where he now sat enduring the painful treatment he was subjected to. He had burned himself but the worst part was his throat and chest. He could not speak for he would cough and not stop until he wanted to wretch, his throat burning so much it sent tears to his eyes. And so, he remained silent, and allowed himself to be cleansed and bandaged. They would have bathed him had there been time, but thirty minutes was all they had.

"Stay close to us, Hwindo—we will watch your back," said Angon as he worked. "You are not fit for this but fifty Sand Lords are a challenge for one patrol—we need you, however much it pains me we cannot tuck you into a bed and sing you to sleep," he chuckled nervously, his eyes briefly dancing over Fer'dán, who scowled as he tied Fel'annár's wet hair upon his head.

"Fel'annár," called Angon, taking the novice by the shoulders and turning to face him. "Can you truly do this?" he whispered.

"I must," whispered the novice. "Water—and food," he added encouragingly. The truth was that his body needed to sleep but his mind was screaming at him to move. He would not be responsible for holding up the patrol when Sand Lords were so close. Pushing himself up, he stood a little shakily and made his way to the bank, accepting the towels that were handed him. They watched as he dried himself and then sat to tug on his boots, wincing as he pulled them over his reddened feet.

Now, realised Fel'annár—it was *now* that all his training would be needed. His endurance and his strength, his capacity to concentrate, centre himself. There were so many things he needed to remember and think upon. The strange thoughts at the pump, Alféna's eyes, how he had found the tree—the *tree*—and Eloran's strange reaction to him. But no, none of that mattered now. He would not think of those things—he would not think of his body's needs. He would block it all out and see only what he needed to see; the Sand Lords . . .

Narosén was beside him then, a bowl of food in his hands. "Eat and drink, you still have a few minutes," said the Spirit Herder, and Fel'annár nodded, taking the bowl and eating as quickly as he could, all the while his eyes fixed on Turion and Lainon some distance away.

The stew was good but swallowing was painful and Narosén pressed his honey nectar into his hands. "Drink," he ordered.

"*Muster!*" came Lainon's voice of command, and the warriors spared one last, sympathetic glance at Fel'annár, who was now dressed and armed, his hair still dripping wet and his face pale and pinched with pain. They longed for the story the boy would tell of the fire, but there was no time—later, they said to themselves, when all was done and they could rest once more.

"Lorthil," said Turion as he adjusted his harness. "Set a guard—if anything approaches that is not us, evacuate your people," he said meaningfully. "Move South-east—we will find you."

Lorthil nodded and then bowed to the captain respectfully. "Aria lend you speed, and a steady hand."

The Western Patrol moved out of Sen'oléi in single file, under the sorrowful, respectful gaze of the villagers and when Fel'annár passed them their hands reached out to brush over his cloak. Narosén had tied a flask of his nectar to the boy's weapons belt; he had done all he could and so he watched as the novice passed by, barely resisting the urge to pull him back, stop him from walking into what seemed like certain death. He could not lose Fel'annár—the Silvan people needed him—he was not expendable.

'Aria protect him' he whispered. 'His destiny is yet before him.'

They moved through the forest in single file, following the track they had found soon after leaving Sen'oléi. The Sand Lords had moved fast and Turion set a brisk pace. Angon and Fer'dán walked behind Fel'annár, their eyes as much on him as their surroundings, and Lainon would often turn back to check on their novice.

But Fel'annár was oblivious to their attention, for his mind was centred on healing his body as much as it could, blocking his thoughts, eliminating emotion and pain. They needed him and he would not fail them now. With a deep breath, he reached out and pulled on Lainon's cloak and then whispered as loud as he dared.

"The forest is uneasy. Further West," he pointed, and then cleared his throat as it spasmed and threatened to send him into another bout of coughing. He remembered Narosén's honey nectar and reached for the bladder, drinking deeply.

Lainon watched him for a moment, a sinking feeling slamming into him. "Sen'uár ..." he murmured and then repeated louder in Turion's direction. "We may be too late . . ." Whipping his head back to Fel'annár he asked urgently, "How far?"

"A few hours at most," he whispered back, his eyes sad, and Lainon closed his eyes in dread. With a cock of his head, he gestured for Fer'dán to scout ahead. He was back too soon and the news was dire.

"Their track is clear. We are on route to engage, close to or in Sen'uár," said Fer'dán urgently, his eyes momentarily slipping to Fel'annár. "Captain," he added, "their group seems to be carrying wounded."

Turion turned questioning eyes on his novice. Fel'annár shrugged and then whispered. "There was an incident," he trailed off and Turion stared back at him, tucking away the comment for later; it was not the time for stories.

The forest was even quieter now and Lainon repressed a shiver. It was a tense silence, the kind that pre-empted storms and he checked the patrol behind him yet again, before moving to Turion's shoulder. "They are close," he murmured.

"Full alert, Lainon," warned the captain.

Nodding briskly, he turned back to the warriors, resorting to hand signals now. Silence was paramount and Fel'annár reached for his honey nectar again, ruthlessly quelling the urge to cough. Lainon's eyes danced over him yet again, and then resumed his place at the fore. Angon's heavy hand clapped the novice on the shoulder, his silent promise to watch his back renewed and Fel'annár allowed himself a soft smile.

Not even the birds sang and as the minutes passed the warriors changed their step, no longer masking themselves as they drew closer to the outskirts of Sen'uár. They needed to engage the enemy before they reached the village, but they were already so close and still, no Sand Lords.

"Fel'annár," whispered Turion. "Anything?"

The novice closed his eyes and tipped his head upwards, trying desperately to understand what it was he was feeling, putting it into the only words that occurred to him at the time.

"Grief—I feel *grief*," he rasped, his eyes suddenly round and full of unshed tears, some brutal onslaught of raw emotion ripping through him.

"We are too late," said Turion with a sinking feeling and when he looked up once more, there was murderous intent in his flashing, Alpine eyes. There was no more need for silence and with a mighty call to battle, Turion drew his sword.

"We *run!*" he shouted, and the patrol drew their bows and unsheathed their blades as they jogged behind him. Soon, the sounds of battle began to permeate the silence, distant screams, the scraping of metal, the bellow of livestock and whinnying horses. Their wrath spurred them on even faster, until they ran into a thinner part of the forest and it was here that they came across the first terrified civilians who ran chaotically towards them, unsure of where to go as they clutched their wide-eyed children, screaming and shouting for lost family and friends. Turion gestured frantically at them to run in the direction the patrol had emerged from. Women, men and children dashed past them as the warriors sprinted forward, their faces set and their steel flashing, until the thwack of elven arrows heralded the first sighting of Sand Lords.

Smoke billowed into the air as thatched roofs were engulfed and the people stumbled out of their homes, choking and crying as they desperately searched for a way out, but the Sand Lords were everywhere, their black cloaks billowing in the winds of battle like the leathery wings of black bats grappling for prey. They descended upon the Silvans with their jewelled swords and senseless cries of fury, severing limbs and slitting throats, sending a frenzy of terror throughout the disorientated villagers.

Some had no time to react as they were run through, while others ran too slowly and were taken from behind, gloved hands twisting their heads mercilessly with a sickening crack of bone.

Fel'annár saw it all through hazy eyes as he fired, again and again until there were no more arrows and he pulled his long sword in one hand and sabre in the other. He saw them fall, saw the women die such tragic deaths, their panicked children reach even to the enemy for comfort, only to be cruelly slaughtered. He saw it all and he fought—the battle *before* his eyes and the other in his *mind*; do not think—do not *feel*.

Screeches and screams mixed with the sound of scraping metal and the thud of arrowheads imbedding in flesh. A roar of victory from the Sand Lords surely meant a warrior had gone down.

With a ruthless flash of metal, Turion slit another Sand Lord's throat, his lip curling in disgust and then chanced a glance at Fel'annár who was facing off with two cloaked devils that twirled their scimitars deftly in their hands. The novice simply held his stance and watched them, long sword poised strangely over his head, and although Turion wanted to watch, he had his own foes to face. Moving before his next victim, he bore down on the black demon in utter fury, until a panicked cry escaped the strange being and Turion moved in, thrusting his sword right through his opponent's chest, the squish of flesh and organs leaving no doubt in the captain's mind that he was dead.

Fel'annár's blades whirled and swivelled, sliced and parried. There was no confusion, no anxiety even though the colours were back. His mind was sharp and in control, all its skill centred on his body and his senses, despite the death and carnage, the suffering of his kin and of the trees. He felt none of this, did not hear the scream of frantic mothers or the desperate wails of injured civilians, he did not feel the weight in his chest or the pain in his throat. Duck, bend, flex; push, cut, slash and stab. Flip backwards, somersault forwards, side twist and parry; kill, kill, *kill*.

He could feel the precision of his movements, his mind anticipating each and every one of his opponent's moves, killing them all before they could even approach him. They were too slow and he was too fast; not even the long cut on his upper-arm had brought him out of his protected place. He had not felt it, it had not hurt, it was not important.

Something hit him from the right and he was brutally thrown sideways, almost to the floor but he kept his footing and his eyes looked down to his shoulder where a thick black shaft was still quivering in his flesh. He heard someone calling his name as he reached up and pulled the arrow out and then slung it into his empty quiver.

His attention was only momentarily lost as a wave of agony made him shudder. It didn't matter, though—and he turned around, his enemies lying around him upon the ground, dismembered.

Screams alerted him to a group of burning houses and he sprinted towards them, shielding his eyes from the burning flames. He called out but there was no answer and so he ran towards Lainon who was facing two

Sand Lords close by; but before he could help, movement from the corner of his eye drew his attention. An archer was sighting Turion from across the field and the captain was oblivious to it, engrossed in his own desperate battle. Fel'annár was too far away he realised even as he sprinted towards his captain, not wanting to shout a warning lest his opponent take advantage of the captain's inevitable distraction. The shot was nigh impossible he realised but still he was running, closing the gap so that his arrow would be in range; but his own movement over the uneven terrain would surely impede his aim.

There was no time to think and a rocky outcrop loomed before him— that was his answer. He ran faster, and then jumped onto it even as he reached back for the black bolt in his quiver. Fitting and sighting in one, fluid movement, he launched himself into the air, eyes centred on his target and the world went silent as he flew—and released.

He dropped his bow just before his feet hit the ground and he rolled with his forward momentum until he crouched on the ground, taking a second to regain his breath and control the pain in his shoulder. No time though, for there were black and silver boots to his left and he ducked under a flash of metal, and then pushed his sword through the belly of their owner with both hands, slowly pulling back lest the metal get caught on ribs.

In the distance a desperate cry carried over the din of battle, a warrior's cry and Lainon's heart sank as he defeated his last opponent, cruelly kicking the headless body to the ground and then wiping his forehead with a hand that still held a short sword, struggling to regain his breath.

Turning, he cast his gaze around the glade. The occasional scream of a Sand Lord soon gave way to soft crying—it was over and only now did Lainon realise that the sun was setting, drowning the land in bloody red light, the smoke from dying fires almost black as it swirled and danced on the soft breeze. He saw Turion standing awkwardly, bloody sword still in his hand, his chest heaving. He saw Angon crouched upon the ground, his head bowed and beside him, Fer'dán lay in agony, clutching at his bloodied leg. Exhausted warriors and shocked villagers roamed the glade, still numb, unable to understand the enormity of the tragedy of Sen'uár, one that would have been complete had it not been for one, young novice.

Turion straightened himself and then wiped his sword on the cloak of a fallen Sand Lord. Wiping his hand over his face he cast his eyes around him, spotting Lainon immediately and walking towards him. Their eyes met in silent sorrow and deep understanding, and with a simple hand upon the shoulder, they rejoiced for the air they both still breathed.

There were warriors to seek out, and civilians to help. There were bodies to burn and a journey to organise—back to Sen'oléi with as many refugees as they could.

It was Turion who first spotted Fel'annár, who knelt upon the ground beside the burnt cottages some distance away.

"Lainon, gather the warriors and arrange first aid. Once that is done, help *them*," he said softly, his eyes moving from one Silvan villager to the next, schooling himself as best he could for their eyes told stories of utter pain and loss, of grief so deep it hurt the soul—how many times had he seen this, he said to himself. It was the reason he had refused to become a captain, so that he would not have to witness this suffering any more.

With a final nod at Lainon, he walked to Fel'annár, who remained upon the slick ground, the damp, bloody mud seeping through his leggings, his own blood running down his arm.

He held a small bundle, clasped tightly to his chest—a babe realised Turion in dawning grief.

Soft wisps of silken hair tickled his neck and Fel'annár's bandaged hand moved up to smooth it down; his eyes though, did not dare to look for although he knew what it was he protected in the safety of his strong arms, his mind did not want to accept it, for to do so would surely be the end of his own, lingering innocence.

"What have you there, Fel'annár?" came a soft voice behind him. "Will you show me?" he asked once more; kindly spoken words meant to calm and to soothe, a father to his son, a captain to his novice.

Fel'annár did look down then, to the weight in his arms, to the harsh, tragic reality of war. A tiny, pink ear, so pointed, so perfect, peaked out from the downy locks of chestnut silk and his thumb caressed it lovingly. He pulled it to his chest once more, but it was useless, for the warmth had gone.

Turion sat beside him, his eyes turning to Fel'annár, who stared blankly off into the distance, the tears in his eyes making his green eyes look like polished glass.

"His light has gone, child. His mother too, has perished."

"*Why?*" came the soft whisper, as if he spoke to the wind but his face changed not.

"That is the question, is it not? You ask yourself how this could ever be allowed to happen. Why the enemy should benefit from taking a life such as his—what is the *purpose?*"

Turion paused for a moment, drawing a long breath before continuing. "The answer is as plain as it is simple, Fel'annár. That babe was no warrior, but he *was* a weapon, the most horrific and ruthless weapon, for with his death the enemy weaves its madness amongst us; it debilitates us, takes from us not the blood from our bodies but that of the soul—where true agony resides. It takes from us all the good feelings and emotions and leaves us empty and wrathful, vulnerable to their wiles. It is a most powerful weapon they wield upon us—this, is the *true* battle—the one I told you would not be easy, the one not all of us can wage. Do you *understand* me now?" he asked kindly, his eyes overly bright.

Fel'annár did not answer. He simply sat there for a while longer before, of his own accord, he slowly rose, the cold babe still in his arms, and together, they walked to where their companions were already clearing the battle site, slowly and painfully with the help of those villagers who were still able.

Dense smoke rose from the pyres Angon and the others had prepared, and now they stood and watched as their young novice approached the fires, and gently placed the still body of the child next to those who had been his kin. There were no words of solace, for there were none to be had; nothing could help their companion save the merciful passage of time—this they knew, for they had seen it before and yet, when Fel'annár bent forward and placed a soft kiss upon the babe's head, something seemed to snap inside and the tears they had all shed the first time they had walked into such a battle were back, after so many years they felt it as if they too, were novices once more.

It was when Fel'annár turned that the breath was stolen from their lungs for there, standing atop the pyre was not a broken, grief-stricken novice but a tall, powerful warrior, head tilted towards the blood-red sky, its glow bathing him and he shone, brighter than he ever had. His beauteous face was hard and angular, and his eyes, although still lovely, held a new light in them. The youth in them had gone though, flown away with the spirit of the babe and in its place was resolve, hard and unyielding.

Fel'annár had entered the Deep Forest a novice, but the novice had gone, fled to a kinder world and in his place stood a warrior, strong and powerful.

This was his baptism, his passage to warrior hood.

The dead were being sent off in silence, for no one had the heart to sing, and as night fell, the pyres burned and the Silvans cried. The warriors of the Western Patrol mourned the loss of two of their warriors and only when they had been prepared and sent to Aria, did they collect the bodies of the Sand Lords, piling them up mercilessly over to one side, as far away as they could. If it were up to them they would have left them to rot, but the stench would have been offensive.

Fer'dán lay still upon a blanket, a Silvan healer kneeling over him and Lainon standing behind, his face blank and his eyes eloquent.

Opposite, Fel'annár sat on a boulder, his shoulder bare and bloodied as another Silvan lady bathed it in a foul-smelling liquid.

Turion was setting up a perimeter guard, even though there was no sign of the enemy. He was taking no chances and soon, as night fell, small fires littered the village clearing.

The warriors huddled together, with Fer'dán lying off to one side. His leg had been slashed wide open, barring bone and ruining the surrounding muscle. Miraculously it had not been severed, but the Alpine warrior had many months of recuperation before him. His life as a warrior was over for now. However, they still had to get him back home, first to Sen'oléi at first light, and then home to the master healers and his family.

Angon accepted a cup of tea that another warrior passed him and he breathed in the hot steam, closing his eyes and allowing it to comfort him. A cry pierced their quiet talk—another death—another Silvan had succumbed to injuries - lost to the barbarity of the Sand Lords. He just wanted to understand and before he knew it, the words were tumbling out of his mouth.

"Why, Captain. Why are there not more patrols, more outposts? How many deaths will it take for our king to protect his people? Does he not see? Does he not *care?*" he asked. His tone was one of anger but also of incomprehension, and Turion took no offence.

"Angon. I share your view on this matter, but it is not the fault of our king. There are those on the council that believe the Silvan people should fall back—leave the forest to the army, allow us to work unhindered in the field."

"*Unhindered?*" answered Angon in mounting anger. "Since when are the Silvan people a hindrance—in their own forest?" he asked with a scowl. "Of course, by '*those*' you mean the Alpine purists? The ones our king seems incapable of controlling?!" His voice had steadily risen in his anger and those close enough to have heard his words stared on, their eyes gleaming in the night. Turion's scowl was enough to tell Angon he should curb his tongue and the Silvan warrior lowered his head. "Forgive me."

"Are there so many, Captain," whispered Fel'annár, accepting a cup of tea from Lainon gratefully, "so many purists that think that way?"

Turion took a deep breath before answering and when he did it was hushed.

"It is not a question of how many, Fel'annár, but who. It is Lord Band'orán, Or 'Talan's brother no less, that promotes these ideas. His influence is a powerful tool, one he uses most skilfully."

Fel'annár had much to say on the matter, especially after what he had lived through that day, but something in Turion's eyes told him not to proceed. It was not the time and certainly not the place and so he simply nodded that he understood. And he did, only that it sickened him and he wondered—how much longer would the Silvan people hold their tongue? How long before grief ended their patience?

He reached for Narosén's nectar, shaking it with a scowl for there was barely enough left for one more swig. He finished it, and then cast it a baleful glare. He looked up at Lainon who was staring back at him and in his hand, a fresh flask of the miraculous brew. Fel'annár reached for it with a look of utter relief on his dirty face.

"Thank you," he whispered with a respectful nod.

"No," said Lainon a little too quickly. "Thank *you*," he said fervently, but then strangely said no more and Fel'annár was left with the distinct feeling the Ari had wanted to say more.

His shoulder twanged painfully and then all the hurts of his body finally began to complain. His chest hurt, his throat was agony, his shoulder sent white hot sparks of pain down to the tips of his fingers and he was utterly exhausted. It must have shown, for a strong hand was pushing him down onto his bedroll and Fel'annár had not the strength to fight against it. Flat on his back now, his eyes caught the retreating silhouette of Angon, before searching for the nascent moon; he would never forget this day—never forget the tragedy that brought with it a new kind of wisdom, one that would change him from this day on.

The following day, the warriors of the Western Patrol broke camp quietly, following Turion and Lainon's gentle orders. There were only eight of them left and the loss and impending news their captain would break to their families was a heavy burden.

They had fashioned stretchers for those that could not make the walk to Sen'oléi, amongst them Fer'dán, who lay in a daze, oblivious to his companions' worried eyes.

They were tired and sore, they limped and their faces were pinched and pale, but their troubles seemed frivolous in comparison to the Silvan refugees of Sen'uár. They had collected as many of their belongings as could be saved and wrapped them in the colourful cloth that had once served as table linen and blankets. It broke Fel'annár's heart even more for they were a simple people, quiet even in their grief. It would have been so easy for them to lash out against the warriors, or the king himself yet they said nothing at all - as if there was no fight left in them.

Finally on their slow, painful way, the warriors took turns in scouting around and guarding the sorry caravan and those left with the main group helped where they could. There were many women and children, but much fewer men but they all struggled with their children and their most precious belongings.

Most of their carts and wagons had been lost in the battle, but one had been salvaged and it now rattled over the forest floor, piled high with all manner of personal effects, even furniture. Fel'annár's jaw clenched in mounting anger and Turion's warning stare at Angon from the night before was enough to keep him silent, but on the inside, Fel'annár was indignant, his mind bursting with unanswered questions.

They stopped at midday and even Fel'annár was required to stand guard, despite his sorry state. He still couldn't speak properly and his flask of nectar had long ago been depleted. His shoulder was on fire and his whole arm felt rigid but it was the exhaustion that was truly impeding him. He had braved the flames to rescue Alféna's children—Eloran and the twins—and no sooner had he returned, than he was marching to Sen'uár where he had fought the longest and most difficult battle of his life, one that had truly shown him the ravages of war.

Running a weary hand over his filthy face he rubbed it in irritation and stood, starting when he found Lainon standing before him.

"Is the way clear?" asked the Ari almost conversationally.

"Yes, Sir. Nothing to report."

"Very well. We should arrive in a few hours," said Lainon unnecessarily. "There are things we must discuss."

Fel'annár's brow twitched as he turned to face his lieutenant but this time, there was no insecurity. He knew he had done well. Whatever it was that Lainon wished to discuss, it was not about his shortcomings.

"We fought a hard battle at Sen'uár, the kind the Sand Lords use against us to whittle away at our resolve, make us doubt the wisdom of what we do . . ." he trailed off, his face turned to the fore so that Fel'annár was left staring at his profile, wondering if the Ari had read his mind.

"I am angry, Lainon. I cannot help it. The plight of these people, is a tragedy; Angon's words yesterday . . ." he whispered.

"Many of us agree with him, Fel'annár," said Lainon, cutting off whatever the novice was going to say. "Many of us know that political—*cultural* division is giving the enemy the edge they need and that while our lords squabble amongst themselves, the Silvans are being slaughtered. Even Turion knows this, Fel'annár."

"But last night . . ."

"Angon spoke too loudly—'tis all."

Fel'annár nodded his understanding. "I am faithful to our king, Lainon."

"We *all* are. But sometimes, even kings can lose faith, Fel'annár—given the right circumstances."

Fel'annár stared for a long while, processing the information. He had always thought of the king as a strong, untouchable symbol yet to consider him vulnerable was strangely unnerving. '*Given the right circumstances*' he repeated to himself—and he found himself wondering what had happened to their monarch that he would lose faith. His throat was burning and he coughed miserably.

"Come," said Lainon, turning on his heel. "We leave, and when we are back, clean and fed—you," he poked Fel'annár in the chest, "have a story to tell us."

"The fire," began the novice.

"The fire, and the *outcrop*," he said meaningfully. "Turion was most impressed," he drawled as he walked away, leaving a blushing novice in his wake.

⚬⚬⚬⚬⚬

By late afternoon, the refugees reached the village of Sen'oléi, closely guarded by what remained of the Western Patrol. Lorthil stood duteously together with Narosén, Sarodén the forester and the entire population. They carried blankets and had prepared pots of steaming food, and those with knowledge of the healing arts stood ready to usher the wounded to the village hall, their faces solemn and the children quiet.

No sooner had they emerged from the forest path, than the villagers moved forward, approaching the women and children and leading them away to their own homes, their faces open and saddened, arms outstretched in silent, solemn welcome. Fel'annár battled with his own tears and tried not to watch their interaction too closely for it moved him too deeply. A heavy hand on his shoulder jolted him out of his misery and he half turned to catch Angon's profile as he moved away to help a villager. He smiled softly for the Silvan veteran was fast becoming a steadfast friend, despite his initial antagonism.

The refugees had gone into the cottages and flets of Sen'oléi, or to the village hall, where the healers had organised themselves as best they could. Lorthil, as their leader, was now in charge and had placed his foresters around the perimeter for tonight. Turion had sent two warriors into the woods to scout with an apologetic squeeze to their shoulders and then turned to the rest.

"Dismissed," was all he said, before adding, "I will be with Fer'dán in the Hall—Fel'annár, with me," he finished.

Lainon saluted his captain, and then turned to the warriors.

"Come. Set up a camp by the river, let us see to ourselves," he said quietly.

"Fel'annár, you will allow Talúa to help you," said the Captain, a warning in his eyes, but Fel'annár was having none of it.

"Sir, look at them, they need her much more than I do," he rasped, his voice coming back to him slowly.

"Fel'annár," said Turion, his voice rising enough to startle the novice. "You wish to be a captain yes? Then listen to me carefully. These people need a healer yes, but they need *us* to keep them safe—you are not expendable, you are what stands between them and certain death. It is a tactical decision, nothing more," he lied.

Fel'annár's eyes were wide but he nodded his understanding and shut his mouth as the healer unbuckled Fel'annár's harnesses and tunics, and finally revealed his wounded shoulder. Talúa frowned and tutted.

"This is infected," she said, her free hand moving to his forehead and then tutting again. "He will stay with me for a while, Captain. I will send him to you later, perhaps."

Turion nodded, his eyes lingering on Fel'annár for a moment longer. "Join us when Talúa gives you leave," he warned, before turning on his heels and striding away.

Fel'annár huffed and the healer smiled as she worked. "Heed your captain, warrior. We do need you, we *will* need you," she said, her eyes gleaming in the half light as she worked.

He awoke, fuzzy and disorientated, wondering when he had fallen asleep. He turned his head to the side and then startled, for sitting there, was Alféna, Eloran's mother. She smiled down at him, and then turned to pour him a glass of water. Sitting up slowly, he accepted it with a grateful nod and drank. It was then, with a furious blush, that he realised he was naked and Alféna smiled.

"Your clothes are already dry, I'll bring them for you," she said kindly. Alone for a moment, he realised his arm had been bound in a sling and that he had managed to acquire a most colourful set of bruises. He felt better, in spite of the fuzziness in his head, but he felt a little too hot and he knew he needed to sleep but he was loathe to do so here, in the Hall. He wanted to be with the patrol and so, when Alféna returned with his clothes, he dressed as best he could, and with a furtive glance around him, made for the main door.

The wounded lay in makeshift beds scattered across the floor, attended to by their families and friends and they watched now as Fel'annár passed. Some had a smile and a thankful nod for him, while others simply stared, and Fel'annár could not rightly say what they were thinking.

The patrol had set up camp in their usual spot close to the river, and soon Fel'annár was standing before them, one arm in a sling and the other carrying his weapons. They smiled up at him from around the fire, shuffling closer together to make room for him. Even Turion and Lainon sat with them tonight, and a pot of bubbling stew sat enticingly over their fire.

Carefully depositing his weapons off to one side, he slowly lowered himself to the ground beside Angon and Lainon, grateful for the warmth the fire lent him and he shivered a little.

"Talúa allowed you to leave?" asked Turion with an arched brow.

"Alféna made no objections," he rasped quietly and Turion frowned at his novice, saying no more for the moment. The boy seemed well enough in spite of the light sheen of sweat on his brow, that and the atrocious timber of his voice.

They ate quietly and soon, tea was being brewed, the hot steam sending the rich aromas of chamomile and tisane into the air.

"An itinerant patrol is due in tomorrow," began Turion quietly. "They will stay here for a while, until these people can organise themselves once more. I wonder though, if Sen'uár has been permanently razed from our maps—the final count is sixty dead, including Sar'hén and Vor'ón." The warriors looked down, deeply saddened by the terrible death toll. Angon's words from the day before were in the minds of them all, yet no one gave voice to them.

"We will honour them when we are home. Their sacrifice will be remembered," he said softly, with conviction.

"May Aria embrace them," said one Silvan warrior, holding his wooden cup before him. The others did likewise and then drank, allowing the silence to blanket them once more.

"Captain," began Fel'annár. "How did the itinerant patrol know to come? When did you send for help?"

"I asked Lorthil to send someone to the nearest outpost after the fire—seems he got lucky and ran across them. Perhaps they had already been drawn in our direction by the smoke," he said and Fel'annár nodded as he sipped on his tea.

"Fel'annár," began Lainon. "Tell us of what you have learned on your first tour as a novice." His eyes danced over the warriors, perhaps to check if his change in the conversation had had the desired effect. They were shaken by the loss of their companions, angry even at the powers, and Turion was strangely quiet.

"So many things," said Fel'annár with a rush of air. "Where to begin?" he croaked.

"Is this what you expected it to be? the life of a warrior in the field?" asked one warrior.

"Yes, and no. It is as hard as I thought it would be in some ways, yet in others it is much, much harder than I could ever have imagined. No amount of training or reading could have prepared me for—for this," he said with a wave of his hand.

"Most first tours are not this eventful, Fel'annár," said Angon. "Mine was downright boring." The others smirked, perhaps remembering their own experiences as novices.

"I thought you were a liability to this patrol," continued Angon quite unexpectedly, and there was something in his tone that made the others listen carefully. "I treated you as I would any other novice—and therein lies my own lesson," he smiled, glancing at Fel'annár for a moment before continuing. "So you see, you are not the only one to have learned something. I have come to understand that what we do, what we have all been doing for so many years—is not all for nothing, it is not futile. We were simply waiting." He trailed off strangely, and when he spoke once more, his strange mood had left him. "You are no ordinary novice, Green Sun. You are a warrior by rights, a Silvan fighter, in spite of that ridiculous hair." He smirked, waving his hands about his own head as if he were shaking it out.

The warriors chuckled, but Fel'annár simply smiled. He had set out to serve as best he could, to learn and not make a fool of himself and he had achieved that—and so much more, and for the first time in his life, he was proud—of *himself*.

And so, their quiet conversation slowly drifted away as one by one, they settled down to sleep, and some of them to dream of better times to come, when common sense prevailed over politics and power games, and these lands were made safe.

Chapter Sixteen

BAPTISM OF FIRE AND WATER

"Trees are conveyers of the Spirit, but some - the Sentinels – can inter-
pret its will. A Sentinel to the forest is as a Listener to the Silvans."
On Elven Nature. Calro

Fel'annár had awoken to an already bustling camp. They had left him
to sleep he realised. He smoothed down his hair and pulled on his boots
with difficulty, cursing the sling he was forced to wear. The lingering clouds
had dispersed, allowing the timid winter light to warm him and somehow,
everything seemed new to him. Why he would think that he could not say.

Approaching the fire, he nodded at Angon and Lainon who crouched
before the flames, talking quietly. Lainon nodded, and then tipped his head
to the food that stood covered over to one side. They had even kept by some
breakfast for him and he smiled softly at the thought.

"How is Fer'dán?" he asked as he began on his breakfast, crossing his
legs and steadying his plate awkwardly with his elbow, and then eating one-
handedly.

"Not good," said Angon. "I will spend some time with him today, speak
to the healers."

"But he will be alright?" asked Fel'annár, as he ate. He didn't expect the
answer he got.

"Not alright, Fel'annár. At best, he will be able to walk, but he will never
again serve as a warrior in the field," said Angon curtly, anger clenching his
jaw.

Fel'annár started and looked at the Silvan warrior in shock. "And at the
worse?" he asked.

"He may yet die—who can say," said the veteran warrior, as if he were already bolstering himself for that possibility. Angon and Fer'dán were good friends, that much Fel'annár knew.

The positive mood with which he had started the day was tempered and he ate more slowly, wondering what Fer'dán would do if he could not serve in the field—what he himself would do should such a terrible thing happen to *him*, Aria forbid.

"Lieutenant," said Fel'annár, swallowing a chunk of bread with difficulty before continuing, "what should we do today while we wait for the itinerant patrol?"

"Nothing—rest, care for your kit, your weapons. We are leaving tomorrow, for home."

Home—home for Fel'annár was Lan Taria but he supposed he would have to go back to the city barracks. The fact remained that he was free—for the entire day. A bath! That was the first thing on his list – well, perhaps a cautious dip, he amended. Then he thought he would wander around for a while, enjoy his freedom. Later, he would visit the Halls, see Fer'dán and seek out Eloran and the twins—he had not seen them since his return from battle and there was a question he would seek to answer. It was a good plan, one that would take his mind off the grief that surrounded him.

Picking up his pack, he walked towards the river, and with a quick glance around, he rid himself of his clothes and walked gingerly into the frigid water, wincing as his scrapes and burns stung on contact. Unwinding the bandages around his chest and shoulder, he sank lower with a sigh of utter relief, one which turned into a long groan of bliss when he tipped his head back and doused his hair.

Ducking his head below the surface, he allowed himself to sink to the sandy bed, open eyes watching as the particles settled and another world opened up before him. The water was crystal clear and he smiled as he observed the fauna; small, colourful fish darted between the swaying plants that brushed tenderly over his ankles, their gills pumping water. It was another reality in which the inhabitants breathed water, not air and yet it was just here, inside his own, familiar forest—it was a strange thought, but it fit so well with his own dilemma.

A world inside a world.

Surfacing, he basked in the weak sunlight, feeling its warmth upon his wet skin. It was a moment of bliss he could not prolong though, and soon enough he was washing away the last vestiges of battle as best he could with his injured shoulder.

He dressed slowly and then re-bandaging his hands but his shoulder would have to wait. Sitting now against the bark of a willow he allowed his mind to wander where it would. He thought of the river bed and the other world he had reached out to just moments before. It was certainly not the first time he had studied a river bed, of course, but something about it had caught his attention today and only now, he began to understand why. It was the perfect analogy, for Fel'annár lived in Ea Uaré, he breathed air and yet, with a simple duck of the head he could immerse himself in water and see what lay beneath it, move into another perspective. He sat up straighter, the dawn of understanding pulling him from the weight of fear and incomprehension.

Everyone could do that; it was a simple case of diving beneath the water—but what if there were elves who could not dive? What if some strange being existed that could not touch water—they would never see what lay beneath, never experience the wonder of it.

Was that what happened to *him*? Were the colours, the feelings and the light of the trees simply another slant on the same world? A slant that not all could see yet existed nonetheless?

With a deep breath, he relaxed back and closed his tired eyes. A great sense of relief flooded him then and he smiled because it was a plausible explanation; not magic, not supernatural but simply another facet of the *real* world. It was a comforting thought.

The first time it happened, he had sensed danger long before it had shown itself, and the second had been in battle with the Sand Lords. The third time had been when he had seen the sentinel, and then when he had saved the children. Finally, just before the battle of Sen'uár he had known exactly where the enemy was.

'*It is a gift.*'

Every time it happened, something good had come of it, in spite of his fears.

'*Do not be afraid.*'

Could he use this new perspective to his advantage? Perhaps it was not a danger to his plans but a tool. It sounded absurd even to his own ears. What was he to do? Speak to the *trees?* he snorted in genuine mirth, but then a thought popped into his mind.

'*Why not?*'

He started, and then struggled to decide whether or not that thought had come from his own memory of Narosén's words. *'Trees do not speak, Fel'annár'*, he ground out to himself in exasperation.

'Trees do not speak, they communicate.'

He stood abruptly, spinning around and pinning the tree with a wide, disbelieving glare, and then strained against the cough that threatened to double him over. *'It was me and my own thoughts'*, he said to himself, a dialogue with myself, nothing more.

Chuckling out loud now, he sat back down and leaned back once more, this time more confidently, a challenge to himself almost. It lasted but seconds though, before his body went ramrod stiff and he froze where he sat.

'Child of the trees . . .'

He scrambled to his feet once more in a flurry of hair, only just resisting the urge to run, anywhere, far away from where he was now but he forced himself to think. Narosén, Narosén would help him and with that, coughing and raking his now shaking hand through his wet, unbraided hair, he strode into the village in search of the Spirit Herder, for Fel'annár was sure, *sure* that he was, effectively, losing his mind.

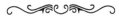

Narosén roared in laughter, deep and strangely addictive, and the Ari's face changed so drastically Fel'annár would hardly have recognised him—he was a study in contrasts, completely unpredictable. Sadly, he himself could not see the humour at all and so he sat before the shaking Spirit Herder, an indignant frown upon his brow as he waited for the mirth to abate, coughing once more and drawing the Ari's attention.

"Forgive me, young Fel'annár." He chuckled as he settled himself upon the ground where they sat. "I *do* understand your worry, do not misjudge me, but nay—you are not losing your mind, child!"

"But how can you *know* that?" asked Fel'annár, "I cannot even identify my own words when I speak them to myself, cannot even understand if those thoughts are mine or those of some other . . . *entity* . . ." he said, waving his hand in agitation. "'Tis as though I were *possessed!*" he exclaimed indignantly and then coughed again.

"Nay, stop, Fel'annár." Narosén giggled, which soon turned into another wheeze of laughter, sending his body crashing back into the tree behind him. It soon passed though, although the chuckles continued for a while longer. Finally though, Narosén leaned forward and touched Fel'annár lightly upon the knee.

"I do not claim to have this gift but I do know something of it—I too, can sense them, but not in the way you do."

Fel'annár listened, intrigued now by what the Ari said. "So you truly believe it is an ability—to hear them, I mean?"

"Something along those lines. Aria has a hand in this, that is all I know for certain, that and the fact that this is a *good* thing, child, something you must use to your advantage, in your service to this land—you are blessed," said Narosén finally, serious yet joyful at the same time, and when he saw that the boy would say nothing, he continued.

"Captain Turion seems fond of you," he said, watching his young companion from the corner of his eye.

"And I of him. He has been good to me. In truth both he and Lieutenant Lainon have been the best tutors I could ever have wished for." And it was true, albeit it was the first time Fel'annár had said as much to anyone.

"It is not a frequent thing, I believe, to have two commanding officers that take your training and welfare so to heart—they see something in you," said the Spirit Herder, too casually perhaps, indeed Fel'annár afforded him a sideways glance before speaking.

"And I do not wish to disappoint them, Narosén. I just want to understand this. If I am to have it for the rest of my life, I need to understand it, *control* it," he whispered with a sour scowl.

"Did your mother never hint at anything when you were a child?"

"Nay," said Fel'annár. "Amareth has always been strangely quiet in that way."

"Amareth? You mother?" asked Narosén.

"Nay, my aunt. I lost my mother when I was just a babe."

Narosén's shrewd eyes held the striking green irises for long moments before he sat back and lowered his head.

"And what of your father?" he asked casually.

Silence followed his question and the Ari furrowed his brow while Fel'annár smiled ruefully, and Narosén's intelligent eyes seemed to understand. "You never knew him then?"

The Silvan shook his head, before elucidating. "All I know is that he was Alpine, but Amareth would never tell me of him. I have always believed he was some exile, perhaps, that he had done something shameful for no one seems to have known him, or if they did, they would not tell me of him."

"It must have been hard," prompted Narosén.

"Yes. But it is no longer of any consequence. I am what I am. My father played no role in my childhood and so who can say he was ever my father?" he reasoned softly.

"You have a point, yes," conceded the wise Ari. "But you must be curious. You must ask yourself what he was like, or *is* like, for he may still be alive. You must ask yourself why he never played a part in your life." Narosén was walking a fine line, he knew, but he would probably never get another opportunity to ask the boy.

"No," said Fel'annár after a while. "I am no longer concerned with that. I used to feel shame, anger, but those days are gone. I have accepted it," he said bravely, but Narosén had not missed the defensive look, the hardened jaw and the steely glint in his eye. This was indeed, dangerous ground, but what could he say? That the boy was deluding himself?

"Perhaps," he said simply, but his own expression was clear enough to Fel'annár, who simply held his gaze and nodded faintly.

Fel'annár knew he had not been believed, but at least he had managed to curb any further, uncomfortable questioning. Narosén decided that it was enough for today. After all, there really was very little doubt left in his mind.

Fer'dán had been asleep when Fel'annár went to visit, and he had not missed the worried expression on the healers' faces—it was not good and his heart clenched. Fer'dán had been good to him, had laughed at his antics and had taught him as much as he could. He had felt the deaths of the other two warriors, but if Fer'dán joined them in Valley, his grief would be much deeper.

Emerging from the Hall, he ran into Alféna, giving her a soft smile. "Have you seen Eloran, Alféna?" he asked.

Alféna nodded and pointed to a path. "He will be that way, playing in the trees no doubt." she smiled fondly and she suddenly reminded him of

Amareth. "He looks up to you, Fel'annár. I do not know what happened that day when you saved my children because he will not speak of it. It must have been hard for him I think, to not want to recount his adventure."

Eloran's terrified face came back to Fel'annár as she spoke, when he had grabbed the children and the boy had cowered against the trunk of the burning tree, his face set in a mask of *terror.*

"It *was* hard, and he is still young—although he will not want to admit to that," he said with a fond smile. "We leave tomorrow—I want to say goodbye."

Alféna nodded and then reached into the pocket of her skirts.

"I want you to have this," she said, holding up an amber stone. It was small but beautiful, for there was a water mark that swirled around it. It was transparent and opaque, a gift of nature that she held in the palm of her hand, and then gestured for him to take it.

"I can't ..."

"You must. It is an honour stone and you are *Silvan.*" Her smile then was wide and beautiful and tears welled in Fel'annár's eyes. "This is for my children – that you may always remember my love and gratitude, and that others may know that you are honoured."

Fel'annár bowed his head and then reached out to take the stone between two fingers. "I don't know how to wear this," he said.

Alféna smiled. "Step closer."

Fel'annár did and she took the stone from him. Reaching for a side braid, she pushed the tip into the stone until it came out the other side and then rebraided the end. She brushed a hand down his arm fondly in silent farewell and then, with a soft smile and a nod, she was gone.

An honour stone – he had read about them but had thought the tradition lost. He would ask Idernon when next they met and he breathed deeply, the deep emotions Alféna had evoked only slowly receding.

He soon found Eloran perched high up in the boughs, alone. Hoisting himself up with some difficulty, he climbed and then called up. It would not do to startle the boy.

"May I join you?"

Eloran did startle, flinching involuntarily and Fel'annár frowned at his strange reaction.

"It's a lovely day. Why do you spend it alone up here?" he asked, accommodating himself on the branch.

The boy shrugged. "Everyone's busy and our visitors are so sad. I want to help but I am just in the way," he complained.

"I know the feeling," said Fel'annár. "I still feel it sometimes. When you are younger than the rest, they will always use it as an excuse to exclude you."

"How old are you?" asked Eloran with a slight blush.

"Fifty-one."

"What? How is it that you are already a warrior?" he asked, his eyes wide and disbelieving, but not in a bad way.

"I am still a novice, Eloran, but I am considered young, even for that."

"But then there is only twenty years difference between us," the boy said, almost to himself, his eyes sipping to the side. He was calculating something.

"Yes," said Fel'annár with a smile. "We will be great friends, Eloran, you will see."

The boy's face snapped back to the novice before him and he smiled, open and unafraid for the first time. "You think so? We'll see each other again then?" he asked enthusiastically and Fel'annár's heart melted.

"I will make sure of it," he smiled, but then he remembered why he had sought the boy out and his face straightened.

"Eloran, I wanted to ask you a question."

"What is it?"

"That day, up in the tree, when I grabbed your brother and sister. You started, you shied away from me—you seemed—*afraid*," he trailed off.

"I *was*," said the boy hesitantly.

"It's alright, Eloran—I was scared too, I was just wondering . . ."

"No," he whispered, his brow furrowing deeply. "I don't think you understand—you see," he said and then moved so that his mouth was at Fel'annár's ear. "I was scared—of *you*."

"Of me? *Why?*" asked Fel'annár with a scowl, completely perplexed.

"I won't tell anyone, I promise."

"What do you *mean?*" whispered Fel'annár, a sinking feeling slowly invading him.

Now it was Eloran's turn to frown, as if only now he was understanding something. "You have strange eyes."

"Well, they are very green—and a little slanted, but—why would that scare you, Eloran?" he asked softly.

The Boy's mouth worked of its own accord for a moment but no words passed his lips. He took a deep breath and then somehow found the courage to look into Fel'annár's *strange* eyes.

"There was light behind them, like a *green sun*," whispered Eloran, as if he were sharing some great secret.

Fel'annár swayed backwards until his back hit the trunk behind him, staring incredulously back at the boy. Had the boy meant the fire had reflected strangely in his eyes? Or perhaps the tears in them had created some strange, optical effect—what an odd thing to say, mused Fel'annár. But try as he might, he could not shake the idea that the boy spoke quite literally. He remembered the shining light, the pulse of blue and green energy as he stepped on the impossibly narrow branch . . .

Eloran was tugging on his sleeve and his eyes snapped back to his young friend. "It scares you too, doesn't it?" asked the boy in dawning understanding. "Didn't you know?"

Fel'annár shook his head. "I didn't know," he said dumbly, "and yes—I am scared too."

"It's funny to see, but I didn't know you then and I do now. You're not a bad elf, you are not a Deviant spirit or a forest banshee," he clarified with a smile. "You are Fel'annár of the funny eyes, novice warrior. I think I may be like you when I am older—a warrior – like my father."

Fel'annár had not seen his father and knew then that he must be dead.

"That stone was his. He wore it always and my mother has kept it safe. I am glad you wear it now."

"You will be a good warrior," said Fel'annár with a smile, his heart warming to the idea that perhaps he had had some part in the boy's wish to serve.

"So, we are friends then, Fel'annár? We'll see each other again?"

The novice smiled wide and mischievous. "When I am captain, I will seek out a warrior by the name of Eloran—perhaps he will want to serve in my patrol as a novice."

Eloran smiled so wide Fel'annár thought his face might split in two and then gave him a thumping salute and together, they giggled at their improvised plan.

Walking back to the settlement, they parted ways with another salute, this one more solemn. "Don't forget, warrior—I will find you," said Captain Hwind'atór seriously, and Eloran squared himself and saluted.

"I will be ready, Sir."

The Western Patrol packed up camp while Turion spoke to Lorthil. Their main concern was how far South the Sand Lords had dared to travel. Lorthil was not surprised it had happened, for their previous incursions had gone unpunished and he begged Turion to convince his superiors of the need for an outpost. He was right, Turion knew. This part of the forest was not adequately protected and he would do all in his power to change that. He would have to instil their need on General Huren, for decisions such as these would need to be taken at council.

"Lorthil," began the captain, "I will speak to my superiors; this entire quadrant needs much more protection than it is getting. I cannot guarantee you *will* get it, but I do promise to try my very best."

Lorthil stared back at the captain, before nodding slowly. "We will await news then," he said calmly. "But I do not think they understand, and I do not think they care enough to even try."

Turion's face remained inscrutable but eventually, he too, nodded slowly and then bowed. "We thank you for your hospitality, Lorthil."

The leader bowed back and then his eyes travelled to Fel'annár, who was adjusting the strap of his quiver. "We shall speak highly of your service to the Silvan people, Captain. We will tell Erthoron so that the Battle of Sen'uár may not be forgotten."

Bowing, the captain moved back to his patrol, while Lorthil and Narosén approached the unwitting novice, waiting for their presence to be addressed, and when the boy did, finally, raise his eyes to meet him, the two Silvans bowed from the waist, eyes glancing over the amber stone in Fel'annár's hair. It was a silent tribute to his bravery, or so Angon thought as he watched the exchange, smiling wickedly at the furious blush that slowly blossomed on their novice's face.

"Remember, Hwind'atór," said Lorthil with his hand over his heart, "remember this place for this is your home." It was the greatest of honours a Silvan could bestow and Fel'annár smiled solemnly, bowing back to the leaders of Sen'oléi, a place he would never forget for it was here that he had come to understand himself. He would return, one day when he was captain, he thought.

Alféna walked towards him with Eloran at her side. Standing on tip-toes, she kissed Fel'annár on the brow and then stepped back to allow Eloran a word. The boy simply smiled and then saluted, and Fel'annár returned it.

"Until we meet again, warrior," said Fel'annár, to which the boy answered, "I will be ready, Captain."

Turion's brow arched imperiously and Lainon simply watched, smiling softly. And with that, the Western Patrol moved out in single file behind their captain and lieutenant. They were homeward bound, as fast as Turion could push them.

Lorthil's words lingered uncomfortably in Lainon's mind. He would speak to Erthoron, the Silvan representative, he had said. They would surely send messages to the king and before that could happen, the Western Patrol must be home; Lainon needed to warn Aradan and Handir.

He might be wrong, but he would wager good coin that the leaders of Sen'oléi suspected more than they let on.

There was no more time left.

Chapter Seventeen

WHEELS OF DESTINY

*"Many things had been lost with the advent of the Alpines, amongst
them the bearing of Honour stones. Our Alpine commanders forbid our
brave warriors to wear them and so they kept them in pouches or boxes,
their pride hidden away; dormant."*
The Silvan Chronicles, Book III. Marhené.

The journey back had been surprisingly uneventful, soured only by the
ailing Fer'dán, who had not improved at all. They had passed a small village
and as luck would have it, Lainon had been able to send a letter to Aradan
by messenger. In it, he had briefly explained his suspicions that Narosén and
Lorthil would soon recount the events that had taken place and their novice's
part in it. Their plan must now be put into action or risk failure even before
it had begun.

As they journeyed on, the troop remained mostly quiet, for although
there were many stories to be told, their hearts were not in it, for Fer'dán's
fate was still uncertain. There would be time enough, they reckoned, and so
they pushed on, enduring as best they could the brisk pace Turion had set.

The village of Oran Dor boasted a master healer, and Turion handed
Fer'dán into her care, for the journey home had been agony for their warrior.
He would have a better chance of recovery here and so, with sad goodbyes,
they left him behind. They had also been provided with horses and the
warriors were ecstatic—yet none more so than Turion and Lainon.

Closer now, and the weather was biting cold, despite the radiant sun
that bathed the forest in a myriad of golden hues that sparkled in weary
green eyes and Fel'annár smiled for the beauty of it, despite his own lingering

discomfort. Yet his smile was no longer that of an innocent young lad, fresh out of a remote Silvan village, wonderstruck at the sights and sounds of the city outskirts. It was the smile of one who was wiser, more experienced, less naive.

The months he had been away, towards the West and ultimately to the North, had been exciting and yet shocking; satisfying yet melancholic, and something else he had not expected; it had been *frightening*.

He had heard the keening wails of Deviants and the guttural roars of Sand Lords; he had killed scores of them in every imaginable way, and yet only when he had finally witnessed the death of innocents and the suffering that lay in its wake had he truly begun to understand the nature of horror and the growing rift between Silvan and Alpine elves.

He had learned so much: about life as a warrior in the wilds, about discipline and leadership, about nature itself and his own growing perception of his nascent ability. He had learned to control his emotions and had not once thought of his illegitimate begetting, and of course, he had learned to braid his hair in pure Ari fashion.

The forest became more populated the further South they moved. Foresters, farmers and children walked here and there, even waved at the dusty warriors as their horses took them through the glades and dells. Any who watched them pass understood the hardship they had seen for it was plainly written on their faces, and confirmed by ripped and tattered uniforms. They had seen battle and endured, and the citizens of Ea Uaré watched them proudly.

"My Lord! Welcome home!" someone shouted from afar. Wondering who they hailed, Fel'annár turned his head, only to find an elf looking straight at him, his hand over his heart.

Fel'annár stared for a moment, before looking behind him, in search of the Lord, but there was no one there, only a puzzled Angon who stared back at him, perplexed. Fel'annár pulled a face and shrugged his shoulders, and then turned to the fore once more, his eyes taking in the new sights and sounds. They were close to the city now, and the familiar surge of excitement grabbed him and he smiled. He was still able to enjoy life, he realised, despite the things he had seen and done, of his grief and his fear.

At the front of the line, Lainon and Turion shared a worried glance. There was no doubt in their minds as to what had just happened. They were not even at court yet, and someone had already mistaken Fel'annár for a member of the royal family.

"We cannot go any further, Turion, 'tis madness," whispered Lainon.

"By rights he should reside at the city barracks," began Turion thoughtfully, "but you are right, of course. We are pushing our luck. The boy already has a reputation, *The Silvan*, remember? I wonder," he said thoughtfully, "I wonder if you could provide the boy with a bed for a few days. Your adopted village is not far from here. You would be close enough to attend your duties in the city, yet far enough to reduce the risks of Fel'annár being recognised. Can it be done?" asked the captain, his gaze resting heavily on Lainon.

"Yes," said the Ari cautiously. "We would have to take him off active duty, register him as wounded perhaps. He could regroup once the Tar'eastór party is ready to depart."

"Then that is what we must do," murmured Turion. "We must speak with Lord Aradan and Prince Handir no sooner we arrive. See to it, Lainon, and send word to the barracks."

With a nod of agreement, it was decided, and soon enough, a puzzled Fel'annár left together with Lainon amidst heart-felt goodbyes and boisterous hugs. There were promises shared too, of serving together once more, for the impact the young novice had made upon them all, although especially on Angon, went much deeper than anyone realised at the time.

The next day, Lainon had ridden with the sun, bidding Fel'annár rest until the evening, when he would be back with news from the city, and so, he sat in nothing but his breeches and a light shirt, his feet dangling in the slow trickle of the stream that ran parallel to the humble Silvan settlement on the northern outskirts of the city. Here, the residences were nestled in the trees, and Fel'annár decided he liked this. He marvelled at the crafted stairs that wound around the thick trunks, the ropes and pulleys that connected one platform to the next, and to their water supplies below. It was ingenious and he resolved to find books on engineering and village planning.

The water was cold, a sure sign that winter was deepening. It was still cloudless though, and blessed sunlight still kissed the land, but the chill was biting and he soon took his feet from the water and crossed his legs.

Why they had left before their arrival in the city he could not say and his disappointment had been all too clear to his mentor. Fel'annár was experienced enough to know that there was a reason for it, and he also knew that Lainon would not speak of it until he was ready, for the Ari was often tight-lipped, preferring the significance of silence to the clumsiness of words. He would wait—after all, surely he would be better off residing in this village than in the cramped barracks. He just wished he knew what was going on.

Was he still a novice? Where would he be sent now, and with whom? And why, why did Lainon not speak plainly with him?!

As he leaned back into the tree behind him, a sense of peace descended upon him and he decided that his first tour had actually gone well. Better, perhaps, than he could have hoped. Aye he had felt clumsy and inadequate at the start, but he had overcome and proved himself to his fellow warriors. Surprisingly too, his own illicit begetting had played no part in his life at all. There had been no antagonism, no mention of it and he had managed to forget—forget he had no father and no siblings, no mother or grandparents—only Amareth—and he smiled.

They love you.

He scowled, for there it was again. Was that his own mind, or was it the tree at his back?

Glancing back in annoyance, he felt the urge to chuckle and again, he wondered if it was his own mirth, or that of the tree. It was exasperating and then he remembered Narosén splitting his sides when Fel'annár had run to him, shouting that he had lost his mind. He did chuckle then, before sitting back once more, absently caressing the rough bark with his hand. Peace was upon him once more and another thought popped into his head.

Patience.

Now he knew. That had *not* been him, and finally, Fel'annár accepted the truth. He *could* hear the trees.

He *was* a Listener.

It was already past the lunch hour when Lainon met Turion before the great doors that led into the fortress and Thargodén's court. Clasping forearms, they walked purposefully towards Lord Aradan's office as they talked quietly.

"How are things at the barracks?" asked Lainon with a wry smile.

Turion's face was sour for he missed his life in the countryside. But that had changed the moment he had been invested as a captain and accepted as a member of the Inner Circle. Turning his head towards Lainon, he huffed and the Ari smirked; the question had, after all, been rhetorical.

Knocking upon the carved oak door, they strode into the well-appointed offices of Prince Handir. A roaring fire crackled and hissed off to one side, and orange light illuminated the beautiful artwork that hung from the walls, one of them a portrait of Or'Talán, first king of Ea Uaré. Lainon stood transfixed, so much so, that he failed to respond to the councillor's welcome.

"He was, indeed, extraordinary, was he not," said Aradan solemnly.

"Forgive me, my Lord, 'tis just, the resemblance is . . ."

"*Striking*," finished Turion.

"Is he truly that alike?" asked Aradan softly. "Prince Handir saw him from a distance and stated there was indeed a likeness."

"Then he must have been far away indeed, my Lord. King Or'Talán had the blue-grey eyes of our King Thargodén, but Fel'annár's eyes are—*green*—suffice it to say. But that is the short of it, Councillor. No one that knew our Lord Or'Talán could ever ignore the Silvan's true house, the nature of his lineage," said Lainon.

"Where is he?" asked Aradan as he approached them slowly, his shrewd eyes anchoring on them both.

"He stays with me, in Dorolén, not half a day's ride from here," explained Lainon. "We thought it best to keep him away from the crowds, my Lord."

"Well done," said the councillor, before bowing to the figure that now joined them.

"Prince Handir," gestured Aradan and the two warriors bowed formally. Lainon's eyes lingered for a while on his ex-charge, remembering that this was Fel'annár's brother—the thought seemed utterly absurd to him—the news was monumental and he suddenly doubted they could ever pull this off.

"Captain Turion, Lieutenant Lainon. At ease if you will, this conversation is private. Aradan, seal the doors."

Moments later, the four elves sat around a small round table, fine wine before them, their faces cast in partial shadow, and where the warriors' worked leather creaked with their movements, Aradan and Handir's robes swished softly as they accommodated themselves in their plush chairs.

Swallowing his first sip of wine, Aradan sat forward, his long fingers stroking his chin as Handir spoke.

"Prince Rinon leaves two days hence, to the East where he is expected to stay for at least two weeks. It must be enough," said the prince seriously, no preamble, no pleasantries, no—*curiosity*, realised Lainon. Either that or it was well hidden beneath the prince's practiced mask of statesmanship.

"As for my father, he expects me to leave for Tar'eastór ten days from now," he said, leaning back and taking a sip of his wine.

"The King was not loathe to release you while Prince Rinon is abroad?" asked Turion.

"Prince Rinon's visit is to the local villages, not the outposts further North. It is not a dangerous mission; indeed, it is not a military mission but one of trade. He saw no conflict of interests; it is all set."

"It seems to have been easier than we had foreseen," added Aradan, "and I must admit that makes me wary. The only setback so far has been the Crown Prince's desire to meet The Silvan, and that has been easily set aside for now, for said Silvan is, supposedly, still in the North. You did well to keep him away from the city, Lieutenant," finished the councillor with a nod of approval at Lainon.

"I must report a—*surprising*—development," said Turion, placing his goblet on the table before him.

"Oh?" asked Handir with a scowl, sharing a momentary glance at Aradan. "Has something happened?"

"Well," said Turion, "you could say that, my Prince."

"Come, Turion, do not leave us in the dark," said Aradan, worry now clearly etched on his wise face as he sat forward, his shrewd eyes searching those of the Captain, noticing his tired eyes.

"The Silvan, he - he has a *gift*."

"A gift," said Handir flatly, his eyes straying to Aradan once more.

"There is evidence to suggest that he, eh, has some sort of—*green magic*—my Lords." His voice had been soft, as if his tone could somehow take away the import of his words.

"Green magic," repeated Aradan, his voice equally monotonous.

"My Lords," began Lainon, his eyes seeking and attaining Turion's permission to continue. "All we know at this time is that this gift has manifested itself for the first time on this mission. It is some sort of, *sensitivity,* to the trees. He senses danger well before the rest of our warriors, and he knows things that others cannot."

"There is nothing certain at this point," continued Turion, "but it is something you both should be aware of. So far, he cannot control it, and there may be further developments we are currently unaware of."

A deep breath preceded Aradan's next words. "The king too, has a measure of ability with the trees, although he is not a Listener. Alright, now is there anything *else* that may interfere with our plans?" he asked, a hint of sarcasm in his tone.

"Yes," said Lainon. "We suspect at least one elf may have an inkling as to who Fel'annár is. It was not immediately obvious to us, but we cannot rule out that possibility."

"What did you do to draw attention to him?" asked Aradan somewhat curtly.

"It is not about what we *did*, my Lord," said Turion a little too abruptly, "but what *Fel'annár* did. The boy," began Turion. "The boy is extraordinary. He is young and inexperienced in all things and yet he fights as the warriors of old. There is a quality about him that inspires—love and—*loyalty*. Our entire patrol expressed their wish to serve with him again, in spite of his rank as Novice, and, if I may, that includes my good Lieutenant Lainon— and *myself*," he said. There was surprise in his words and in his eyes. Lainon glanced back at his friend, his strange, slanted eyes glinting in the shadows as only silence followed the Captain's words.

"Well, Lainon? Is this true?" asked Handir. Although his tone had been neutral, his voice seemed to echo around the room unnecessarily loudly.

"Yes, yes it is true. Yet even if you were to demand of me an explanation I could not give it for I cannot explain it myself.

Silence, again.

"What happened out there?" asked Aradan, sensing there was much more to the tale than the warriors had offered up.

"It is a long story, my Lord," said Turion. "I will submit my full report later today before General Huren. We have important tactical information and news that should be conveyed to the council. There has been a great battle."

"Is it that serious?" asked Handir, bending forwards so that he could better read the captain's eyes.

Turion stared back at the prince, his face blank. "Sixty civilians slaughtered, two of my most veteran warriors and a village razed to the ground, my Prince."

Utter silence followed Turion's words and Handir sat back, and then slowly closed his eyes. It was the first sign of empathy they had seen from him. It was not much, but it was a start, Turion supposed.

"Well now," said Aradan, his tone bringing them all back to the present. "Commander General Pan'assár has requested to see you both tomorrow morning, briefing for our upcoming journey."

"Pan'assár?" asked Turion, clearly surprised.

"Yes," said Aradan. "*He* is to lead Prince Handir's caravan."

"But, what about Captain Turion?" asked Lainon with a scowl. "I had assumed . . ."

"Then you assumed incorrectly, Lainon. When a member of the royal family travels, it is the Commander General who oversees the journey personally."

Turion looked to the floor and closed his eyes for a moment, and when he looked at Lainon there was an apology in his eyes. "Pan'assár is Alpine—with a capital A," he said, his tone somewhat dark and sarcastic.

Lainon stared back at Turion. It was true then, what he had heard. Pan'assár was the Commander General, their best warrior and leader, but those that served under him spoke of his cold demeanour, his cutting manner and often times cruel words. He was respected but feared, obeyed yet not from the heart, but from the mind.

"But he knew Lord Or'Talán, was one of the Shining Three - he will recognise Fel'annár," said Lainon, a note of alarm creeping into his voice.

"We could not avoid it," began Aradan. "It is custom and had I contested that decision I would have raised suspicion. We must work around this. The caravan is large and armour will be worn. We need to keep the boy away from the front."

"He will need protection, help—someone to make sure he is not discovered before he can be told the truth," murmured Turion.

"Idernon and Ramien."

"What?" asked Turion distractedly.

"We must send Idernon and Ramien as the caravan's novices," explained Lainon.

"Can novices be sent on such a mission?" asked Handir.

"Yes, it is not unheard of," said Turion. "But Pan'assár will not like it, especially because they are not Alpine."

"See that it is done," said Aradan.

"Who are Idernon and Ramien?" asked Handir.

Lainon smiled. "*They* are *The Company*," he said with a sly smile, to which Handir cocked his brow, and Lainon left him wondering.

Chapter Eighteen

CATHARSIS

"So avid were we for but a spark of hope that would shake us from our long sleep, a glimmer of something that would awake in us the splendour of this Silvan nation. It came suddenly, in the shape of one amber river stone that sat defiantly upon the end of a warrior's braid."
The Silvan Chronicles, Book III. Marhené.

Fel'annár stood in his new uniform. Black breeches and heavy boots and then a knee-length brown leather tunic. The vambraces were black, like his boots and the buckles made of silver. The straps of two harnesses crossed his chest and from his leather-clad shoulders, a bow lay to one side and the pommel of a broadsword to the other. There was something else though, something he knew he should not wear but that felt wrong not to. Alféna's Honour Stone sat at the end of a side braid. It would be hidden for the most part but would surely be visible when he walked or moved. It was a risk he was prepared to take for how could such an honourable thing be deemed inappropriate? It sounded to Fel'annár like the purposeful destruction of Silvan culture, repression of their identity.

Lainon and Turion had said nothing on their journey back but Fel'annár knew that other commanders would not be so indulgent. Nevertheless, in this one thing he would defy them.

Walking towards a lone beech tree, he placed his palm against its trunk as he remembered Lainon's words from the day before. They were off on another tour, only this time he would be required to leave Ea Uaré for the Alpine kingdom of Tar'eastór in two days' time. It would be his longest journey yet, and he was unsure how he felt about it. He would be walking into the very seat of Alpine power; a Silvan novice that looked like an Alpine. It was begging for trouble - madness. And then his training would be disrupted for Lainon was assigned to the prince; he would have no time to spare. There was something else, though. Tar'eastór was surely the birthplace of his father. The thought was mercilessly suppressed; he would never think on that again.

His father was dead, even if he still lived.

There were advantages too, he told himself. The greatest warrior ever known resided there, Commander General of King Vorn'asté's army – the mighty Gor'sadén, one of the Shining Three. He had read the stories, devoured them as a child and remembered them now as an adult. He was a living legend together with Pan'assár and the deceased Or'Talán.

But then what did that matter? He would probably never even *see* the elf, let alone talk to him, ask him of the battles he had waged, the strategies he had employed.

He chuckled out loud as one finger brushed over the rough bark.

'Have faith.'

Faith? It was not faith that would help him – it was himself, it always had been.

'Aria sees you.'

Does she? And why can I not see *her*?

'You do.'

Fel'annár pulled his hand back from the bark, as if it had burnt him and he frowned as the words echoed in his mind. He was distracted from any further thoughts as the corner of his eye spotted a group of children huddled together, obviously masterminding some devious plan—Fel'annár knew for he had done just that with Ramien and Idernon so many times in his own childhood, when being warriors was still a fantasy in the distant future.

They played some game it seemed for they crouched in the bushes, plotting and planning as they waved their tiny hands and whispered furiously between themselves, casting furtive glances his way—as if he could not see them. They were talking about *him*, he realised, and a smile blossomed on his face for the first time that day.

Looking around for any sign of Lainon, he was, once more, drawn to the children as the whispering became louder, and before he knew it, one boy had broken from the main group and was slowly creeping towards him. The boy's face was rigid, eyes wide and searching as he made his skittish way towards the imposing blond elf.

"Greetings, warrior," said Fel'annár seriously. "What are you tracking?" he asked, and the imp stopped dead in his tracks, his head whipping back to his friends in mounting panic, as if he had suddenly been caught in quicksand.

The whispering was back as they flapped their arms, signalling to their friend that he should continue his quest and so, bolstering his courage, the young one continued his tortuous way forwards under the puzzled yet amused gaze of Fel'annár.

Soon enough, he was just a few feet away, staring, his mouth hanging open. Before he had been scared but now, he was curious, for the boy's eyes strayed from the large green eyes to the thick locks tightly secured in a high ponytail at the back of Fel'annár's head, and then to the amber stone at the end of an archer's braid.

"Are you, a—are you . . ."

"Speak child, I do not bite; well not usually," smiled Fel'annár lop-sidedly.

The children behind snorted in laughter and shoved each other roughly, but their eyes never left the scene before them, admiring their friend's bravery no doubt.

"A—are you—are you The *Silvan?*" he asked in awe.

Fel'annár was taken aback. How could this child possibly know the nick name he had been given? He was new to this village, nobody knew him in Dorolén except Lainon, and the Ari had not used that name here, he was sure of it.

"Yes," he answered simply, and to his utter surprise, all vestiges of fright and apprehension disappeared, replaced now by the biggest, toothy grin Fel'annár had ever seen on the face of a child. His eyes sparkled and he squealed in delight, bouncing on the spot where he stood, all pretence of being an imposing warrior and tracker gone in the wake of childish delight.

The other children ran forwards, almost crashing into their courageous friend for it seemed they would not be left out, and of a sudden, questions began to bubble from their giddy mouths.

"Is it true, are you The Silvan?" they asked excitedly.

Frowning yet smiling, Fel'annár nodded. "Yes, that it what some people call me. How did you know?" he asked softly, desperately trying to quell his mounting trepidation.

"Everybody knows The *Silvan!*" another boy shouted. "He is the mightiest Silvan warrior of our time, daddy has told me so!" he exclaimed.

Fel'annár was dumbfounded, but before he could ask, another child spoke up.

"It's all true, *look!*" he shouted, making the others giggle with glee as he slowly reached out to touch one of Fel'annár's Ari locks. It was enough to bolster the courage of the others and soon enough all five were touching his hair, until one little hand strayed to a short sword and Fel'annár stopped him. The boy startled, but then smiled when Fel'annár smirked.

"You see! He is the handsomest warrior of them all. Mummy says you are our champion, that you will protect the Silvan people and our forests! Will you?"

The sinking feeling that had assailed him moments before was back, and he answered dumbly, his mind not entirely on the child before him. "I will do all in my power to protect my people, child, for whatever difference it can make."

The sound of someone clearing their throat drew Fel'annár's attention back to the present and he turned to meet Lainon's amused gaze.

Straightening himself and his tunic, Fel'annár saluted formally to his superior as was custom when wearing one's uniform, and from the corner of his eyes, he could see the boys mimicking him. He tried to mask the grin that threatened to ruin his solemn stance but to no avail and he looked down in embarrassment.

Lainon had not meant to frighten them, but he certainly was not used to children, and his stern gaze was enough to send them running, squealing and laughing as they scampered into the trees, their voices shouting over and over.

"*The Silvan! The Silvan!*"

Fel'annár turned his perplexed face to Lainon, whose own expression was blank, all emotion channelled, it seemed, into his next words.

"News travels fast."

"But *why?* I mean, many warriors have saved the lives of civilians, kept them from danger. Why do they talk of me?" Fel'annár asked, pleaded almost. "I have no rank! When I was their age I wanted to be a *captain*, not some lowly novice!"

"Perhaps it is not only the *Silvans* that speak of you?" he said cryptically as his hand patted the trunk of a nearby oak. Fel'annár swallowed, and quelled the cold shiver that ran down his spine for he had not quite reconciled himself to the idea of being a listener.

"Fel'annár," said Lainon as he began to walk, "the Silvan people are ruled by their respective village chiefs and Spirit Herders, as well you know. They have representatives at court, but there is no one person they all feel identified with, one they can claim as their own. A brave warrior with the qualities you have already shown is the perfect candidate; *you* have been chosen, in a sense, not collectively but individually—by many. Does that make sense?"

"No, not really," said Fel'annár. "You are saying they need a leader? A *Silvan* leader?"

"Yes, yet more than a leader they need a protector, a symbol of their waning identity. They are marginalised by the Alpines and they are hungry to state a claim, to show they will not be pushed into the background – not in their own homes. That honour stone is a testimony to that, a lost custom that Alfena has brought back into use, and you wear it – are proud of it, as well you should be."

Fel'annár kicked half-heartedly at the dust, uncomfortable with the conversation and so he turned his gaze on Lainon once more. "Lainon. How am I to continue my training in Tar'eastór? Well you know the Alpines won't take kindly to me and you will be busy with our prince.

"Are you telling me you're scared to be left alone with them?" smirked Lainon.

"What? No, I'm not *scared*. I just want to learn, not waste my time in petty argument, to be constantly proving myself to others."

"Well you will hardly be *alone*," said Lainon drolly and something in his tone had Fel'annár's eyes back on him. "There are three other novices travelling with you. One is an erudite, the other is a brute and the third has butterflies in his head…"

Fel'annár's form straightened slowly as the frown on his face dissolved. "The Company? They are coming to Tar'eastór?"

A smile was Lainon's only answer.

"How, how is it possible? We have served in different patrols for the last year. The chances of this happening are …" he trailed off as realization sank in. "*You* did this?"

"And *Turion* did this – he cannot accompany us but he made sure you would not be alone in Alpine lands."

A disbelieving smile had stuck on Fel'annár's face and he shook his head as his eyes danced around the glade, as if he could not quite understand.

"Lainon. I bless the day Turion sent me to you. No one," he whispered harshly as he turned to fully face the lieutenant, "no novice could ever have a better master, a better friend." Fel'annár stepped forward and clasped the Ari's forearms with his strong hands. "You must join my Company, for only those I consider my brothers can be a part of it, only those closest to me . . ."

"I would be honoured then," smiled Lainon, and then laughed. "You will have to find me one of those fancy names!"

"Fear not, for I already know what I will call you," said Fel'annár slyly.

"Oh? And what would that be?" asked Lainon with a quirk of his brow.

"You are an elf of few words and great deeds. You speak little but say much. You, are Dim'atór, the Silent Warrior."

Lainon stared back at Fel'annár blankly, before slowly smiling and nodding. "It is well chosen. I shall be Dim'atór, Dima the Ari!" he proclaimed pompously and Fel'annár grinned at this little-known side of his mercurial mentor.

"Welcome then, brother of *The Company*—now we are four."

Lainon nodded humbly, his eyes resting calculatingly on Fel'annár. Every time he looked at the boy, every time he gazed upon this young elf that would, one day, be his superior, he just wanted to tell him the truth about his family, his lineage, and then help him accept it so that he could get on with his life, finally know who he was, his family, and the sad story behind his own existence, not to depress him but to give him closure and set him upon the path towards his destiny, one he knew was marked by greatness.

"Warrior Fel'annár."

"Sir," answered The Silvan, the smile still on his face. "Look to your left."

Fel'annár's smile slipped as he complied, eyes swivelling to the tree line, but before Lainon could say more, the boy was loping forwards, his long hair streaming behind him until he crashed into Ramien's chest, and then was hugged from behind by Idernon. They were all safe, despite the odds.

Lainon took his time as he walked towards them, noticing Carodel the Silvan bard player did the same from the other side. Soon though, all five stood together, and Fel'annár spoke.

"Brothers! We have made it! Look at us! he exclaimed proudly as he pushed and pulled on his friends' leather jerkins playfully. "And *you* Carodel! Did you three serve together?" he asked.

"Aye," said Idernon with a wide smile, one mirrored on Ramien's face – until it slipped and the Wall of Stone frowned, eyes resting on the strange twists in Fel'annár's hair and then the amber stone in his braid. "What—is *that?*" he asked with a jab of his finger.

"Those, *novice*, are Ari locks—anything to object?" asked the Ari'atór as he stepped forward, his eyes narrowing dangerously, and even though they twinkled with mischief, Ramien swallowed thickly, stepping back in respect, scowling when Idernon snorted.

"Nothing to object, Lieutenant. They are very fine locks," he said lamely and then smiled stupidly. Fel'annár and Idernon chuckled, but then the Wise Warrior carefully took the honour stone in Fel'annár's hair between his fingers, admiring its beauty.

"You have stories to tell," he murmured. I have rarely seen these in the hair of our warriors – I thought it a thing of the past," he said, almost to himself, but Lainon heard.

"And perhaps, it is a sign of the future," said Fel'annár.

Idernon and Lainon shared a glance, a soft smile pulling at their lips.

"We must tell you that we have a candidate for The Company," said Ramien, glancing at Carodel and then turning to Fel'annár.

"What have you done to deserve such merit, Carodel?" asked Fel'annár as he clasped forearms with the bard player and smiled.

"That is a long story," said Ramien, "suffice it to say we have served and suffered together – we would tell you of his merit later, with wine and a song. I think though, that you have your own story to tell," said the Wall of Stone, his eyes searching those of Fel'annár and then glancing warily at Lainon.

Fel'annár smiled, somewhat enigmatically, for where to begin? "I do, but that too must be told with wine and song," he smiled, his eyes slipping sideways and to Lainon.

"Surely *not?*" blurted Carodel, and then smiled falsely, embarrassed that his words had come out wrong. "I mean that is wonderful, I just hadn't expected . . ."

"For an Ari'atór to join you?" asked Lainon drolly. "And why not? Are you not here for the same reasons as I? What has rank or race to do with it?" he asked, not unkindly.

"Nothing," replied Carodel boldly. "If you are here for the same reasons as I, then you are most welcome in my eyes, but of course that is not for me to decide. If Fel'annár says it, then so say I."

Lainon smiled. "Do I intimidate you, novice?" asked the Ari carefully.

"Yes," was all Carodel said, and it was enough for them all to chuckle for it was true, the Ari'atór was a strange-looking elf who was unnerving at best, and downright terrifying at his worst.

"They need names!" said Idernon slyly and Fel'annár smiled as he answered.

"*If* – you are deemed worthy," he smiled slyly, "then Lainon here is Dim'atór, The Silent Warrior for he speaks little and says much, and you, my friend Carodel, are Lorn'atór—The Bard Warrior," he finished with a flourish.

Lorn'atór bowed, as did Dim'atór, but the Ari could not help wondering at this game they played, for it was surely that—and yet there was something in the young ones' demeanour that contradicted that idea. He resolved to observe their dynamics, discover what it was that made him unsure of the nature of it.

"Well, well," said Idernon, holding his arms out to the sides. "Three Silvans, one Ari and one . . ."

"Half-blood," finished Fel'annár, not angrily but with a rueful smile on his face. "I am honoured. May we fight and serve together for many centuries!"

Lainon placed a heavy hand upon Fel'annár's shoulder. "Come," he said, a lieutenant once more, and Fel'annár nodded, falling into step with his superior, the rest of The Company right behind him.

Before long, they stopped and Lainon turned to face Fel'annár.

"*Attention!*" he commanded, and despite his puzzlement, Fel'annár squared himself, aware that the rest of The Company had moved away. He barely resisted the urge to look behind him for his neck prickled—elves were approaching from the tree line but protocol demanded he stand still, eyes to the fore.

A sparkle of metal caught his attention and before he knew it, Captain Turion stood before him in full, ceremonial uniform, the one that marked him as a member of the Inner Circle. His combat decorations shone upon his right arm and Fel'annár battled with his hands so as not to reach out and stroke his fingers over the carved metal that spoke of mastery in swords and knives. He wondered if he would ever wear such a glorious thing, if he could ever make himself worthy of such finery.

His awe soon gave way to the realisation that he was to be formally invested as a warrior, now, in this very glade, by Turion no less. Indeed, he was called upon to repeat the vows of service to Crown and land. It was a solemn vow but Fel'annár's joy was so great even Turion could not hold back a soft smile. When it was done, Turion saluted formally, to which Fel'annár replied in turn.

A novice no more - a warrior at last.

But Turion had not finished. Taking one step towards the newly-appointed warrior, the captain produced a leather band, at the centre of which stood a finely carved silver symbol; two crossed arrows.

Fel'annár's eyes bulged and then shot to the captain.

"You have been granted Master status with the bow. Congratulations, warrior," he said formally. "Not many can make such a shot in the air," he said, his head cocking to one side and allowing his smile to finally blossom. "Your feat was duly noted."

Fel'annár blushed and then bowed in humble gratefulness, for never in his wildest dreams had he imagined being a master so early in his career. It was unheard of. He closed his eyes slowly, as if the darkness could, somehow, slow down the rush of emotions—happiness, pride, determination, resolve. He thought it was the happiest day of his life so far, one he would never forget.

His eyes slowly slid open, and of a sudden it seemed to Fel'annár that the whole world had changed, or was it him that had changed? His body hummed and his mind cleared itself; everything around him was now startlingly clear, as if some small piece of a puzzle had slipped effortlessly into place. He was startled by honey-coloured eyes that stared at him—too close. He could see himself in them, and yet not entirely. Blood of his blood, but not his mother, whoever *she* had been.

It was Amareth, his aunt.

"My son," she whispered, her eyes wide and misty. A gentle hand reached up and cupped his cheek lovingly.

"Amareth," was all Fel'annár could say for a moment, for she was, in everything but the womb, his mother. "You came."

"For you, for this day," she said softly.

"You have never left Lan Taria, or so they say," said Fel'annár in wonder.

"I am not a traveller, Fel'annár," she smiled, but he could see her words for what they were. There was a reason she had never left their village, one he had never understood; even now she would not explain, just as she never had about anything of import in his life. It was frustrating and it curbed his exuberance, soured the joy he felt at her presence.

"Already a master archer, I see," she smiled in pride and Fel'annár returned it.

"I cannot believe it myself but yes," he said, brushing his fingers over the silver symbol reverently to better appreciate the workmanship, or perhaps to convince himself it was still there, that it was all true.

"Fel'annár!" came a shout from behind Amareth, who stepped aside to make way for a charging Thavron, who promptly crashed into his friend, rattling them both as they embraced and thudded each other upon the back.

"My favourite forester!" shouted Fel'annár.

"My favourite warrior!" shouted Thavron of Lan Taria. "You have made us all proud for do not think we have not heard of your deeds in the North!"

Fel'annár's face paled a little and his smile slipped.

"Oh, enjoy it while you can—you are a hero! you are The *Silvan!*" chuckled Thavron as he held Fel'annár out at arm's distance. "Your hair— what have you done?"

"What has Lieutenant *Lainon* done, you mean. It's an Ari style," he said somewhat defensively.

Thavron smirked, hugging his friend once more and then latching on to his arm. "Come, say hello to everyone for there is a party tonight, just for you. We will dance and drink, eat and frolic into the night for we are *Silvan!*" he proclaimed with a flourish, and more than one voice shouted *'Aye!'* as they passed.

True to Thavron's word, woodland fiddles soon echoed throughout the secluded glade and family and friends began to celebrate, the crowd ever growing as others from Lainon's village, and even further afield, joined the festivities.

Merry jigs were accompanied by lively percussion—drums of different tones and timbers wove complex movements that were sometimes slow and romantic, and at others, rhythms that set the feet to tapping and the girls to swaying and smiling at the boys. Likewise, the lads' eyes roved over the pretty lasses until they fixed on their next dance partner, only to reel her away in a swish of fine clothes and silky hair.

And while some danced the night away, others stood and talked. Every corner of the glade was occupied by small groups of elves that conversed as they drank and then drank again, their eyes occasionally straying to the music and the gaiety of the younger members of their society, and especially to Fel'annár and his group of faithful friends.

In one such group, Amareth stood talking with Lainon. The Ari had taken it upon himself to inform her of Fel'annár' progress, yet only to the point of not trespassing on his young friend's privacy; indeed he said nothing of Fel'annár's budding gift with the trees.

As he spoke, he was reminded of a much younger and lighter Amareth, a woman who still enjoyed life. Now, however, he found her light much diminished. She was still alive, for it was not so much grief that afflicted her, but *time* and the events it had brought with it that had curbed her enthusiasm for life, leaving in its wake a quietly dignified woman who spoke little and transmitted less to those that did not know her.

"Lainon!" shouted a well-dressed elf from afar, his face flushed with the dance and the wine and Lainon prayed to Aria he would not approach now, for if Calen had a loose tongue when sober, it would verily flap if he were into his cups, as he suspected was the case.

Hence, Lainon's smile was a little lopsided when Calen finally reached them.

"A wonderful party, my friend! So many have come; so many lovely ladies!" he smirked as he gulped his wine, his eyes gleaming in the moonlight.

"Then have fun while you can, for the night is young and you—are unattached," said Lainon levelly, hoping that would prompt his friend to jump back into the fray. Alas, there was no such luck.

"Your new friend is popular with the lasses. I will have to stake my claim on Elbanié—must be those eyes. I would bet my best belt that is Lássira's son," he said calculatingly as he sipped once more upon his wine.

Amareth flinched and instinctively turned away, and Lainon's body straightened of its own accord.

"The grapes addle your mind, Calen—Lássira was not wed," said Lainon carefully.

"And what does that matter? There are plenty of bastards in this world, born outside the binds of marriage!" scoffed Calen, and Lainon was suddenly rigid.

"I tell you there is no mistaking it—I am not *blind*. Nobody else has those eyes, Lainon. I wonder who the lucky . . ." Calen trailed off, his eyes growing impossibly wide as he slowly turned to Lainon.

"Lainon," he said seriously now, no traces of his growing inebriation. "Lainon you don't suppose . . . I mean you know what they said of Lássira—Silvan lover of the king . . ."

"Don't be ridiculous!" said Lainon a little too curtly, indeed he could see Calen flinch at his steely words and so he calmed his mounting anxiety. "Calen, that is ludicrous and you would do well not to repeat that; it could cause much harm."

"You are protective of him," said Calen again, his gaze now shrewd and sharp. "Lainon, we have known each other for many years—do not take me for a *fool*. I know what I say and if his father is not—*him*—his mother *is* Lássira."

"Then for the friendship we share, Calen, do not repeat your conjectures," said Lainon in a tone that brooked no retort. "Fel'annár has no parents, nobody knows who they were and that is the end of it—do you *understand* me, my friend?"

Calen held the Ari's dark gaze for a while before answering him.

"I *understand*, I understand *perfectly*."

"*Promise* me," said Lainon, his eyes boring into Calen's, hypnotically almost. "I will not discuss this again with you but be warned. My loyalty to the king is far greater than my friendship with you."

Calen swayed backwards as if he had been slapped, a hint of fear in his bold eyes. "You cannot mean to hide this," he whispered, eyes overly bright in his shock.

"I will not discuss it," repeated Lainon, his jaw clenching and Calen stepped down, nodding curtly. With one last, lingering stare at Amareth's back, he bowed and left.

Amareth let loose a mighty gasp of air, and Lainon turned apologetic eyes on her, but before they could discuss it further, Erthoron, the leader of Lan Taria and Silvan representative at Thargodén's court joined them.

"Amareth, and Lainon - it has been a while, Lieutenant," he said softly, his eyes moving from one elf to the other and then scowling. "What has happened?"

"Fel'annár is in danger of being identified," said Lainon. "He is too much like his mother."

"Wait until he travels into the lands of the Alpine proper," sighed the village leader, "for it will not be *Lássira* they associate him with."

"I know," said Lainon, "I know."

Another figure approached then, Turion, his exquisitely carved breastplate catching the light of a waxing moon.

"Lady Amareth?" he asked tentatively, to which she nodded, but said nothing. "I am Captain Turion, it is a pleasure to meet you."

"Thank you, Captain. I believe you have been Fel'annár's commanding officer."

"That is correct my lady, although for this upcoming trip I cannot accompany him. He will be with Lainon, though."

"Turion," said Lainon urgently, for he realised the captain did not know she had not yet been told of their plans. Luckily though, the two had worked together long enough to understand each other's non-verbal communication and Turion nodded subtly at Lainon. It was time to tell her.

"My Lady," began Lainon. "There is something of great importance you need to know."

Amareth scowled in puzzlement but her nostrils flared, and Lainon immediately knew she was nervous. With a brief glance at Erthoron, he continued.

"First you must know that Turion is aware of the facts and is sworn to our cause."

"Our cause?" asked Erthoron quietly, his eyes darting around them.

"Yes. You see," began Lainon, "from the moment Fel'annár became a recruit, you surely knew the consequences, did you not?" he asked, his eyes falling heavily on Amareth.

After a moment of silence, she nodded. "Yes," she said quietly, "Yes, I knew, and Aria is witness to my doubts but—I could not hold him back," she said pleadingly. "I knew it would only be a matter of time but I could not keep him in a remote Silvan village—he is too—*important*."

Erthoron looked into his cup and Lainon simply nodded his understanding.

"We too, know this and - we have a plan—so that both Fel'annár and the king do not find out from others, so that his existence is not used against Thargodén by those that would lead our land to ruin."

"You tread dangerous ground, Lainon," warned Erthoron.

Lainon nodded before continuing with his explanation. "The day after tomorrow, both I and Fel'annár ride to Tar'eastór as part of Prince Handir's escort."

"You would take him there – into the very lands of his father? Are you mad?"

"Not mad, my Lady. We would tell him of his heritage, before we arrive."

She stood silently. There was shock on her face but if Lainon had expected her to object – he was wrong.

"Better that he is abroad then – he will be safer," she mumbled.

Now it was Lainon who frowned. "You see the danger then? That his existence may be used against the king, hinder Fel'annár in his military career?" Lainon had not expected her to be quite so understanding.

When Amareth spoke her next words, they left Lainon, Turion and Erthoron speechless and with the fine hairs at the back of their necks standing on end.

"The real danger is not to his military career, Lainon – is to Fel'annár himself. If he were to stay here – he would be hunted down and destroyed ."

It was Turion who put an end to the shocked silence.

"What is it that you know that we do *not*?"

It was Erthoron who replied. "Captain. We always knew that should Fel'annár step into the light, there are those that would do him harm and yet, so too did we know that he *would* leave."

Both Lainon and Turion's eyes widened at the implications. "Who told you this?" growled Lainon. "Who *dared* to threaten you?" he trailed off, his eyes widening in sudden realization, turning abruptly to Amareth. "It was the same one, wasn't it? The same elf who told the *queen . . . who*?" he whispered.

"We do not know their names but they were Alpine," said Amareth. "They said they spoke for many at court, that a royal bastard would not be tolerated."

"Band'orán's followers, I would wager on it," said Lainon urgently. "This is unexpected. Band'orán knows there was a child, that Fel'annár is here, in Bel'arán; perhaps we should . . ."

"*Never!*" growled Turion. "Now, more than *ever*, I am determined to do what is right for the boy. We cannot cage him in, we cannot stunt his destiny. This must end, and it ends with the *truth*. No sooner you are on the road, Lainon, and you *tell* him. Aradan and I will see to the rest, to the king." He would brook no argument it seemed and Lainon nodded curtly.

Amareth nodded, but there were unshed tears in her eyes. "The king? When he hears of what really happened, he will fade, Lainon. He will weaken and they will take advantage. They will place Band'orán on the throne as they have ever wanted to do."

"That is a possibility, Amareth," said Lainon calmly. "But think of this. The king may not react as you say. He may take an interest in his son. Not all the Alpines at court are disloyal to Thargodén; the majority are with him. It is the *Silvan* people who float in the middle of this, Amareth . . . do you not see? Do you *all* not see? Fel'annár is The *Silvan*. He has already won them over and will only become stronger in their eyes, albeit he is blissfully unaware of it as yet. It might just be enough to deter Band'orán's followers from threatening his life for if they do, the Silvan people would not tolerate it and that—is not in Band'orán's interests . . ."

Turion, Amareth and Erthoron stared at the Ari for long moments, before the village leader finally broke the silence.

"Well-reasoned, Lieutenant. Well-reasoned indeed."

"Lainon," said Amareth, her hand lightly touching the lieutenant's forearm. "I would have your promise – that you will see him through this. You cannot begin to understand just how much this will affect him. I – *we*," she corrected, "have led him to believe his father was an outcast, that he did something passing ill to be ignored in death, not because we said as much but because we said nothing at all. It was the only way to keep him safe, keep him in Lan Taria while he was young and vulnerable. I wager he thinks his father dead because that is the only way he can understand his absence. Fel'annár is a tough boy but he *will* flounder, Lainon, of that I have no doubt. Deep down he wants what he never had – he wants a father but he will never admit to it."

"And now I am to tell him his father is the *king*," said Lainon flatly. He breathed heavily and cast his gaze to the trees above. "You have my promise, Amareth. I will watch out for him, I will make a brother of Handir if I can, protect Fel'annár from Thargoden's line in Tar'eastór."

"It seems an impossible task for just one elf," murmured Erthoron, "even for you, Lainon."

But Lainon smiled then. "I am not alone, Erthoron. I have The Company," he said and his eyes slipped to Amareth. Her own lips parted and then the corners tugged them upwards.

"I trust you, Lainon. I have always trusted you. You are the only person that can do this. I cannot – never could. He will hate me for keeping the truth from him, he will struggle to understand my motives and that is my sacrifice, one I will never regret making – for my people, for Lássira, for my son."

Turion raised his goblet in silent salute and Erthoron nodded. Lainon simply watched her and wondered. If Lássira had been anything like this woman, Ea Uaré would have had a formidable queen at Thargodén's side had hatred not stepped between them and torn them asunder.

Lainon knew then, the true nature of his goal – he would bring them back together – not the king and Lássira, but the king and the son they had created between them, for of that union, great things would surely ensue.

Chapter Nineteen

CULMINATION

"Change had come to the Silvans in the form of an honour stone, worn defiantly by one Silvan warrior. To the king, that change came from the trees. It was the beginning of a new dawn for Ea Uaré."
The Silvan Chronicles, Book III. Marhené.

"There is a missive from Erthoron that must be discussed, my King. We should meet first thing tomorrow to discuss it, if that is acceptable?" prompted Aradan.

"Of course," came the monotonous answer, soft and apparently unconcerned.

"With both princes abroad, my Lord, I have asked Colophon to assist us with their administrative duties."

"Good," came the equally unemotional response.

"Very well, my Lord," said Aradan, hesitating for a moment before turning, leaving the introspective king to himself and his thoughts.

The heavy oak door clunked shut and Thargodén closed his brilliant blue-grey eyes for a moment, before opening them once more and turning to the window behind him.

Winter was advancing and with every day the weather became colder and the landscape waxed brown and grey—so like himself—he mused. Cold and grey, withered and exhausted—alone.

Rinon and Handir were abroad—everyone had gone—and he remained, rolling as would a boulder with the inertia of an empty life, one that made no sense except to administer the land his father had colonised and then prematurely left in his care. It was his only motivation to continue in Ea Uaré. It *was* enough, but he was profoundly unhappy.

To his three children he meant nothing, their respect for him fuelled only by his status as King. He had lost them in all the ways that mattered, their regard for him spanning from civil to downright cruel.

Any attempt he had made to be the father he had once been, to show his love for them had been countered by their disappointment in him, for precipitating their mother's departure to Valley. He had left them bereft and they would not forgive him.

He *had* lost them and his only hope for happiness was when he too, finally stepped upon blessed soil and kissed the hand of his true love and, perhaps, the child they had created together, the one that had served to save her life, to deliver her into the healing lands of Valley.

How long would he have to wait? How long before he could allow himself to disconnect from this place, leave behind his children, and set foot upon the Last Road?

But he could not, for however much they reminded him every day of his sins, of what he had done to them, he could never leave them behind. He could never do what the queen had done. There was nothing in this world that could move him to sever his connection with his children.

He looked down, his nostrils flaring subtly for a moment before raising his eyes once more, only to settle upon a small book sitting between two larger tomes upon a dark, dusty bookshelf.

Slowly, he moved towards it, his hand reaching out tentatively until his fingers brushed over the small, weathered book. His index finger hooked over the top and softly, he pulled it out, until it finally rested in his white, manicured hands.

He looked away for a moment, but his eyes were drawn back to the diary, and with a heavy breath, he opened it.

There, upon the ancient paper, was a drawing, one he himself had rendered, partially obscured by a dried flower. It was brown and brittle, where once it been a supple, vibrant green—just like her eyes. She had gifted him with this, revered flower, one that symbolised eternal love to the Silvan people. He had cherished it once and yet now, to look upon it was to be reminded of what he had lost, the eternal death of his heart.

Finally, he allowed himself to admire the features that had mesmerised and captivated him since he had first seen them, tears welling in his burning eyes and his heart clenching painfully. One shaking hand reached out to trace the outline of the face, the wave of chestnut locks, the slant of her legendary eyes, the strong brow and the high cheekbones.

"*Lassiel.*"

Thargodén's finger brushed softly over the full pink lips, marvelling for a moment at the characteristic shape of them. "Will I ever see you again?" he whispered, a lone tear finally escaping him. It burnt a trail down his pale face, like the shallow cut of a sharp blade, the one that stabbed him in the heart every day when he thought of her.

He closed the book with a harsh, angry thud and strode to the shelf once more, replacing the diary in its almost hidden home. Turning, his face was stern, the tear swiped away angrily as he came to stand before the open balcony of his rooms.

The Evergreen Wood rolled away into the distance, its beauty calming his grief enough to make it bearable once more.

'Strange,' he mused, stepping onto the mighty plateau and walking to the very end of it so that he seemed to be hanging over the forest, the trees below and around him. There was a song on the air, from the trees he was sure—he had not heard them for so long.

Concentrating, he tried to discern the feelings they evoked for only in that way could he understand them. He wasn't a listener but he was sensitive to their moods.

Pity, sorrow, forgiveness, understanding, excitement.

Excitement?

Furrowing his brow in concentration, he tried again. The same emotions came through clearly but there was more . . .

Joy—why would they sing such a thing? Their land was assailed by Sand Lords and Deviants, the people and the trees were suffering. Why would they sing of bliss? It was almost offensive.

Patience, understanding, reprimand, *joy* . . .

He shook his head in frustration, trying one more time, and then a thought occurred to him. Were they mocking him for his moment of self-pity?

Fool, grief, pride, victory, *Lord* . . .

"What . . ." he said aloud. Turning suddenly on his heels, his skin prickling as he strode back inside, he made urgently for the door of his study, flinging it open until it thudded against the wall behind.

"Aradan!" he shouted, before turning back into the room and to the window, trying one more time to understand the strange song of the Evergreen Wood.

Patience, pride, courage, Forest Lord.

Thargodén's eyes bulged. Did they speak of *him*? Had they called him Forest Lord?

"My Lord," hailed Aradan as he entered slowly, concern written on his face for Thargodén had not shouted in many, many years.

"Aradan. Do you hear the *trees*?" asked the king urgently.

"No, I never could, my Lord," said Aradan carefully, trying and failing to read the conflicting emotions on his monarch's face.

"Do you *hear* nothing at all?" he shouted in frustration, and all Aradan's senses were alert. Thargodén never lost control, never shouted, never expressed deep emotion, be it good or bad. Whatever had happened must have been transcendental.

"I do not, my Lord. Thargodén—what is it?" asked Aradan, his face pulled into a deep frown.

"I will tell you what they say, Aradan," whispered the king, his eyes glinting in the failing light, a look so intense on his face that Aradan shivered in mounting dread, resisting the urge to step backwards.

"They speak of joy, of bliss, they speak—of a new lord; one they have named as their own."

Aradan's eyes widened of their own accord, before he found the wherewithal to ask the first of many questions that had jumped into his mind.

"A new lord? What does that mean—there is *danger*? Someone seeks to *overthrow* you, what . . ."

"No!" shouted Thargodén again, ripping his intricate crown off his silver locks and placing it unceremoniously on his table. "Not a usurper, a lord, a Lord of the *Forests*."

Aradan straightened, the skin of his scalp tightening painfully and sending his ears to sitting low on his head as suspicion began to take hold.

The king's unnerving eyes were now riveted on Aradan and then he rounded on his Chief Councillor, until his frantic face was but inches away from him. It was then that Aradan knew he had not been able to mask his suspicion, for Thargodén's face was a terrible sight, one he would never think to cross.

The flashing eyes narrowed and when the king spoke, Aradan could do nothing but obey.

"Tell me what you know, Councillor. Tell me *everything* you know."

Epilogue

It is with the passage of time and the coming of bad things, that we learn to suffer, and with our suffering comes a deeper understanding of the world.

Some become bitter and wrathful, oblivious to the plight of their brethren, while others feel their emotions, their worries and predicaments. These are the special ones, the ones that see it all and do not wallow in self-pity and revenge. These are the ones that must step forward and teach us harmony, for without this one thing, life is but the spark of a project—where no certainty of joy can exist.

Harmony . . . we still had it in the Deep Forest, but in the city, that was a different matter. Power and wealth is a drug few can rid themselves of, and Band'orán, uncle of Thargodén king is a particularly extreme example of this. He is not alone in his prejudiced ways and the Silvan people are slowly but inexorably falling into the category of 'lesser being'.

We were not pleased, and yet we had no leader to bring us together and fight for our lost place—our home—one that was claimed by the Alpine rulers of Ea Uaré. It was an impossible situation that must, eventually, come to an end, and the nature of that end was yet to be seen.

We sit now, upon the dawn of a new cycle. The woods are silent no more for they are expectant, their song yet timid but clear all the same. The natives of the Deep Forest can sense it sometimes and they talk now of change.

At Thargodén's court though, the elves do not speak of such things for they are inconsequential. Here, they talk of politics and trade, of foreign relations and diplomacy.

The forest, you see, is their garden, something to be cared for so that they may sit and enjoy her bounties and this—is what separates them from the true Silvans.

The forest is not their garden, it is their house—their home; nothing else matters as much as this one thing—Aria's creation.

The king though, had heard the trees that day for the first time in many centuries, a sign, perhaps, that not all was lost; there was still a spark in the dying embers of Thargodén's soul, Aradan said, one that may become a flame should it be given kindling.

The enemy has no ken of these things, though. It does not care for justice or awakenings. The Sand Lords become bolder for their incursions are poorly contested and they are encouraged. The Deviants are still in their mountain dwellings for winter lingers upon the land but when Spring returns, so too, will they and more will join them, for there will always be mortals who wish to be immortal.

Ea Uaré needed unity, needed a strong leader to push back the enemy and perhaps even vanquish it, but with the Alpine and Silvan people at odds, and a king who had yielded his will to grief—unity was but a dream—a dream shared by four elves who had dared devise a plan to change what seemed inevitable. They had set out to change history, and this was the dawn of their endeavour.

Marhené.
The Silvan Chronicles Book III

END OF BOOK I

Coming soon: The Silvan Book II—Road of a Warrior

Acknowledgements

This book would never have seen the light without the encouragement of M.Y. Leigh. No author could aspire to ever having such a wonderful reader, reviewer and friend.

Thank you, Dan, for your input on maps, and the wherewithal of cardinal points. Thank you, Siân for your encouragement, and Curious Wombat for making me a better writer.

Thank you Naledi and Ziggy for inspiring me in the first place. Thank you Illeandir, Sierra and Cher for trudging through those chapters. Thank you, Greg, Sunny Treasures, Monster Cupcake, Thefangirlofhp, Sapphirerose14, Powerpuffrogers, Kuroneko714 and SunLillyJackson for being such wonderful readers.

Pilar, Dona, thank you for putting up with my rants and monologues and finally, thank you J.R.R. Tolkien, for inspiring me to write about elves.

I'd love to hear from you:

Blog: www.rklander.com
Twitter: @rklwrites
www.facebook.com/rklwrites
Email signup: http://eepurl.com/cQuHxf

11470904R00129

Printed in Great Britain
by Amazon